Dry River

Dry River

Alicia J. Rouverol

Bridge House

British Library Cataloguing in Publication Data
A Record of this Publication is available from the British
Library

ISBN 978-1-914199-44-8

This edition published 2023 by Bridge House Publishing
Manchester, England

Cover design © Andy Broadey

An excerpt of *Dry River* was first published, in a slightly
different form, in *The Manchester Anthology 2013*.

This is a work of fiction. Certain long-standing institutions,
agencies, and public offices are mentioned, but the
characters involved are completely imaginary, and
timelines have been changed to suit the novel. Any
resemblance to individuals, dead or living, is coincidental.

For my brothers,
Jonathan and Geoffrey,
and my cousin,
Deb

As for man, his days are as grass: as a flower of the field, so he flourisheth. For the wind passeth over it, and it is gone; and the place thereof shall know it no more.

Psalms 103:15-16

CONTENTS

PART I

MILL VALLEY, CALIFORNIA
2007

Five Years Ago

October 2007

Chapter One

That business about my marriage; it went something like this: I decided to walk to the library, up the winding hill and in the shade of redwoods, where it was lovely and cool and the ferns had not yet faded. It was mid-October and the season had changed. The kids were in the stroller; Mark was two, Jacob not yet four. He still had a penchant for running ahead, so he was just young enough that it was maddening having him walk. And I was especially on my guard after that last incident. So I insisted Jacob stand behind Mark on the back end while I steered that tank-of-a-stroller up the hill.

A man overtook us. He smiled, taking in my load and said, "Well, that's a haul up the hill. Where on earth are you going with that?" This made me laugh.

"To the library," I said.

"Do you want a push? I could just push it. I mean, I'm going up there too. It's not like it's a problem."

"Nah," I said. I didn't let just anybody hold onto my kids' stroller.

He fell into step with me all the same. He was dressed in jeans and a short jacket and had blond, close-cropped hair. He was almost exactly my height. I was thirty-eight and he looked my age or younger and not like the typical Mill Valley lawyer or banker type. His stride was quick, his pace energetic, and I liked that about him, instantly.

"You live around here?" I asked.

"Yeah, down by the old library."

"Sure, I know the area. What takes you to the new library?" My world was obvious; the stroller said it all. But I was curious about his world.

"I'm a builder," he said. "But I do my own design. Like

an architect but a lot cheaper." He grinned. "I'm taking a look at the library – they're thinking about expanding."

"Oh? Like another wing, or something?"

"Sort of. I'll find out what they're thinking in about fifteen minutes. I'll let you know what they say," he said. "These your kids?"

"Yeah," I said, with a laugh. "Why, have any kids of your own?"

"Ah! No, I know better than that madness." He said this, but then he couldn't take his eyes off my boys. Jacob turned around to face him. His eyes narrowed; the man narrowed his eyes right back at him. He didn't do all the usual things like ask what their names were or pretend to engage them just to get my attention. Just then Jacob leaned his belly against the strap designed to hold him in, but the snap was jammed.

"Hey, don't lean too hard on that, cowboy, or you'll fall out. You need to fix that strap," he said, reaching forward to free it and re-fasten it. "You okay with this?"

"Sure."

Jacob held the strap beside the man's hand, the big hand and the small one together. His hand was tanned, the fingernails neat. Jacob said, "Who *are* you?"

"My name's Zeke. Ezekiel."

"What kind of name is that?" Jacob said.

"Jacob, honey," I said.

"That's okay. I get that a lot. It's a Biblical name," he said. "Who's your brother?"

"Mark."

"And your mom?"

"Sara." Jacob liked being the little big man, calling me by my name.

"Sara." Zeke turned to me just as the breeze picked up. The sun was warm, the air deliciously cool. "Sara – anything?" he said.

I smiled. "Sara Greystone."

"Greystone, that's a nice, strong name. I'm Zeke Harris."

That night when my husband Tye came home, I didn't mention Zeke, but Jacob did. "He was nice."

"Oh?" Tye said, raising a brow. "And who is he?"

I hid my smile. "A new neighbor," I said. "A builder doing some work for the library." I tore up the lettuce, tossed it into the spinner, but pulled the string too hard. It broke. "Drat," I said, dropping it in the trash; there was no fixing it. It meant another expenditure. "Yeah, it was really a hassle getting the stroller up the hill to the library. I won't do that again." Actually, I was already thinking about doing it again.

"Okay day?" Tye asked. He leaned against the counter, and stared past me to the magnolia tree outside. It was holding onto a few blossoms still.

"Sara?" he asked, to my silence.

Because by then we'd become increasingly silent. Whole days would pass without our saying anything of real import. It was all logistics: the kids' day at preschool, Jacob's dental check, Tye's IT boss insisting the client had fifty-four new requirements they'd missed.

Jacob was bouncing around in front of us, though Tye didn't see him. Tye was watching my face. I looked away. I didn't say that this chance encounter made my day because there was no sense to it. There was no isolating this feeling, there was no knowing if there was any deeper feeling there at all. Or just curiosity.

The next morning, Tye got up at 6:00 am, which he had been doing a lot of recently for work. I followed behind, trying not to wake the boys. We were still getting up together at that point. The mornings were always rushed, because we had to fit in what we could before they woke;

11

it was the only real time we had to talk: "*Are you getting the dry cleaning, or am I?*" "*I made the appointment but had to cancel; Jacob had a field trip that day.*" Sunlight cast shadows on the wood floors. As he padded down the staircase in his slippers, Tye kicked some of the toys at the base of the staircase by mistake.

"Shhh!" I said, as if he'd just dismantled the entire house.

"Sara, it's not going to wake them."

Tye began making his lunch to take to work, while I fixed his eggs. He scanned the fridge. I pointed him toward last night's leftovers. We were in the California economy now: we recycled food daily. He poured his coffee, took a seat in the alcove by the window, and stared out of it. I slid the plate of eggs across the table and took a seat opposite him, so he would have to look at me. I remembered my folks' talking things over when I was growing up, my dad hunched over the table, his face steadily watching my mom's. But Tye seemed so distracted all the time.

I'd been thinking about money lately – or the lack of it. We were making it, but barely. "Do you think I should go back to work?" I asked. It wasn't just the income. I hadn't practiced Law in five years. I missed the Public Defender Office, missed the intellectualism of the East. Since coming back West, I couldn't seem to find a strand of it embedded anywhere out here in this granite rock.

"I don't know, Sar. I think it would be more difficult. Can we do more difficult?" He took another sip of his coffee and turned to watch the hummingbird outside as it fluttered and dropped from sight.

We didn't run into Zeke again until a few weeks later. The boys and I saw him at the market, perusing the blood oranges at the fruit stand. When Jacob spotted him, he called out,

12

"Hey, Zeke! It's my birthday!" It was days away from Jacob's birthday, and he was obsessed with it. Zeke looked over and lifted back his sunglasses. Strips of morning sunlight fell across his face from the lattice awning above us.

"Hey," he said, meeting my gaze. A buzz shot through me. "Which one?"

"It's my fourth," Jacob said, and continued to chatter. Zeke listened patiently, while Jacob described his upcoming climbing party at the park. He ended his monologue with an invitation.

"Jacob," I said, "Zeke probably has other things to do."

But Zeke said, "When is it?"

I laughed, blushing. "It's this Saturday at 1:30. Really, you don't have to come."

"Are other adults coming? Or is it kids only? Do I need to rent some kids?"

"No, my brothers are coming, and my mom and dad. A couple of old friends, a few neighbors." I trailed off, thinking, *What would Tye make of Zeke being there?*

"So it's a climbing party," Zeke said. "What else do the kids like to do?" He seemed genuinely interested.

"Well," I said, "one week they play 'store' and the next 'bank' and recently it's been 'park,' making a park in the backyard."

"The boys right down from me play Iraq," he said.

"You're kidding, right?" I hadn't heard about kids playing "war" in ages, not since moving to Marin – the land of the politically correct. Largely white, heavily moneyed, the county was a Democratic stronghold. I couldn't believe he'd just said this. We'd only been back a few years, but I'd already grown accustomed to the homogeneity.

"That was a joke. Actually, though, I think their father is in the Army."

"Like that makes it all right?" I said, with a laugh.

Jacob pulled at Zeke's jacket. "Are you coming to my party?"

Zeke didn't answer, but he didn't say no. Then I did something I hadn't done in a long time. I scrawled my number on a piece of paper and handed it to him.

He shoved the paper in his pocket, holding back a smile. "See you later, Sara."

I was out running errands on a Saturday morning a month later when I saw Zeke at the bank. I was standing a few people behind him in line as he was finishing his business at the counter. He leaned forward, set down his sunglasses, and ran a hand through his hair. He wore his clothing well, effortlessly. But he radiated more than this: a sense of intelligent containment, of quiet control. He pulled out his wallet and slipped out his ID, his movements precise. When he spoke to the teller, he didn't flirt as much as engage and pay attention. I was tingling like I was fifteen again.

Zeke walked past me toward the exit. "Sara," he said, turning.

"Zeke. Hey, how are you?" I said, as casually as I could.

"Good. Where are the kids?" He scratched his head, looked away, then back at me. He studied my face, standing quite close to me.

"At home," I said, and stopped there. It was obvious they were with their dad.

The woman before me, dressed in a high-end tracksuit and Nikes, began chatting to the woman ahead of her, spinning her silver bangles as she talked: "I've taken her to every studio in town; the level isn't high enough. I've got to take her into the City for ballet at this point." She sighed.

Zeke followed my gaze and shot me a conspiratorial smile. I smiled back. He stayed beside me as the line progressed. "I didn't call you about Jacob's birthday. I had to be away that weekend."

I nodded. "Well," I said, "I mean, he's four. He invited a lot of people to the party." Jacob, at least, had long since forgotten about it.

He looked at me steadily with his almond-brown eyes. I tried to look away.

"I'll wait for you up front," he said, as I stepped up to the counter.

He held open the door as we stepped out into the cool December air. At the edge of the parking lot, I stopped beside a tree, its branches stripped bare of its leaves. I felt bare; I had no children to cover and protect me.

"The library gig didn't happen," he said. "I got some jobs out in Chicago through a friend, and then I've been traveling the past month." It was cold there right now and he liked it, in a way, but then coming back to California, he knew he really couldn't handle that sub-arctic weather. The man had the gift of the gab, and I was partially enthralled, but partially wondering what the hell we were doing.

"What about you? What have you been up to?" he asked.

"I've been studying for the bar." I had told no one this, not even Tye.

"You're studying to be an attorney?" He raised a brow.

"No, I *am* an attorney. I practiced for years and then we moved out here." I paused, because the "we" made things very apparent. "And now I'm facing the music on taking the California bar."

"Is it hard? I mean, how hard is it?"

"People fail all the time. I failed the North Carolina bar the first time. It was mortifying." I laughed and then pulled back, painfully aware of how hungry I was for adult conversation. "And, of course, I can't blame it on just being out of Law School this time."

15

"So you can't take it again if you don't get it – pass – the first time?"

"Well, I can, it just doesn't look great. It wouldn't *feel* great, either."

"So you're ready to go back to working?"

"It's either that or another kid," I said. It was a nervous joke, and now I didn't know where I was headed. "But I don't think my husband will go there." I gave an uncomfortable laugh. "So it's the bar for me." It was anything but funny. This was the crux of my crisis: a marriage on its edge, my children's departure from infancy, and the fact that I wouldn't be having another child, as much as I wanted one. I knew then that I was deeply in trouble with Zeke. I had just laid out how I felt without working out my defense ahead of time. I was completely exposed. He nodded and listened, and told me stories about the Windy City that made us both laugh. I was sharing what I was because of who Zeke was. I'd broken my own silence. Even I wasn't fool enough to miss what that meant.

At home that evening, after dinner, I went upstairs with Jacob to put down Mark. He slid under his covers and I sat beside him on his bed, one foot off the ground, and read him the Mike Mulligan book, which was his favorite. He kept stopping me to examine the steam shovel, pointing at it, as he did every night. Jacob crouched beside us, listening, picking at the sole of one of his footed jammies. He kept pulling at one of the threads to undo it.

"Don't undo it, honey. You want to keep it intact."

He stared up at me. "In what?"

I smiled. "You don't want it to come apart, do you?" I turned out his brother's light, checked the nightlight, and then took Jacob into his room.

"Bedtime, sweet guy. Let's go."

16

"Okay," he said, climbing into bed. I read to him, but he wasn't settling. He kept chattering, running his finger along my cheek, his brow furrowed, as if he knew I was distracted. I stroked his head for a long time in the dark, until he fell asleep.

After the boys went down, I told Tye I was studying for the bar. We were in the alcove off the living room, and I was sitting up on the little sofa cushion on the built-in bench, stretched out reading. I set down my reading glasses, took a sip of tea, and announced it as if I was dredging up some sort of dirty little secret.

"You are?" He set down the high-tech rag he was reading.

"Yeah, I think it's time."

"You mean, you want to go back to work?"

"Yes. Why? Is that a bad thing?" Zeke had thought this was a great idea.

"Sar, how are we going to manage the kids?"

"How are *we* going to manage the kids or how am *I* going to manage the kids? What you're really saying is 'Sara, you need to manage the kids. What do you think you're doing going back to work?' "

"I didn't say that."

"Tye, you all but said it. What do you expect me to do, hang up all that education, all those years working in Raleigh?"

"Oh, come on, you didn't work that long." He stared at me flatly. His tone was chilling.

I shivered and pulled the red wool blanket beside me over my lap. I felt cold now, a hard naked cold, a my-husband-wants-to-fuck-me-over cold. I didn't feel clean anymore, the way I had earlier that day, exposed to the essentials of who I was.

PART II

CHAPEL HILL, NORTH CAROLINA
1997

Fifteen Years Ago

August 1997

Chapter Two

You think you know someone at a first meeting – I did. I believed I knew Tye Bradshaw. He wasn't a lawyer; this much I knew.

I met him a few years out of Law School, when I was twenty-eight. I'd been single for a while after a hard break up, so I suppose you could say I was ready. The man I'd dated before him – when I was twenty-three and working at Trisha's office – was a successful attorney. Josef Albert was older, by seven or eight years; owned his own loft in LA, which even if I had one, I'd have barely inhabited it. He took me everywhere. Mexico, Hawaii. But mostly – when we weren't working – we stayed at his apartment, making love on his sleigh bed. He wasn't a futon guy; he came from too much money, too much stock and education. His parents were both attorneys; they loved me, of course – I was planning to go to Law School by then, so why wouldn't they love me? But Josef and I talked shop all the time, and when he drank, nearly nightly, we argued; we were never far away from the Law, or far enough, which meant a constant infringement on our personal life. This would not lead me to take wedding vows, much as I knew he loved me, much as I loved him. But that was only my official reason for ending the relationship. Josef's adoration scared me: it meant I had to "show up" in a very real kind of way.

Tye and I, by contrast, met at a bird store, examining birds.

The stakes, you might say, were not especially high.

The mall at Chapel Hill – the town where I lived at the time, in 1997 – had multiple levels and housed a cinemaplex and in the far corner a shop selling birds, which drew all the bird enthusiasts in the area. I wasn't a birder myself, mind you. But Amelia, the daughter of a friend of mine from Law School, who I sometimes sat for, had been asking for a bird for months. Lisa – my closest friend from the program – also sat for her; we'd been vying for who might buy Amelia a bird first. I knew nothing about the feathery creatures and didn't have time for an Internet search, because I was out of school by now and deep into preparing my cases at the PD Office in Raleigh, and work was all I did.

The bird sounds inside the small shop were not deafening so much as chaotic and overlapping, a peculiar kind of music with no rhythm to it. Cage after cage lined the wall, feathers of every color, a yellow finch housed beside a cockatoo; some birds slept, while others hopped about, peering at you peering at them. I stood transfixed before a multi-plumed parrot.

A tall man with black curly hair almost shoulder length poured over the binoculars behind me. He put down a pair, stepped back into me and onto my foot. "Sorry," he said, wheeling around to face me.

"No worries." I didn't take my eyes off the birds as I spoke.

"You in a bird quandary?"

"Yeah." I laughed. "Why, do you know anything about them?"

He slipped his bag onto the other shoulder, and said, "Yes, actually, I do. I know a lot about birds."

"What do you know about them?"

"What do you *want* to know about them?"

I told him what I was after: a bird that wouldn't die on a six-year-old child, a bird that she could hold, a bird that would fly around the living room and go back into its cage on its own.

"Go for the simple parakeet."

"But that's so… uninteresting."

"Doesn't matter. It'll do the trick. Choose some pretty feathers. Go for what will work."

He was practical, he was clear.

"So how do you know about birds?"

He'd gone to the coast for years – to the marshlands, where he spent hours watching them, days at a time, because birders pride themselves on the numbers of days spent in the field annually. At first he went with a Sierra Club group out of UNC, then he began birding on his own. He liked the solitude on the coast, walking the shores, waiting for flocks to fly overhead. He told me all of this with a far-away look, as if he were on the coast, actually watching the birds.

He gasped. "That's a Jamaican Yellow-Billed Amazon! I can't believe they're selling it here. They're not supposed to be pets." He turned his full attention toward a parrot with bright red plumage beneath its yellow beak in a cage on the other side of me.

"It's not boring, bird watching?"

"God, no." He pulled his gaze away from the bird finally. "Think of the variety. Think of the colors. Plus the coast here is gorgeous."

He'd grown up in Maine in a small university town, where his dad taught. Maine was pretty wild and he'd spent a lot of time outdoors, until he left home for college in North Carolina – kind of glad to leave home, he said, with a laugh. He had a periodic tic above his right eye as he talked. His forehead was broad, his skin fair, and he had piercing blue eyes – Black-Irish coloring. He wasn't handsome as much as attractive, in an affable way. He was attentive, and listened, if with a slightly vacant stare.

Then the oddest thing happened: a weird piercing

scream came up out of nowhere and the birds started screaming with it, and the shop attendant yelled, *"Fire!"* Tye grabbed me by the elbow and commandeered us out of the store and down the central walkway of the mall, where men and women raced past us, faces taut, teenagers huddled in corners, disbelieving. An elderly man careened around a potted plant, bumping into a woman with an infant. No one seemed to know where the fire was located.

"Is it real?" I asked.

"Do you want to stick around to find out? Come on, let's go out this exit."

We pushed through a fire alarm door and slipped out into the unbearable August heat. I gasped, the wall of humidity outdoors oppressive in its own right after the air conditioning left your bones actually cold.

Back then, in the 1990s, Chapel Hill was not hugely developed and you could step outside the mall and you were almost in the country. It was the New South – not yet the New New South – and kudzu hung on the trees marking 15-501, a sense of wildness right beside a suburb – nothing I'd experienced growing up in the Bay Area. Railroad tracks and old mills and tiny fried chicken restaurants buried beside brand-new BP stations and university research facilities. You never knew where you were, caught in the past or moving forward into the present.

"Want to have a coffee?" he said.

I blinked, trying to catch my breath, staring at the people as they streamed out behind us. "Uh, sure." Sirens screamed in the background.

It wasn't real, of course, the fire. As we sat drinking coffee, watching the firemen in long coats on a warm August morning, I stole glances at the man across from me. He wasn't overly impressed by me, or didn't make a show of it like so many men. I liked that about him. He stirred his coffee with the wooden stick and paused, paying attention. He watched the college kids as they swung through the doors, the heat of summer, even at this early hour, blasting in on us. The bell kept jangling, flagging the intense bellows of hot air before they would hit us. He was an observer, I noticed; and he was observing me.

"Why didn't you study birds?" I asked, when we moved away from the door. We sat now in the far corner of the café, away from the foot traffic and the blistering heat.

"Why didn't I—?"

"You know, you could have been an ornithologist."

He scanned my face, as if expecting judgment, but there was something in Tye that made you unable to judge him, even then.

"It never occurred to me." He sat back, half smiling, and crossed his arms. "I didn't want to take something I loved and corrupt it by trying to make a living at it."

"Yes, but that would be like my saying, 'I love the law, that's why I can't do it.' Does that make any sense?"

"Do you?" he asked. "Do you really *love* law?"

"Yes, I do," I said, and gasped. "Think I could have made it through Law School otherwise? It's just horrible. You have to love it or there's no point."

He wanted to know what it was I loved about the law and what kind of law I practiced. He sounded skeptical, as if it wasn't possible to be passionate about something you did for a living. He liked his IT job in Raleigh – Raleigh was where all the conventional people lived and worked, I knew – but no, he didn't love it.

He told me they'd brought him on board just as the TV station was going online, so he got to launch its first website. His boss was thrilled. But now that Tye was past the initial challenge, it had become a bit of desk job. In Maine, where he'd grown up, he'd spent a lot of time outdoors, which was where he really wanted to be most the time.

"But what about you," he said. "Why Law?"

I studied my cup before taking the very last sip. "I guess you could say I believe in the concept of fairness. I think there is a right and wrong – not in a moralistic, self-righteous way, but in a human fairness way. If that makes any sense. And being an attorney is one way to work toward that kind of fairness."

He nodded, watching me. But he didn't respond, at least not at first. He tapped his stirrer on the edge of his mug, then leaned back again. He was a man whose waters ran quietly, like the bay where he birded, the water mirroring the sky. His T-shirt stuck to him in places from the perspiration, even inside, where it was air-conditioned. He pulled at his shirt slightly when he spoke. Was he nervous, or was he just hot?

"It's good to believe in something," he said.

"And you?" I asked. "What do you believe in?"

He paused. "Birds," he said. "I believe in birds."

The site of our first date wasn't what I expected, and I guess that's also what I liked about him: he wasn't what I expected. He didn't ask me to go birding. He wanted to go walking, which surprised me, because it wasn't overtly romantic, like a traditional date, but instead was simple and clean. And that is what our courtship felt like: simple and clean.

That afternoon, I leaned against the massive loblolly by the side of the road that ran between Chapel Hill and Durham, waiting at the head of the path that wound miles into the woods and led to the river. He was late, or I was early. But I didn't mind. No one was in a hurry back then; I didn't work on weekends and so Saturdays were pretty relaxed. I crouched down onto my heels, digging at the soft red clay soil with a stick, thinking about the last date I'd gone on and how poorly it went. Dating: it was always a bad idea. Better to meet someone at work, where you actually saw someone in the context of your lives...

I heard crunching, the sound of boots on twigs, and started.

"You okay?" Tye towered above me and I squinted up at him.

"Yeah." He took my hand and pulled me to my feet.

We began walking and though it was noon there was more than a breath of air for a change. Summertime in North Carolina is brutally hot, especially in August, which was when most smart people went away, down to the coast to Emerald Isle, or left the state altogether if they weren't from around here. Tye didn't go away often, he explained, but sometimes took trips to the coast for his short birding expeditions, mostly day trips, or went to see his parents in Maine. (I was, for the record, relieved he hadn't asked me to go birding.) His jeans clung to his hips as he walked, a steady tight rhythm, his long shoulders reaching upward, squaring off because they were sharp and angular. I liked his movements, the steadiness of his motion, and how he watched the sky, and not just for birds but for its vastness, I imagined. (These were the things I told myself then.) He seemed drawn to open space, and I wondered how it was that he could sit at a computer ten hours a day. He seemed distant, though, like he was somewhere else.

As we walked along the path toward the river, we talked about my work and his and birding and how often he went (not often enough, he said), and about the severity of the heat there in comparison to my homeland and his. We came up a short incline, where a boy and his mother stood pressed against a birch tree, its bark stripped away, the trunk a stark white against their dark clothing. I knew instinctively something was wrong by how the mother held the boy against her belly, arms locked behind his back. He was arched slightly against her arms, stiff.

The mother looked up at us, aghast.

We both followed the woman's gaze.

A copperhead, six feet in length, was coiled, ready to strike.

No one moved for what felt like minutes.

The copperhead, its diamond-patterned back and short, forked head, began to slither away from the mother and son, pressed to the tree, along a path just inches beside them.

Tye grabbed a long-pronged stick. He bent down, shoved it under the snake and then – with remarkable force, lobbing it underhand like a tennis player on the court – flung the copperhead broadly into the woods. The snake – having coiled the moment the stick touched him – sprung loose from his coil just as he flew up and over the path, beyond the edge of the cliff, where the river ran, and vanished out of sight.

I stared at Tye in utter amazement. I couldn't have done what he did.

The anxiety dropped from the mother's face; she unclasped her son, who let out a gasp of air and began sobbing – he was only five but old enough to know he'd been in danger. "Robby, it's okay, sweetie, everything is fine." She picked him up, held him close, her hand holding his head tightly to her ear. Her eyes glistened in relief, and she mouthed the words, "Thank you," to Tye. He nodded, dropped the stick, and it was only then that I saw the tremor in his arm, the tension of the act, releasing.

I stood beside him, placed my hand on his shoulder, in shock and approval, and smiled. I hadn't imagined him capable of that act; and it left me impressed and more attracted to him than I'd been when we'd first met. The man had fire in his belly after all.

Above us a gust of breeze lifted the high limbs of a loblolly pine. A few pine needles dropped on the path before us. Tye took my hand and in silence we walked to the river's edge.

On our next date, we went for lunch in town and then afterward to a city park where Tye did the exercises at each station and I pulled a law journal from my white cotton handbag. I stretched out on the cement bench, held the journal at arm's length and began reading. He dropped down off the nearest bar and sat on the bench beside me. He lifted my head onto his lap, drew my hair from my face, and looked at me steadily.

"What are you reading?" he asked.

"*Modern Law Review*. Does that make me a deathly boring date?"

"Hey, I was doing pull-ups on the bars over there. Does that make me a complete loser-hosehead?"

I laughed. "Would it really interest you? Most people I know find law journals deadly."

"Try me."

"Okay," I said, "it's on public interest immunity. 'Volte-Face on Public Interest Immunity.' "

"Public *what?*" he said. I laughed again.

Then he pulled my head up to his and kissed me. I realized in that moment that this was a man I might love, and that perhaps he might love me back. It had been a lot of years since that kind of love had come my way, and as I stared up at a hazy blue summer sky, I lost sight of all but his face, framed by that expanse of blue, his dark eyes like saucers, watching me, watching over me.

When the light began to grow lower and a car pulled

out over the gravel drive leading to the park, we knew it was time to go. He pulled me to him again and I softened, because I could soften, then.

"Where are we going?" he asked. "And are we going together?"

That night we went to his house. While Tye cooked dinner, I took a stack of magazines and read through them, skimming swiftly, one after the next. It came of all that reading in Law School. I'd gained speed as a reader, and when I needed a break from the heavy texts I had to absorb night after night, magazine reading sprung me free from all that. It was still a strategy I relied on if my workload got heavy at the PD Office. The competition between the deputy PDs wore me out. "Law School was fucking tough, but this is like tight-rope walking," I said, as I dropped the stack of magazines on his wooden floor and rose to my feet.

He nodded in agreement, even if he didn't share the experience. "I'm not missing any of that," he said. "In case you're wondering."

I laughed. "Which? Grad school or the Law?"

"Here, put this down," he said, pulling another magazine out of my hands. Then he enclosed me with his arms and I felt the tension melt away.

Later that night we went back to my house; I needed to be up early the next day for a big deposition. I never expected this would be the first night we would sleep together; it was so uneventful, in a way. It was fall and breezy, the rain pulling down leaves, leaving patterns in the light that shone from the streetlights of Chapel Hill. My apartment wasn't insulated and sometimes, on a night like that night, it felt almost cool. We huddled beneath my comforter on the futon I'd bought at a yard sale months after I first arrived in the South. Tye's black hair looked

28

even blacker in the dark with the light shining above it. I wound my fingers around a curl. He watched my face intently and when we kissed I knew this would be the moment. Making love with him was light and easy and I felt carried away. He was tender, but firm, and I liked his certainty. I'd been with a few men before grad school, but Tye was the first man in a long time who actually seemed to care about me. Tye had been with a few women, but only a few, and he brought to lovemaking a certain innocence.

Afterwards, we lay on the futon and he stroked my hair. I was dozing, and he said, "Sar?"

"Hmm." I was nearly asleep. The reverse of the standard female-male, after-lovemaking moment, where he rolls over and nods off.

"You awake?"

"I am now." I smiled in the dark. The windowpane, shook by another gust of wind, rattled.

"Does it bother you?" he said.

"What?" My voice was dreamy; I was barely paying attention.

"You know, the fact that I'm not in a grad program, or likely to do one. Do you care?"

I squinted at him. Patterns of leaves, branches waving in the breeze, fell across his face. "Why would I care?"

"I don't know. I just didn't know if this is an issue," he said. He was all of thirty-two at the time, but clearly sensed something I wasn't seeing.

"What do you like about him? About your relationship?" Trisha asked me once. Trisha was the attorney I had worked for in LA, who inspired me to go to Law School. We still talked from time to time, even after I moved to Chapel Hill.

I was standing, phone pressed against my ear, in my upstairs apartment a few blocks from downtown Franklin

29

Street, watching the leaves fall from overhanging maple and oak and birch, row after row, beside the large lovely wood-slated homes. It was a fantasy world, so far from Albany's urban tarmac and screaming interstate noise.

"I don't know, Trish," I said. "He's a good guy. What's not to like?"

He was, as I think on it now, a good guy against the backdrop of a good life. Nothing filled my head at the time but the latest law case controversy or lecture I'd just gone to on campus, or music from the shows I went to almost nightly. I was filled, and it didn't take much more to fill me up. We had sex on my low-to-the-ground futon, and I had a good time and most of the time didn't care whether it was perfect or not. He was a good man, and a good man, I must have assumed, was good enough.

Six months later, we began talking marriage. Six months after that, in a sparsely attended civil service at Chapel Hill's City Hall, we signed the certificate. Both sets of parents met for the first time that day and awkwardly exchanged small talk while we spent the short time after the service chattering with our friends: Emily from my graduate program, his friend Roy from the TV station, who were our witnesses. We held a slightly larger reception – with staff from the PD Office and other friends from Law School, like Lisa – at Duke Gardens, under a bow of wisteria that hung in trails, clumps of purple flowers that swayed in the breeze. I still believe that was the happiest day of my life. Marriage – our marriage, I thought – would take us to some place other than where we'd landed, that sweet place of affection. We were only at the beginning; from here, I assumed, the love would deepen. We would grow into our best selves together, over time.

I suppose I mistook kindness for love. As it turns out,

they are not essentially, or exclusively, the same thing. Had I confused agape – the selfless love for mankind – for eros? What I didn't understand is that it takes both of these to make a marriage work.

We had travelled to the wedding of a friend out in Charlottesville, Virginia. It was the following year, late August, and the heat had subsided. The drive had gone smoothly: no fights, no hiccups, no wrong turns. Tye was in a chipper mood, which he'd not been in for some time due to a difficult situation at work. We arrived at the site of the chapel. On the path leading to the church stood a broad, leafy Japanese maple. The sight of it made me think of our reception, the way weddings can remind you of your own. Duke Gardens featured a number of Japanese maples. I glanced at Tye, pointed to the maple. "It's gorgeous, isn't?"

He threw me a sheepish grin. Tye wasn't one for overt references, but I was fairly certain he'd gotten my drift.

He parked my car on the side of the road. We had changed into dress clothes at a service station on the way up, an old, white-planked affair that looked scrubby on the outside but featured kindly owners inside. When Tye asked for the bathroom, explaining we were bound for a wedding, they let us into the back area to use their own. They threw in a bottle of wine at the till. They'd misunderstood and thought it was *our* wedding; Tye and I laughed the whole way out. We left the station in high spirits, as if everyone was conspiring for us to enjoy the weekend.

"So what do you think?" I asked, when I got out of the car onto the dusty roadside. "Will it pass?" I was in a blood-red gown, nearly the color of the maple.

"It'll do just fine." He raised a brow, code for we-should-have-done-more-than-just-change at the service station.

31

Inside the chapel we congregated toward our friends. These were Tye's set; I sometimes felt that I didn't belong in their world, but they were always congenial when I joined in. Elizabeth, a friend from the TV station and Roy's partner, slid over on the empty pew. "Take a seat," she said.

Tye, in his best dark suit, waved me in and I moved onto the bench beside Elizabeth. It was wooden seating, hard on the bottom, smooth to the touch, and inviting. Tye sat beside me and clasped my hand. He wasn't always overtly affectionate, so when he was, I relished it.

Elizabeth grinned. "That drive was ungodly this morning, but look at this place."

It was archetypal, old Virginia architecture: peaked ceiling; wooden posts and arched doorways; beaded, solid-wood doors; a stately organ near the pulpit. I laughed in delight. Tye squeezed my hand, this time because the ceremony was about to begin.

When the singing began, I was taken by surprise. A gospel group shook the building with "There is Love." The sounds reverberated through the chapel. I felt the hairs on my arms lift, and I shivered. The bride was openly weeping as she proceeded down the aisle; she wasn't accompanied. Roy had told us the story: she'd lost her parents in an accident and besides, he said, she didn't believe in being given away.

When she joined the groom on the stage, a silence fell in the church. I thought of my parents, I thought of Ephraim and Barley; I wondered if this couple knew what was ahead, if her weeping in some way articulated some fundamental understanding of the difficult path. We knew Hannah, but hadn't met Harry the groom. Roy had known him for years: the man looked equal parts terrified and overjoyed. He wiped his brow when Hannah reached him.

Elizabeth whispered, "Jesus, that nearly took me down."

I glanced at her, nodded. Tye was looking straight ahead. Did this moment resonate for him as well?

The ceremony was brief; from the back of the church, Elizabeth and I stretched toward the front of the congregation, straining to hear the vows. "Did you catch any of that?" I asked Tye.

"Not a word," he said, his face rosy from the heat in the chapel, or from excitement, I wasn't sure which.

Outside we showered the couple with rose petals from lace bags that had been placed on every pew. The champagne was poured into plastic glasses as they fled the church, and at the reception in a hall 200 yards down the road, Tye's friends sang and bellowed into the night. At 2 am, we turned out onto the grassy field behind the reception hall. The newlyweds had left long ago to drive up the coast to Martha's Vineyard, having booked a tiny lodge for the wedding night somewhere along the way. Roy and Elizabeth, Tye and I, sat wrapped in woolen blankets, hunched on patches of damp grass where we had watched the moon rise earlier in the night.

Roy handed a bottle of Scotch to Tye, who managed successive swigs. He had always been good at handling liquor. I'd stopped drinking a few hours before.

"God, poor sucker," Roy said, about Harry. He narrowed his gaze on Tye. "So is it awful being married?"

I laughed. "Oh, that's cruel. Put the guy on the spot!"

"No, it's not," Tye said, squeezing my shoulder.

I scanned Elizabeth's face, cast grey in the moonlight. Did she care about being married, or did it mean absolutely nothing?

She pursed her lips, as if she'd heard me. "It just isn't for everyone," she said. She reached over to Roy, interlaced her fingers with his. His hands were splayed behind him, legs outstretched beside her. He turned to me. "And is it for you, Sara?"

33

"HA," I said. "I get your game." I gazed at the Japanese maple near where we had parked. The tree, its limbs reaching over the cobblestones like a shroud, left a wide, deep shadow, and I longed to be under it with Tye. "Come on," I said, and dragged him to his feet.

We stumbled over dewy grass toward the maple, and when we stood beneath it, he pulled me close; I felt him envelope me. The night had grown cool and quiet.

"Let's go," he said, grabbing my hand. I squeezed it back.

PART III

MILL VALLEY, CALIFORNIA
2007

Five Years Ago

November 2007

Chapter Three

The afternoon of Jacob's fourth birthday party Tye and I were in the kitchen, preparing the food. He was slicing celery, explaining yesterday's crisis. There'd been an IT meltdown: the system had crashed and the CEO had a board meeting that weekend in LA, so the heat was on.

"I should be used to this by now," he said, "but he's such a jerk, and I hardly ever see him anyway. It's not like he actually appreciates what I do. I'm pretty good at getting things up and running again, and you know the flunky they hired below me, well, I just can't count on him for anything. Every time I tell him to do something, I have to double-check it... Are you even listening?" He set down the knife, exasperated.

"You know, I can't really focus on it right now. I'm going a million different directions." There were balloons to blow up and Mark wanted to nurse, Jacob was having his usual pre-party meltdown. It was Saturday, 1 pm; the party would begin in an hour.

"Okay, but next time you get upset at me for not listening..."

I set down my knife. "Go on," I said, and glanced distracted at the clock.

"So I told him that Bruce – he's our CFO – couldn't run the numbers."

"Meaning...?"

"I told him the system was down."

"Was it? It was down, right?"

"Well, for a time." He smiled. "But then it came back up."

"So he *could* have run the numbers for him?" Now I was confused. "Did you not tell him the truth?"

"Well," he laughed. "It was true at the time, but then the system came back up. By then Bruce had already left. What was I to do, call him on his cell and have him come back downtown?"

I blinked. "Yes, but Bruce could have gotten him that report. And if they figure it out, won't it be clear – obvious – that you didn't go the extra mile?"

Tye didn't seem to think it was an issue; he'd already told his boss they couldn't deliver. It was a moot point.

It sounded to me like bad politicking, but then I'd been out of the work force so long, what did I know? I pulled out the vegetables and placed them in bowls, lay plastic wrap across the tops, and set them in open cardboard boxes on the island in our kitchen. We knew people who catered their children's events, but it felt like outsourcing my job, so I refused on principle. But the money was a piece of it; it was a piece of all of it.

"What?" he said. "What's wrong?"

Mark began fussing in "the jumpy" – a plastic seat suspended with rope from the doorway – so I put him on my boob as I leaned against the island. I noticed the time.

"Shoot, we've got to get going. Jacob, come get your shoes on. Tye, can you handle Jacob? Do we have everything?" The party bags, erect in a cardboard box like sailboats lined up at the dock, stood ready by the front door.

"Yes," he said, in a clipped tone.

In the car, Jacob chattered in the backseat; Mark was gurgling. The roads were congested. Marin County, where we lived – the county north of San Francisco – clogged up on the weekends. Hillsides teaming with redwoods encroached above us; Tye wove expertly through the valleys, the dappled sunlight falling across the tarmac before us. He spoke about public lands here in the West –

37

how everyone wanted access, but there wasn't road enough to get to them. I stared out the window, feeling depressed. I hadn't yet told Tye that Zeke might be coming; I felt inordinately preoccupied, and being in the dark about my own emotional landscape left me feeling untethered.

We arrived at the park before anyone else. Tye hauled the boxes of food and cake from the car. I placed Mark inside the A-OK corral with some toys. My son stared up at me from his contained sea of grass, blinked, and smiled. I laughed with the purest of joy.

It was warm and breezy out. Tye was taping the paper tablecloths onto the park tables, but they were flying up as quickly as he held them down. Jacob stretched one end over a corner and the tablecloth began to tear.

"Jacob, *stop*!" Tye said.

"Tye, he's just trying to help."

"He's being a pain in the ass."

"He's being a kid." And then I stopped myself. "Here, let me help." I taped down the last tablecloth, trying not to think about whether Zeke would show.

My mom and dad pulled up, and behind them Larry, my older brother. A woman with long blond hair, in a mid-length skirt and boots, climbed out of the passenger seat of his gold-colored truck. He'd brought his new girlfriend; he rarely brought anyone to family events. My dad walked toward me carrying a big box and smiling, his legs bowing in the proverbial tradesman/plumber walk. Tye relieved him of the box, and they chatted, my dad staring into the distance as they spoke. They didn't have more than about seven words to share, though to his credit, Tye tried to bridge that gap. My mom followed behind at a faster gait; she was much leaner, particularly since the illness. She handed my dad his over shirt, smiling sweetly as he took it, their rapport so easy.

Buoyed by the sentiment, I said to Tye, "Oh, that neighbor we met a couple of times might be coming."

"Who?"

"That guy Zeke. Remember I told you about the man we met at the library – that builder who lives in our neighborhood? Jacob invited him the other day when we ran into him at the market."

Tye shrugged. It was a complete non-issue. The party invite list wasn't on his short – or even his long – list of significant events in those days.

Fran leaned against the gift table, its tablecloth torn at the corners from the wind, and wistfully told my mother how she and Larry managed never to meet at High Sierra or at any of the fall and spring Strawberry Music Festivals they'd both been at for a decade. "We met in the classroom, if you can believe that."

She was a teacher and, like my brother, a musician. Her voice was lyrical, and when she talked, Larry couldn't take his eyes off of her. He augmented her stories until she laughed. When Jacob began pulling at my dress, I took his hand and together we ran hard up the grassy slope and into the wind. I wanted to blow my envy and frustration away. It was my son's birthday after all. At gift opening time, I let him carry the presents to the blanket at the A-OK Corral. I knew what would make him happy. That much I did know.

I kept watching the road as cars pulled up, though I didn't know what Zeke drove. He didn't show that day.

Two weeks later I went down to see my mother. She was doing okay since the illness, but she tired easily and her spirits dipped frequently. She was eager to spend time with

Mark; she felt she'd missed so much with her recovery. We set up Jacob in the other room to watch a video, which we did religiously when we came down. It was a special treat for him and it gave my mother and me time to visit.

In the living room, she spread out quilts from my grandmother on the floor. I loved examining the threads and patterns, and rode my finger along the seams as we talked. I told her about Tye's sharp reprimands with Jacob, how much they troubled me.

My mother was on her knees on the quilt with me, her face still as I spoke. "Well, I think you're both right on this one. No, he shouldn't need to use force. But you countering him in front of the kids won't help his cause any."

I told her I was trying not to.

"Did you talk about it later? Did you make a plan of how you want to handle it next time?"

I told her we hadn't.

"Why not?"

"Because I'm tired of bringing everything up. It wears me out."

"Will he talk about it when you do bring it up?"

"Sometimes." There was a lot I was not saying.

She pursed her lips, picked up a building block from the quilt and handed it to Mark, who was piling them up now. I was trying to read her face and then something flickered across it.

"Sar, is your marriage going okay?" she asked in a quiet voice.

"I don't know, Mom." In the past six months – after phone calls with Trisha in LA and Emily – no one had asked this essential question.

Mark spun around on the floor, his face wide open without a hint of sadness or uncertainty. My mother squeezed my hand but said nothing. Then his sock snagged on a nail in one of her floorboards. I leaned over to roll back my son's sock until it was just so.

My mother walked me out to my car and held Mark as I assembled the diaper bag and got everything in the backseat. She was chortling to him, and he was pulling at her curly grey hair – Ephraim's hair, I saw now, increasingly resembled hers.

"Any news from Eph?" I asked. I'd purposefully stayed off topic.

"He's moving out. For now, anyway."

"Wait, I thought Barley was leaving?"

"She didn't want to leave the house."

Barley had done an about-face and insisted she didn't want to leave the house, my mother explained, which put the onus on Ephraim to move out. Barley argued that it would be too hard on the kids if she, as primary parent, were in a different residence. And Ephraim – being who he was – had complied.

I got the kids in the car seats and then stopped to face my mother.

She put her hand on my arm and said, "Don't say it." Barley had helped her after her illness, when I'd had months of morning sickness and couldn't drive.

"Are you worried?"

"I think *he'll* be okay. It's the kids." She was tight-lipped, the prospect painful.

"Do they understand what's going on?"

"Not really, at least that's what Barley says."

"That's a good thing, Mom," I said, in a moment of compassion for my sister-in-law. The deeper I felt myself drawn to Zeke, the angrier I had become at Barley.

She nodded grimly.

I said nothing. I couldn't imagine what Barley was

going through now. I didn't want to. It was too terrifying a place to go in my mind. She was living a double-life, still seeing that man, still dancing around my brother.

When Larry called three days later, I decided my mom was rallying the troops. He rarely called and only came to visit after both Jacob and Mark were born. Perhaps now, five years in, he believed we were actually staying. I was feeling low after seeing my mom and was glad for the visit.

Larry pulled up the steep driveway in his gold-colored pick-up. Our house was in the foothills of Mill Valley; we could never have lived there if we weren't still renting.

"Should I put a block under this?" he asked. He'd always been obsessive about his vehicles. I reassured him the car wouldn't go anywhere without him actually driving it. He laughed.

Larry was the sibling who was always left out – the textbook middle child who had vanished. Ephraim had been our mother's favorite, and I was determined to be in on the game. You could see it in our professional choices. Larry was the one my parents asked the least of and perhaps gave the least to. He didn't seem to care. He didn't seem vested in being central to our family, or he'd just given up and let go.

"How's it going?" he called out, with more enthusiasm than I was able to return.

Jacob was inside napping; Mark had just woken up. We parked ourselves on the bench in the sunny part of the garden. He didn't teach on Tuesdays and had to pick up some supplies at one of his favorite stores over here. I told him he didn't need an excuse to be here, and he smiled.

He stretched out his legs. "Can I light a cigarette?" he asked.

"Sure."

He lit up, blew the cigarette smoke away from my son. He tapped one foot against the knee hiked up in his lap, as if on edge.

I asked him about his music classes.

"They're great. Really."

"Still doing the carpentry and eBay?"

"Yeah." He talked for a few minutes about his music classes and then he said, "Hey, I need to ask you. How did you know you wanted to marry Tye?"

I paused. Did it look so obvious?

"I'm thinking of asking Fran to marry me," he said. And then he blew out some smoke, took a finger and poked at the flap on his boot that was beginning to come off. He laughed. "I know that's crazy, given who I am – where I am. Would she even want me?" He looked straight ahead wistfully.

"Larry, that's terrific!" I said. "Of course, she'd want you." I wanted to counter his self-reproach. I didn't know if she loved him, but I wanted her to for his sake.

They'd been seeing each other for a few months. She was ten years younger, which he acknowledged maybe wasn't so brilliant. I did the math: I was thirty-eight, that made him forty-one. "Thirty-one isn't so bad," I said, trying to encourage.

He smiled.

This wasn't Larry, my brother. He wasn't a smiler, he didn't blush. He also didn't tell me things, or hadn't in a long time.

"Have you told Ephraim?"

He shook his head. "It seemed better not to. With his divorce and all, seemed hardly a good time."

It'd taken Ephraim every bit of the last three years to sort out his marital life. It was clear Barley wasn't coming back, though it wasn't clear whether this new relationship – the man she'd ostensibly left him for – would amount to much of anything. But wasn't that the way? Most people don't really fall in love when they are having marital difficulties, I believed; they are just looking for a quick way out. I figured it was the body's way of reading the mind.

"I think you should tell him. He's a big boy, he should be glad for you."

"Yeah," he said, and his entire expression lifted. "Took me awhile." He cleared his throat, remnants of years of smoking. "I've loved other women. Here and there. But how do you know if it's the right one to marry?" He laughed and said, "Jesus, what a stupid problem to have." He leaned over his crossed legs, blew out more smoke.

"I don't know, Larry."

"She's who I think about," he said, looking over at me. "I think about her all the time." He teared up. "Shitty time to get married, though. She lives in a shit-hole apartment in Oakland with her son. It's all of twenty-square feet. I don't even know where we'd plant ourselves. But does it matter so long as we really love each other?"

I felt a lump in my throat. I looked away briefly, watched a blue jay settle on the fence until I could collect myself, and then said, "Larry, I think that's lovely." I reached over, picked a nasturtium, and deposited it in his lap. "Here you go. Congrats, Bro."

He picked it up, turned it slowly in his hand, and then the smile deepened.

Mark was struggling to get out of my arms, so I stood up, put him down on his feet. "What do you love about her?" I asked, as I held my son by his hand. I wanted to know why people fell in love these days, people who were remotely my age, what caused them to fall in love, and more than anything, what kept them there.

"She's just herself," he said. "And you know, she loves me exactly the way I am."

Larry stayed for several hours. I hadn't really expected it. I made him a couple of cups of coffee, which he sipped while smoking out on the back patio. We visited while I attended to the boys and threw in a few loads of laundry. He talked about the work in the schools; it was getting slim now, so few actual positions that he was going from school to school. I couldn't imagine how he was making ends meet, but he didn't seem troubled by it. Larry had dropped out of California College of Arts & Crafts years ago. He'd gone for a semester, studied music and never finished. Then he picked up odd jobs, played in a few bands, until the music in the schools gig had materialized. He was never dissatisfied; didn't seem to worry about the next paycheck, or didn't talk about it if he did. When it was time for him to leave – to catch the store before closing – we walked out to the driveway together. The afternoon light crept in through our half-open blinds; Jacob was in front of the TV, watching a video. I brought Mark out with me.

My brother stood beside his truck for a moment, ran a hand over his tire, checking a nub to make sure it wasn't a nail. He pulled his clean hand through the hair that curled around his ears. "Has it been okay for you, Sara, coming home?"

I scratched my head. "Yes. Hard in some ways; it's not the place I left behind." I was glad to be here today. I was glad for his visit, and told him so.

"You okay with," he paused, "all this..." He swept his hand toward the house, my domestic life.

"Well, I'd rather own than rent. But I don't think we can. Not now. It's out of sight here in Marin. We'll never own here."

45

"None of us'll own here. This is fucking Marin." He laughed. "Sweetheart, I got news for you, this ain't Kansas anymore…" And this time he let out a loud raucous laugh that made me laugh with him.

He grew serious suddenly and looked right at me. "What I meant was being home. After the PD Office." He'd come out for the wedding; he knew my world then.

I shrugged. "It won't be forever." That is what I kept telling myself, but the night before I'd dreamt of the PD Office.

Larry stood for a moment at the back door. "That man of yours gonna let you outta the house?" The sun slanted behind him, capturing the flecks of grey in his hair. He took a drag on his cigarette. "I guess I just didn't peg you as the 'stay-at-home' kind. You know, you had that career and all."

"Yeah, I *had* one is right," I said, trying to make light of it. Of course, he couldn't know how hard those words cut me, and I couldn't fault him at all for it.

He threw me a grin, stubbed out his cigarette, reached over and gave me a hug. I hugged him tight. Much as I admired Ephraim, this was the brother who had my backside.

I didn't tell him I'd met Zeke, but I wanted to and thought seriously about it. I wanted to know if he felt about Fran the way I was beginning to feel about Zeke.

46

PART IV

CHAPEL HILL, NORTH CAROLINA
2001

Eleven Years Ago

October 2001

Chapter Four

We'd been married three years the night we went out to hear music and I discovered how differently Tye and I walked in the world. It was October. The heat was still prevalent during the day. Sometimes it cooled down at night; but not tonight. It had been Indian Summer and the magnolia blossoms were still fragrant, leaving an odor that permeated the air in the residential part of Chapel Hill. But we were bordering Carrboro, and while it wasn't rough per se, it was further out from the university and more like city life.

In the alley behind Cat's Cradle, there were dark corners beside the dumpsters, where people could have been shooting up drugs or mugging people, although nothing like that much happened, most of the time. Tye found a spot in the far corner of the lot. We slipped out of the car and joined the stream of bodies lining up outside the club. We stood behind two youngish kids. She had a razor cut, her profile exposing her dyed-orange hair, her black skirt intentionally torn at the hem. The man beside her wore an earring in each nostril. The girl turned around and beamed at us. Tye was tall, 6' 4" tall, and remarkably slender, and because he wore his hair long still, people took him to be much younger. He smiled back.

I was tired. It had been a long day in Raleigh at the PD Office. I'd had a run of good "wins" lately, but our appeal on the Susan Holeman case had been denied. The Court of Appeals had found no error in law, so a new trial was now the only avenue. It had taken me a year to locate new evidence; I had just found an old neighbor of Susan's who might be able to testify, but he was elderly and infirm. That morning, I'd put in the motion to reopen the case. I was feeling the strain, even if it was Friday night and Tye and I were about to cut loose.

"You okay?" he asked.

"Yeah, I'm okay."

My mother had phoned the day before to tell me about the birth of my brother Ephraim's twins. I'd not been able to get him or my mother by phone; and I wanted to hear about the birth. I assumed all was fine, but Barley's first pregnancy had been a challenge. The whole thing – in combination with those damn roads (everywhere I drove in California, I saw sky; but the lack of visible sky in North Carolina left me feeling hemmed me in) – had me missing the West.

"Do you want to stay for the show?" Tye asked.

"I think so."

Ordinarily, I was as enthusiastic as he was about going out to music. We both knew people in the club scene. As a computer geek, Tye knew virtually all the sound people and fixed their equipment on the side. He did it as a favor, and because he liked having an entry to that world. We weren't celebrities, but we were known in this world.

Inside the club, the lights above the bar glowed, where men in jeans and ratty T-shirts, and women in short skirts and leggings or straight-legged jeans, waited for drinks to fuel up for the night. It was a twenty-something crowd. Now that we were in our thirties, we were on the older side of this scene, but neither of us wanted to give it up, maybe because that would have meant acknowledging losing something. Tye returned from the bar, stopping to talk with a guy who nodded enthusiastically while Tye yelled in his ear, then he joined me where I stood on the dance floor near the stage. It wasn't really a dance floor, no one danced; they just swayed. The Cradle only offered rows of chairs if it

49

was a folk crowd because the folkies liked to sit down. Beside me, Tye sipped his beer out of the red plastic cup until a girl slinking by bumped into us, and the beer sloshed across the front of both our shirts. He shook his head, took the sweatshirt from around his waist, and mopped off my chest, then his. Sometimes he got mad at that sort of thing, because he was protective of our space as a couple and had a chivalrous streak. But tonight he only glared at the girl silently, and she mumbled what might have been "sorry," though not loud enough over the din of the music for us to hear. The strumming on this number was long and hard. Slowly people began to sing; I knew the song too and the next one and the one after that, and then I began to smile.

"Glad we came?" Tye yelled.

I nodded. There was no point to talking, the sound was deafening now. I pointed to his ears, and he shoved his earplugs into place.

Tye used to talk about the silence in your head when you're listening to ear-deafening music wearing earplugs. Sometimes he took his out because he didn't like the sensation. He said it gave you a feeling of insularity, even when surrounded by others. The sound enveloped you, and after a while it was like you weren't even there, like you'd gone somewhere else, alone. At the close of the first set, the music receded near the end of a song, and I began to feel myself recede, rocking back and forth, standing in one place, everyone swaying to this slower, twangy song. Ordinarily I liked the feeling, but that night it made me feel sad.

At set break, Tye motioned that he was going backstage to help his buddy Eric. Most times I liked his comings and goings, but that night I felt adrift.

"Lisa's here," Tye said, when he joined me later. "Did you see her?"

She was leaning against the wall beside the pinball machines. Lisa was tall and slender, with short blond hair; her long legs were crossed at the feet, suggesting their illustrious length. Dressed in a smashing jumpsuit, she looked a fraction of her age, whereas I was feeling every inch of my age. I didn't feel like going over. She'd been spending a lot of time at ours lately, and I was beginning to feel she had become too much a fixture in our lives.

"Sar, what's wrong?"

"I think it's Ephraim," I deflected. "I tried all day to get him when I wasn't in the courtroom."

"Can you call him tomorrow?"

I nodded.

"Look, we're out; let's have a good time. Lisa!" he called out.

Lisa spun around. "Tye." She smiled broadly, and raised a brow coquettishly.

"Here, come on," Tye said. They began talking about the club that had just opened below one of the stores in downtown Chapel Hill. Lisa was still single and flirty with Tye, especially after a beer or two. Tonight I turned the other way and pretended not to notice. I checked my watch. It sounded like the music was starting up, and I was about to tug on Tye's sleeve.

But it wasn't music at all; shouting had erupted from the outside the club in the dark recesses of the back parking lot. Someone threw open the door, the sound of the door ricocheting off the inside wall. I wheeled around. Outside the club a tall guy was throwing fists heavily at a shorter, stockier man, who was ducking and swooping and, when he didn't move quickly enough, taking it on the jaw. You could hear the grunting, the sickening thud of fists against skin and bone. Sweat flew off them as they swung and dipped. It was still warm out that night and the humidity was high. The heat only added to the feeling of pressure, as the crowd forming around the men began to jeer.

"Jesus," I said, walking toward the door.

"Sara, wait."

"We should call the cops, Tye."

"Sara, it's a club – this stuff happens all the time." But we hadn't seen this ever at the Cradle. There was blood dripping from the shorter guy's face. He was slurring as he yelled, spitting between each blow. The last one was brutal; a string of blood spattered across the man's T-shirt.

Lisa towered behind me. "What's going on?"

"We should call the cops, don't you think, Lise?"

She furrowed her brow. Two attorneys and neither of us wanted to bring in the law. Then she sidled up next to Tye. The tall man grasped the short guy by his shoulders, picked him up and slammed him against the brick wall. His eyes bulged at the pressure, before he closed them.

"Jesus, somebody stop him!" I yelled.

The club owner flew through the open door. "Stop this fucking *shit*," he said. "Your ass is *never* coming back here if you don't stop, Jamie."

Jamie dropped back and the other man slid down the wall until he hit the ground.

Blood trailed along the brick wall behind him. I didn't recognize the tall man, but we knew the man he was beating up; he was a regular at the club. I stepped around the corner, pulled out my cell (not a lot of people had them then), and dialed 911.

Tye followed me around the corner. "It's over, Sara. There was no point to that."

"There is a point. I'm a public defender. I work in the law. I can't stand by and do absolutely nothing."

Siren wails lifted into the sky, dark and hazy from humidity. I smelled the mingling scents of magnolia and dumpsters. The air felt thick and I was sweating from the stress as well as the heat. I turned around and walked back into the club.

In the car ride home, as Tye took the curves too swiftly, I wasn't saying anything. I kept feeling uncomfortable about the way Lisa hung around Tye, how she had sidled up to him as the fight had begun. I pushed the image from my mind.

"Is he going to be okay?" I asked finally. "The short guy, the one we know."

"I doubt he had a concussion. He was probably just badly bruised." My husband's mouth was a solid line. "Look, you know what, that could have gotten really ugly. That's why I didn't step in," he said, defensively.

"I'm not blaming you, but it's not how I handle things. It's a professional issue. I'm a public defender – honestly, I shouldn't even be going to clubs." It was 2001, only weeks after 9/11, everyone over-sensitive about security and safety. We were all tense.

The car headlights traced low arcs across the windy road. Thin strips of land fog curled against leaves and trees and a thin speck of sky. I thought about the time growing up when we saw a boy fall and crack his head open after racing on his bike down the hill. We were in San Jose on the edge of Milpitas, when it was still country, decades before Silicon Valley grew up, and there were orchards everywhere. We were with our cousins, my brothers and me, hovering at a safe distance across the street until the ambulance and the boy's family arrived. A pool of blood stained the tarmac around the boy's head. His parents were there beside him, so he wasn't unaccompanied. But the boy didn't make it. He was the first kid we knew who died. Back then we were children, so no one expected us to call the ambulance. But I was an adult now and a public defender, and it was my job to intervene. The line between work and home life was already blurred on this case.

I was stressed at the prospect of a new trial, and I told Tye this. Susan Holeman wasn't likely to get off this time either and I knew it. I knew what I couldn't change.

"Sara, you're not going to win every battle."

Maybe it was the beer, maybe it was the fight we'd witnessed, or my irritation at his lack of backbone during the bar incident, but I couldn't hold back. "That's not the point, Tye. These kids will see their mother – when they see her – behind bars. That alone is damaging. One out of every four African American men is behind bars right now."

"You've told me that statistic a dozen times."

I sailed right over his comment. "And a case like this, where she's actually innocent, only adds to that statistic. These kids won't stand a fucking chance. And everything we're doing right now is not going to make a difference." I knew it already.

Tye's face was solemn.

"I can't just stand by and be an observer," I said.

He blinked. "So that's what we are – what we were tonight?"

"Yes, we were observers. We weren't taking action."

"Meaning, what? Meaning we didn't want to get caught in the crossfire so we're morally wrong?" He screwed up his face, like he didn't buy it. "I think you're being too critical," he said. "We were just out having some fun tonight. It's not a crime."

"No one said it was a crime. Just a question of taking a stand and not being afraid to get involved."

Tye was silent. The car swerved around the final bend before the road to our home.

I stared out the window. I'd never been an activist but I'd worked on immigrant rights in LA. And I believed in fairness. Tye seemed so disaffected.

It was more than that, though. I felt we were holding onto something it was time to let go of. "I guess we're in different places," I said. "I want to be starting a family – I want to be building our lives – not chasing down college life. Good Lord." We'd talked about kids the year before, the year after we married, but Tye said he didn't feel ready.

"Woah, how did we go from getting involved – or not – to having kids?"

The masked face of a raccoon appeared at the edge of the road, barely visible in a strip of fog. Then it shot across the road. "Tye, slow down – the raccoon!"

He swerved, then brought the car to a halt. "Don't scream like that, Sara. You'll land us in the ditch." He ran a hand over his face. "Jesus."

The raccoon scuttled into the woods, its tail trailing behind. Tye began to drive, the car tires humming against the road. I sat silent again.

"I'm not sure I want to be here raising a family, anyway," I said, finally.

He opened his eyes wide. "Where do you want to be? LA? You can't be thinking of LA?"

"I'm thinking of California, yes. But not LA."

"Albany? Don't say Albany... You're going to kill me."

I let out a short laugh. "No, north of there. Maybe more rural? But I do want to go home, Tye. I don't want to raise a family here." We'd discussed this before, but that night I felt homesick – some mix of Ephraim's twins, too much drink, and the Holeman case.

He pulled into our driveway. The old Mercedes had seen better days. It was gold-colored, but fairly beat up and

55

the seats were torn from his years in college. Pine needles lining the road crunched beneath the car; the scent was pungent as we stepped out. I felt myself shaking all over. Maybe it was stress, maybe it was the conversation. Tye pulled me toward him, leaned with me against the car. I was against his groin, could feel him beneath his jeans. It would have been midnight by now; Cat's Cradle would have just been taking off, but I'd insisted we come home early.

"I need to think about California," he said. "That's big."

"And the family?"

His smell of sweat, beer and deodorant mingled with the scent of pine needles. I nuzzled my head against his, wanting to feel closer, and pressed my chest against his, wanting to find some place where we were connected.

Tye paused. "It's a lot of change. Is it too much?"

"We'll be fine," I said, knowing he was getting close to yes, and feeling the smile spread across my face. I was a little drunk, in truth.

Tye leaned forward, pulled me by the arm into the hallway of our home, and began to kiss me deeply. I slid down against the wall; my hair caught briefly in the cloak rack behind me and Tye's elbow knocked the woodprint on the wall; it swung and nearly fell. We both started to laugh, then his kissing grew harder and deeper, and we began stripping away our clothing in what, for me at least, felt like an almost desperate act.

PART V

PETALUMA, CALIFORNIA
2004

Eight Years Ago

January 2004

Chapter Five

It was six months after we arrived West, and we had just survived our first rainy season. In Northern California the rain begins in early November, and the water drives down in full, unforgiving sheets. West County floods swiftly, easily, the clay soil balking in response to such steady rain. Standing water, surrounded by shoots of bright green grass, stretches for hundreds of feet on end, flanking the lower roads leading from Sebastopol to Petaluma. Bright sunlight rages for days after solid grey skies. We called it "monsoon season." Tye liked the weather, he said it felt like a taste of the East with its seasons, but I found it oppressive.

We were living in a rental, white-walled and carpeted, down a lonely road in Petaluma. Tye had secured IT work not long after we moved west in September 2003, though it meant a long commute to a job in Vallejo. Jacob had arrived with the rains, more or less on time, in early November. So this was new terrain, even for me: the baby, the place. We'd opted for the North Bay Area, because we both wanted to be out in the country, as we'd been in North Carolina. We'd even planted ourselves near an interstate on-ramp. We thought we'd done everything right. Although we'd left behind a decade worth of friends and, for me at least, a vibrant career, if somewhat checkered now.

Since leaving the PD Office, I wasn't thinking about my record-high wins, all the more improbable in light of the limited time we usually had to prepare our defense. I didn't think about all that. Instead, I fixated on cases I'd lost, the ones where I believed we'd get an acquittal, namely Susan Holeman's. The neighbor's testimony had been scant, as it turned out, and didn't constitute new evidence, so we'd not been able to reopen the case. Meanwhile, Susan had had an altercation in the mess hall at the medium-security prison, which meant early release was not looking like a strong option. Most days I tried not to think about the case, tried not to think of it as the unmitigated disaster it was.

In January we had a reprieve – at least in the weather. When the phone rang one morning, I expected it to be my mother. But it wasn't; it was Trish.

"So let me get this straight," she said. "You have been here six—"

"No, not quite six— "

"Okay, five months, and you have not called me? You have not even *told* me you were here? I know you're nursing, Sara, but really. Inexcusable." She had found out from a friend at Chapel Hill, who'd joined the PD Office in San Bernadino.

It was true; I hadn't told Trish about the move. The last time we'd spoken was when I'd called with the news about the appeal.

"Okay, yes. Bad," I said, feeling my heat rise. Jacob was napping. I stared out at the backyard, with its knee-high unmown grass, opened the back door and stepped out onto the porch. "Listen, I'm sorry. It's been hectic. The move, the birth…" She asked about the baby, but Trish had no children, only a niece and nephew.

"So do you miss it yet?" she asked.

"The PD Office?" I sputtered.

"Are you ready to go back? You can practice here. We have courts, too." She laughed. "You should have come to LA. We could have worked together."

I smiled at the thought. It was ten o'clock, and the fog was burning off. I shielded my eyes from the sun. I was six months out of the PD Office; I'd left two weeks before the move. It felt freakishly strange not to be working, but I wasn't ready to leave Jacob.

"Trish, he's three months old. It's too soon."

"When you're ready," she said, "call me. We'll get you through the California bar." I hung up the phone several minutes later. I wanted to be excited about that prospect, but oddly enough, I wasn't.

When the phone rang later that morning, I half expected it to be Trish, reminding me of where I belonged. But this time it was my mother. Ordinarily her tone was so even; generally, little fazed her. "Ah!" She inhaled sharply. "I just can't believe it."

"What?" I said, still in my robe, a product of my sleep deprivation, or so I wanted to believe. Jacob was in my arms and I had curled up with him on the sofa. After Trish's call, I ought to have recognized it for what it was: depression.

"It's Ephraim. He and Barley are separating." Ephraim was the brother I adored. And Barley – much as I hated her name, such a California name – I loved her. And they had three kids.

"Oh, Jesus. This can't be true!"

"It is, Sar." Her voice quivered.

Divorce had never registered in our family as it had in others we knew growing up in California. We lived in Albany, the poor sister of Berkeley, where all the families seemed to be breaking apart. My parents had hit rough spots; we'd heard some harsh fights through thin walls. But no fists were thrown. My mother's Catholic upbringing and my dad's Lutheran background, though they'd long since given up churchgoing by the time we came along, may have kept them from splitting. But I think it was tenacity. Divorces happened in everyone else's family, not in ours.

"No!" I pulled myself off the sofa and stared out the window aghast. "Is it final? Are they getting a divorce? I thought they were fine. Ephraim's always fine."

It was noon. Outside the leaves were in blossom, oak trees lining the road triumphantly, and it was full sunshine; everything about the day countered this news.

"This isn't happening."

"Sar, it is," my mother said.

"I'm phoning him."

"It's not going to make a difference. You can't insert yourself like that. Sar, I'm afraid this isn't about you."

She was right, of course.

"I'm horrified, that's all. I mean, that was the marriage that worked."

"Thanks, dear."

"No, I didn't mean that."

"What did you mean, then, Sara?"

"I meant in my generation, I meant among us. Larry's never held a relationship together for very long. And me..." I trailed off.

"And you? You're married," she said, defying the obvious. "You're holding it together."

"Yeah," I said, but even I wasn't totally convinced.

"Tye's a good man."

"Tye's a good man," I repeated, the ever-dutiful daughter.

A week after I spoke to my mother, I called Barley and she invited me down.

Ephraim and Barley's home was perched on a winding road, the house shoved into a hillside held up by retaining walls, deep into the Berkeley Hills. In fall, their yard was littered with leaves and Barley raked them religiously. On our visits back home from the East Coast, I often found her in the garden, but not today.

I pulled up into the driveway and loaded Jacob into the pack. Barley greeted me at the front door, mug in hand.

"Want some coffee?" she said. "Sorry, I forgot. Nursing." She gave me a hug, then twisted around me to see Jacob's face. "Gosh, he's beautiful. Enjoy this time," she said. "It's the best. Here, come on in."

"The place looks fantastic," I said. The house was Arts & Crafts and on the open market – in any market – would sell for a large sum. It was an Ephraim-style architect's home: you could see it in the order and tidiness and in the structure itself. He'd rebuilt portions of the house because of termites, yet it remained in its original form. He was gone at the office today – I knew this already – but I would at least be able to visit Barley.

We sat at the kitchen table, beside an island made of tile that had hanging pots above it, and baskets filled with onion and garlic, fresh fruits and vegetables. We could have been in *Architectural Digest* or an ad for Berkeley Bowl, the marketplace everyone raved about in the Bay Area. "Let's get you something to drink and then we'll go into the living room. I'll put something down, so that he can get out of the pack."

Barley dug into the closet under the stairs to find a quilt while I hovered in the kitchen. They had loads of kids' paraphernalia – toys that were foreign to me but I knew would become familiar over time. Barley was a pro at parenting. You could tell by the perfectly framed photos held up by magnets on the fridge: her boys as infants, then toddlers; Traci in pre-school; and then a host of professional photos, each child carefully groomed. Christmas photo cards from previous years, theirs and others. But the array was orderly and calm, like Barley. How do you take a life this orderly and calm and dissolve it? I wanted to know. Was it even possible? Why would she want to?

"I told Ephraim you were coming down and he wants

to come home for lunch," she said, when she emerged from the closet.

"He doesn't have to do that," I said, in surprise. It wasn't that I didn't want to see Ephraim; it just didn't fit with what I had in mind, this talking to each of them to learn what was going on and why.

She smiled a smile that told me absolutely nothing. My mother, of course, had been given no more information than anyone else. Jesus, they were close-lipped.

In the living room, Barley put down a series of quilts and blankets. "He can't go very far," I assured her.

"Yes, that's right," she said, as if distracted. Surely she knew this.

I pulled Jacob out of the pack and laid him on his belly, then excavated from the diaper bag a few cloth blocks for him to bat around. Barley and I curled up with my tea and her coffee on an overstuffed sofa beside him.

"You loving it?" she asked.

"Yeah, it's great."

"Miss work?"

"Not much." Well, I missed the PD Office, but I didn't miss the caseload, I told myself.

"That will come later. It doesn't come for a while – at least for me it didn't."

"Do you like having three?" I asked.

"You bet." She laughed. "Best thing I ever did. It's taken a while to get my work life back in order, but I'm there now. I love doing part time. Though, of course, that's going to have to change."

This was the first mention. "How do you feel about that?"

She shifted her weight on the sofa. "I think it'll work. I think it's the right time."

In the silence that followed, I stared at the mantelpiece,

where an oil painting of West County hung. "Is that a Brooks Anderson?" I asked. He was in the North Bay, and our aunt, Soti, and her husband liked his work a lot.

"Yeah," she said. "Soti gave that to us."

"Funny, I don't remember it."

"It used to be in our bedroom. I moved it out."

The items in her home, arranged with such care and delicacy, changed from room to room with such specific, if unexplained, reasons. But Barley had always been lean on words, and I found myself grateful that Ephraim would be joining us. Maybe I didn't know her as well as I thought. Maybe all those Christmas visits while living on the East Coast didn't, in the end, amount to building a friendship after all. Maybe my eleven years back East – the years in which Ephraim and Barley had married and had three children – counted for more than I knew.

Over lunch, while Jacob was napping, we three discussed the state of politics in California, the recent election of Schwarzenegger – a point of discussion for everyone, it seemed. They were polite, each of us asking someone else to pass a dish. Ephraim seemed so serious. I remembered his craziness, his spell of drug experimentation, before he knuckled down and went to Berkeley. He had the most outrageous laugh. As kids, he and Larry would chase me, one holding me down, the other spitting in my face, because I was the "poison baby" and they could get away with it. But that was thirty years ago, so why was I even thinking of it now? – though it was the last time we'd spent much time together. After high school, Ephraim went to Asia, where he became enamored of the shacks in the villages where he stayed. That was where his love of architecture began, in witnessing how structures supported people's lives.

As I passed him the plate of olives and cheese, I wondered about the structure they were in now, and what would happen if they didn't have their marriage intact. Wasn't their marriage – like this home – built to last?

Midway through lunch the phone rang. Barley started. Ephraim watched her from across the table. We were eating on their screened-in patio, beneath the twisted vines of the wisteria.

"Are you going to get that, Barley?" Ephraim asked archly.

We were mid-meal: reason enough not to pick up, perhaps.

Barley reddened, glanced at her watch, then shook her head. "No need," she said.

We returned to our meal, to the conversation about California politics and the budget stasis, but thereafter Ephraim picked at his food and stared not at his wife but at the door beyond her, the closed door leading to the inside of their home.

At the end of the visit, Ephraim walked us out. He took the steps slowly, surveying the yard, paying attention to the ferns draping over the walkway, stopping to pick up one of the twins' toys at his feet.

"Ephraim, what's happening?" I said.

"We're separating, Sara."

"Yeah, but why?"

"She fell in love. Barley's fallen in love with someone else."

A chill ran through me. "How, where?"

"Her work. It doesn't matter—"

"What do you mean, it doesn't matter? How can you say that?"

He stopped at the gate, pulled back the latch, examining that, too. "I meant it doesn't matter where she met the guy. She's not been happy for a long time."

"But maybe she's just not a happy person."

"Not so simple." He pursed his lips, sucked in a breath. "Are you okay?"

"What do you think?" His eyes were still, the irises gone deeper and darker now that we were outside.

"Oh, Ephraim." I put one hand against his arm, which I could barely feel beneath the jacket. It was as if he'd physically retreated. "I'm devastated – for you."

"Yeah, I'm devastated for me, too." He let out a short bitter laugh.

"Does she really love him?"

"She says she loves him, *thinks* she loves him. You know, the usual. But who do we ever really love? I think it's her way out, that's how I've been trying to see it."

We slipped out the gate and down the short steep driveway. His face was grim; his cheeks, clean-shaven, looked deflated in the harsh January light. He picked up a wide blade of grass and split it with his thumbnail again and again.

"Are you going to go to counseling?"

"We have. Didn't help."

I inhaled sharply. "Can I help in any way?"

"I don't think so, Sara. I'm going to get an apartment closer to work, walking distance. She'll stay here for now, and we'll sort it. Somehow." His voice went flat; the animation at lunch had vanished. Everything in his life intact, but this.

Driving home across the Richmond Bridge, I took in its structure and noticed how carefully it had been put in place, one steel girder at a time. The car bounced comfortably over each stretch of pavement, until we reached the base of the Marin side of the bridge and dropped hard into potholes that had grown severe, the cement railing crumbling in spots. The decline in California's infrastructure was staggering. I hadn't come home to the same place. At least the sun was out and the Bay now alive, but its surface was a steely blue sheen because the air was so still. The radio was on low. Jacob had fallen asleep, and so I gave myself something I hadn't allowed myself since coming home: permission to cry.

We were at breakfast the following Sunday. Tye was eating his scrambled eggs and I sat in front of my half-eaten plate, with Jacob at my breast. I couldn't stop talking about Ephraim.

"You can't be serious, Sara?" Tye said.

I'd just proposed that we spend more time with Ephraim and Barley.

"What kind of difference is that going to make?" He reached for another croissant. We couldn't have the lifestyle – we were after all living in a semi-rural duplex – but we could have the food at least.

"I want us to be a support."

"What, you think we'll end up convincing her she loves him after all? Or this new guy is some sort of disaster? Does anyone know anything about him anyway? Who knows, maybe he's more *perfect* than Ephraim. Maybe he earns more *money* than Ephraim." He laughed. Tye was from Maine. To him, everything out here seemed to be about the money.

"I didn't mean that."

"Then what did you mean?"

"Emily says that church and family keep marriages together. He doesn't have church. We're family. Do you not see the logic?"

Jacob gagged at my breast, the flow of milk too plentiful. I pulled him up onto my lap, faced him forward and patted his back. Tye threw him a wry glance, then leaned over to wipe off the table.

"Yes. But…" he said.

"What?"

"What if it isn't right for them to stay together? What if this is the right thing?" He looked past me, his eyes focusing on some distant point.

"Divorcing? You can't be serious. They have three kids, Tye. How on earth can this be the right thing?"

He got up to pour himself another cup of coffee. "What if they simply aren't happy? What if," he said, leaning back against the counter, crossing his arms, "What if it's not the right person? Sometimes, people don't marry the right person."

In a flash, I remembered my dream from the night before: we were out on the Outer Banks, not Wilmington, where Lisa's house was. And Tye was running down the beach after her, sand kicking up in his wake. I shuddered, blinking up at him.

"What?" He shifted onto his other leg.

Why could I not stop thinking about Lisa and Tye?

I paused to scrape the remains of the cereal from the bottom of the bowl, and began to feed my son again. "They ought to have figured that out before kids, no? They should *make* it work. And can she even afford to divorce him?" He had forgotten I was an attorney; I always thought in terms of defending my client. I had appointed myself not just my brother's defense but Barley's. "She's a social worker, Tye. California will kill her. She's going to die on the vine out here on her own."

May 2004

Chapter Six

Several months later, I called my mother and told her I wanted to come visit with Jacob. She hadn't seen Jacob in a few weeks.

She hesitated. "I have an appointment," she said.

"Then I can take you to the appointment."

"Okay," she said, still reluctant. "But it's a follow-up appointment. You need to know that."

My mother sat beside me quietly in the car, content to be a passenger. She held a Kleenex in her hand and occasionally twisted it. "They've done a biopsy," she told me as we drove to Kaiser Permanente. "It's come back positive. A tumor on my liver, and no, I don't want to talk about it."

I felt my stomach drop. "When?" I asked. "When did you learn this?"

"A few days ago." Then, after a long silence, she said, "I'm sorry you came home to this."

"Mom—"

"No, I mean it. It should be a celebratory time with Jacob's arrival, and because of my health it's not, and that's not right. It troubles me." She studied me from the passenger seat.

She'd been to Kaiser for a check-up within weeks of our arrival and learned she had a growth, but hadn't made the follow-up appointments until now. She had told me none of this. "You were still settling in," she explained, "and then there was the birth, and then I had to get past the holidays…" It was impossible to get angry; God knows, I'd just done the same thing to Trish, not updating her on my own developments. But the delay – let alone the news – troubled me. I focused on the driving.

I knew the roads to Kaiser – these were the roads Larry, Ephraim, and I had biked to get to El Cerrito Plaza. When we were old enough, we rode there daily. Now, in its new street-facing storefront style, the Plaza might have reeked of gentrification except the re-model was too poorly done, each storefront a carbon of its neighbor. It was nothing like I remembered: it had been retro for years through the early Seventies, its Fifties architecture outmoded, the Capwells' sign hanging above the central portion of the outdoor mall like a carnival entrance. Now, as we sped past, the Plaza seemed overshadowed by BART, just beside it. A train raced overhead, a wave of late commuters flooded the BART station entrance. I'd never commuted here; so much felt foreign to me coming back now.

"Well, at least I can be here for this," I said, finally.

"Are you glad? Are you really?" She eyed me.

"I am. Shell-shocked maybe," I said. "But, yes, I am glad to be here." We bounced over several speed bumps. I slowed so Jacob wouldn't wake. They had put these in before local services took their first dive in the late 1970s. I could never remember what streets to drive to avoid them. I stopped at the red light, waiting.

My mother stared straight ahead. "How is it being home with Jacob? Do you miss the PD Office?"

"Yes and no. It was pretty grueling."

"You won a lot as I recall."

I smiled.

"What happened with that case?"

"The Broadman one?" I asked. It was a case involving mental health issues on the part of my client and had proved really complex. It had been a spectacular win.

"No, I don't mean that one. You know, the one you worked on for so long."

I blinked. "The Susan Holeman case? We lost."

"But what happened to the appeal?"

"Lost it." I grimaced.

A wave passed over my mother's face. "Oh, Sar. Why?"

I didn't much want to talk about it. We'd just pulled onto San Pablo Avenue. The traffic here was denser than Sonoma County, let alone North Carolina, and I had to pay attention. But that was only part of my reason. Losing the Susan Holeman case still stung.

"It's complicated," I said. "We tried to appeal, but in North Carolina those appeals are tough. Once a decision's handed down it takes an act of God to reverse it, Mom. We were in the wrong state."

"Is this the right state?" My mother's brow smoothed again. "It is, right? You're taking the bar here, right?"

I laughed. "I'm taking a break. I want to be home – at least for a while."

"And you should. I only meant—"

The job market had bounced back after the recession in 2001, but my mother wasn't the only one who didn't trust the economy. She pointed at the broad expanse of pavement beside the massive structure of Kaiser Permanente. "Right here."

I followed her directions, but something in her tone alarmed me.

The nurse drew my mother's blood and I sat beside her and told her about the time they drew blood during the pregnancy and I thought I was going to faint. That started us on sonograms, and I told her about the first one when I lied to the physician and said I could make out Jacob's scrawny little body, but I couldn't see a damn thing, and then the second, when I was certain I could see his penis. I called it his "weenie"; that made her laugh. Then we both laughed,

71

and I felt a kind of visceral relief. Jacob didn't understand what we were saying, of course, but laughed with us all the same. And then she talked about all three of her pregnancies, while the nurse now taking her vitals smiled.

My mother's face was thin but the cheeks held vigor still. Her eyes were solid in color, unflinching in the directness of their gaze. She had a way of extracting anything I might withhold; as a child I had learned the art of minimal disclosure to avoid my brothers' playful tortures. She was loving, mostly, but demanding, ever insistent we take the right stance. Her mind was sharp and feeling, but unsentimental; she would have made a brilliant lawyer. She accepted nothing less than absolute truth; I often felt less than honest in her presence because, by contrast, she was so utterly true to herself. The day I called to say I wanted to be an attorney, she had laughed.

"*What*?" I said, incredulous at her response.

"I always knew you would be a lawyer. You were way too smart for anything else. Thank God you figured that out. It's about time." My mother had passed up nursing for social work – a rare choice at the time – later settling for work at the local bank. I knew she felt she might have done something more.

I held her free hand now, as she and the nurse spoke. She needed another sample; she said she hadn't taken enough. My mother frowned. "Can I give you the other arm, at least?" she said, not hiding her irritation at all. The light poured down from a skylight, eclipsing my mother's face. The needle jabbed her and she winced. The nurse stepped out of the room.

"You okay?" I asked. Her legs twined round one another, my mother looked almost like a child. I thought of her mother, wondering about the mother she had been, and what kind of comfort she had given. Or conversely not.

72

"Yes," she said, through a thin line of a smile. "They have a way of poking. It's just a vein, though. I'm sure they do this, what, three hundred times a day?"

We waited more than forty-five minutes for the doctor. My mother sat on the edge of the table in a blue hospital gown with her thin ankles exposed. The paper cloth of the gown made a whirring sound as she swung her legs, gazing around the room absently at the skeletal chart, the blood pressure tips, and the health report postings. It smelled of disinfectant and the rubber gloves the technician had tossed in the bin. I leaned forward in my seat, Jacob in my arms, trying to keep our conversation going. I wanted to be cheerful. I felt anything but.

The prognosis was good, the doctor said. Six weeks of chemotherapy, then a break for recuperation, then another six weeks of radiation – if she was responding well to treatment. "These tumors shrink all the time," he said, as if we were discussing the laundry, not my mother's health. I took notes and jotted down terms I would research – later. He left the room, his white jacket trailing behind as he escaped. Closing the door created a vacuum and a gust of air blew in; my mother's gown trembled. She changed with her back to me, pulling her slacks over her hips. I noticed the rounding of her shoulders, the curvature in her spine reflecting the daily bend of parenting and the long hours spent standing at the bank. The doctor knocked on the door and we followed him into a small room with white walls and a single desk shoved in the corner; on its surface files were piled and clipboards scattered. We sat in two chairs tucked in beside the desk, my chair so close to his our legs might have touched had I shifted the direction of mine. I was struck by the intimacy of the moment, as he began detailing the particulars of my mother's condition and the treatment, and yet he had not bothered to close the door, or perhaps it wouldn't close with all three of us in there. Above us the neon light glared; the room stank of leftover cafeteria food. He stood up, set his knee on the chair, and reached for a chart outlining the standard treatment schedule, hanging on a nail above the table. I held my mother's hand as he spoke. Now I was the one sitting on the edge of my chair, with Jacob remarkably calm and quiet, in my lap. As the morning wore on, exhaustion had begun to make the base of my neck tingle. I felt a wave of sadness thinking about the poking and prodding and radiating that was to come.

"It sounds worse than it is," the physician said.

My mother, sitting straight up in her seat, smirked. "Sounds worse than it is, eh? Easier to say where you sit, no? I want *your* job," she said.

He pursed his lips, fighting back a smile. His smooth wave of brown hair was flecked with grey. He was efficiently handsome; his gold cufflinks glinted in the neon lighting. He had a thin gap in his front teeth, and I liked him for that, for this slight imperfection.

"Mom…" I said.

He smiled. "It's okay. You're right," he said. "That is easier for me to say. And you know, it's better that you say that. This isn't a time to mince words."

"Okay," she said. "Then I won't. I don't have coverage for this. I don't have full coverage any longer."

I gasped.

"We changed our policy last year," she said. Her voice faltered. "It's a catastrophic plan."

He pulled his knee off the seat and dropped into the chair, his knee grazing mine. I flinched.

"Then some of this treatment will have to be out of

pocket," he said. "I'm sorry. I can't help you with this. You'll have to talk to billing."

I waited until we were back in the car. While she strapped in, I stared out the window at a thread of bougainvillea that danced up the redwood arbor in the lot. "I understand why you didn't say anything after we arrived. I get why you didn't mention it while we were moving," I said, "because I was pregnant. You hadn't gotten the biopsy yet. But the insurance? Why didn't you tell me that you'd gone to the catastrophic plan? We could have helped you out, Mom." Both Tye and I were working then; we could easily have made up the gap, even without stretching financially. I would talk to Ephraim; he and I would need to subsidize her coverage.

My mother said nothing, only held her lips firm.

I turned on the engine to open the car windows and let out a sigh as I scanned the bougainvillea. I stuck my arm out the window to catch the breeze.

"I'm sorry," I said. Because I knew I shouldn't have said it.

"Your father's heartsick. Believe me."

"Is this why he's working still at seventy-two?" My mother was sixty-seven; she, at least, was retired from the bank.

"No," she said, "it's because of the property tax."

"You've owned the house for years, since before Prop 13. Your taxes are frozen, how can it be the property tax? You've got Social Security."

She laughed. "It's not enough, Sar. It sounds strange," she said, "because we've worked hard our whole lives. It's very expensive here – it's the housing. But I guess you're beginning to figure that out." She looked over at me with a curl of a smile. She knew we were trying to buy, and that it felt out of reach.

75

Yes, I thought, it is expensive, and costing more every minute.

That night, Tye was pulling off his clothes as I talked – about the diagnosis, about the treatment. I had held it together during the day, but now I was crying.

"Have they isolated the tumor?" he asked. Matter of fact.

When he was down to his socks, I said, "Tye, this is my mother…"

He glanced up at me and blinked. "You don't know enough yet," he said.

"Don't know enough to be… what? Assured she won't die?"

He pulled off the other sock. Why was my husband at the other end of the room, futzing with his threadbare cotton socks?

He came over to me in his boxers, held my hand and put his other hand on my leg. I could feel his warmth through my nightgown but it felt a mile away. "Sara, it is going to be okay. They've caught it pretty early."

"Yes, they caught it early, but she sat on it for months before the follow up." I shook my head. "Good Lord. I cannot believe this."

He started to say something, then stopped, stared over at our dresser where the mirror caught a reflection of us both. I could see the thinness of his cheeks. I felt like crap at how hard he was working and that Jacob was so wakeful still.

He sighed, loudly. "Here is the really good news," he said.

"And?"

"We're here. We could be in North Carolina still."

I had thought about this earlier in the day. "Yes, but she's still got a tumor."

"Yes, and you'd be flying across the country – it'd be a nightmare."

"Okay… So that is a point of comfort, I *guess*."

I studied his face, every inch of it. The creases beside his thin lips. The birthmark above his left eyebrow. I knew every corner of this man, I had thought. How had I not known that he lacked the essential capability to comfort?

I shivered.

He reached back for my thigh or maybe it was my shoulder. He held me briefly, gave me a kiss on my forehead, and said, "Sar, let's go to sleep."

I spent the next few days on the phone with my mother and then Medi-Cal and Medicare, and finally Trisha, whose law practice was devoted to assisting the under-privileged. Though she dealt largely with immigrants, Trish knew virtually all the resource organizations in the state. "I don't think you're going to find a way around this, Sara," she said, between phone calls to clients. "Yes, contact these orgs. But your mother is not, technically speaking, in desperate enough straits. They are just resourced enough. It doesn't seem fair, I know, but it's true. Your folks are going to have to pick up some cost. You can always plead charity, but it won't necessarily work."

Several things happened that summer that changed the tenor of my relationship with Barley. I suppose it served one purpose, fixating on my brother and sister-in-law: it kept my focus off my own marriage, not to mention my mother's health.

Barley called a few weeks later and said she'd like to come up. Why not? I thought. She was still in the family, after all. I needed to accept the situation. My mother was right, about that at least. Her treatments hadn't yet begun, so I would not be on the road to the East Bay. I told Barley it was a good time to visit.

"I figured we'd throw Jacob in the pack and go for a walk," she said, when she arrived. "I brought one of ours, a proper baby backpack. I can pop it in your trunk."

"Great idea," I said, and then gathered together some snacks for us.

"Can he manage those?" Barley stood over me as I sliced grapes and chunks of cheese and avocado at the kitchen counter. She scanned the four-burner electric stove, solid-state fridge, and pine cupboards, wiping out the twin-stainless sink after me. Barley didn't mean to suggest inadequacy, but her tone often implied it.

"He'll be fine. Mostly, *I'm* lunch," I said – I was still nursing. We both laughed.

We drove to a local park in Sebastopol. The breeze had come up, the air cool in this part of West County, only eight miles from the ocean. But it was still eighty degrees out and the windows were down since we didn't have air conditioning in our car. I cast sidelong glances at Barley as we drove, watching as her silver locks whipped around her face.

Barley was forty-something and wore her hair in a bob that met her angular shoulders. She was tall and very pretty in an exotic way; dark olive skin against her silvery hair. She had a wide-open smile and was generous with it, and her face was expressive, especially when she talked about her work, which was often. Today she was laughing and seemed freer. I wondered what had transpired to lighten her load.

We pulled into the parking lot. Barley slipped out of the passenger side and helped load Jacob in the backpack. "It's a little worn now, but it's still got a few more years," she said, showing me where to strap him in. "We don't have any use for it anymore." Was that line of thinking what ended her marriage?

The park boasted a "Peace Circle," and we headed in its direction. The path led through rocks and native plants to a bench made of redwood with a cast-iron base in the shape of a trunk. It was mid-June and the sun, even at 10:30 in the morning, was blazing hot. We took out our snacks and sandwiches, and drank Honest Tea in bottles, chilled from my icepack. She was in a thin dress with Keen sandals (everyone wore them, it seemed), her tanned legs crossed. Jacob was out of the backpack and on my lap. She slid him onto hers and fed him bits of avocado and Trader Joe's O's cereal as we chatted about the climate in Sebastopol and West County. She asked about my mother, and I told her the treatments were scheduled to begin next week. And then she said, as if we'd already been talking about this for some time, "So Ephraim has told you, right?"

"About?"

"About my friend."

I had to stifle a smile. Friend seemed a bit of an understatement. "Yes."

"It isn't what you think."

Did she know what I was thinking? I waited.

"Are you okay talking about this?" she asked.

I nodded. I ought to have said no. But she'd just driven an hour and a quarter, a significant commitment.

She had met him at a conference six months ago. He was in her field and working in similar areas of social work; they were both interested in "evidence-based practice," which was just taking hold of the field, she said. They spent time together at the conference – "you know, together not romantically, just as colleagues" – then ran into one another on the street in San Francisco on a home-based visit. "I didn't go looking for this, Sara," she said.

Ah, so that makes it all right? I thought.

Jacob was finished eating, standing up against my legs and had begun foraging and popping acorns into his mouth. I suggested we get moving. We left the "Peace Circle" and took a trail that wound through blackberry bushes not yet in fruit to the marsh, except it was now summer and the clay soil had dried up. Buttercups were still in bloom and Queen Anne's Lace – on the East Coast, that's what it would be called; here it was Yarrow. Bees buzzed around us; I scanned the bushes for an active hive, while she rattled on about this man and how she'd not intended to fall in love. I kept thinking, *Does she not remember this is my brother?*

His name was Elijah Griffin. Griffin was not his last name. "He likes to go by both given names," she said, as if this would make me like him more.

"Do you love this man, Barley? This Elijah—?

"Elijah Griffin—"

"Elijah whatever. Do you really love him? Or has he just shown up at a hard time in your marriage?"

She stopped. "For about a year before I met him, Sara, I'd been thinking to move out. I wanted to be alone." Her silver hair glinted in the sun. "I had this fantasy of living absolutely alone—"

"I don't know if I can hear this right now," I said.

Barley kept walking and I trailed after her. The blackberry trail had gone narrow, making it increasingly difficult to walk through. I had to push the brambles away and then make sure they didn't swat Jacob as I passed through them. Barley was silent.

No, I realized, she wasn't thinking of Ephraim as my brother at all. Even those words hurt, saddened me: she wanted to leave her children as well as my brother. Does he even know who she is? I wondered. *Do we ever really know someone else? Or do we just think we do?*

"Why? Why did you want to live on your own?" I said, finally. "I don't get it, Barley. I really don't get it."

She picked up her pace, squinting into the sun. The corners of her mouth turned down. "You don't know this now, Sara," she said, tersely. "You are early into it. But it gets harder. It does. You love your family but it's exhausting, too. Welcome to the world of exhaustion," she said, with a weak smile.

I held Jacob's foot in my hand as I walked to keep contact, or to cool myself down. I wanted to hate Barley for breaking my brother. But as the brambles grabbed at her ankles, nearly tripping her up, I couldn't. She was confused fifteen years into her life with Ephraim. She'd met him while they were at Berkeley. She had been all of twenty-five.

"You okay, Sara?"

"I'm fine," I said. But I wasn't. It was impossible to be fine in the face of my sister-in-law's confession that she'd wanted out for such a long time. "Did you not love him, Barley? Ephraim's a good man," I said, sadly.

"I know he is," she said. "I just wish I still loved him."

We emerged from the path, the last bramble catching at my hair. We had arrived back at the "Peace Garden." I did not miss the irony of its name at this moment.

Barley stopped. She swung around to face me. "Are you really okay, Sar?"

I was relieved to be out in the open again, but I wasn't wild about my sister-in-law's question.

"No, Barley. I'm not. How can I be okay with this? Ephraim is my *brother*. This kills me, this kills *us*. All of us."

Barley's mouth settled into a solid line. We stood there in silence; a hawk circled above us, as if searching for its prey.

"You are not okay with the truth then? What is your truth, Sara? Is yours anywhere," she swept one hand in front of her, as if pointing to the native plants surrounding us, "here? You have never felt something for someone else in the course of your marriage? Never?" She stared me down. The sun was beating down on me. I blinked to keep the rays from my eyes. Or to avoid her stare. Or both.

I paused.

"You have," she said, triumphant.

I wasn't about to mention my colleague Jay at the PD Office back in Raleigh. Or the attraction I felt, however briefly, at a play group just last week. I wasn't going to say a thing. I would not admit to Barley that I, too, was flawed.

That night I waited up for Tye. I'd done the washing up and mopped the kitchen floor, each sweep of the mop leaving behind a tidemark of dust and cookie crumbs. Upstairs I pulled clothes from around the room, picked up socks and T-shirts from the bathroom floor, and dropped them in the bin. It was midnight.

The front door opened. I could hear him drop his briefcase. Footsteps into the kitchen. The creak of the fridge door. And then I heard the sound: the pop of the beer bottle. I didn't worry about his drinking then; it really wasn't a lot. Not compared to his dad. Tye's father had been an alcoholic, although he managed to keep his post at Bowdoin, the small private college where he taught on the Maine Coast. Tye had told me stories about the isolation: his father shutting himself up in his home office for hours, emerging only to bark instructions at Tye; his mother pretending as if nothing at all was wrong. She ran a small sewing concern out of the house, a cottage industry, which she busied herself with even when Tye was home. When Tye came back from school each day, he might have been a latchkey boy. Everyone home, but nobody present. He had adapted, but he'd done so by making the solitude a part of himself.

I went out into the hallway to check on him. "You doing okay?" I was in my nightgown, leaning against the doorsill. But he said, "No, I'm not okay. I've been laid off."

I dropped into a seat at the kitchen table. "Oh, Jesus. You have got to be kidding."

"I wish I was."

"What on earth happened?"

"Vallejo's going down," he said. "Tele-com overnight, bust-town tomorrow."

"Really." My breath left me. I wasn't sure what to say. I went over to him and took him in my arms. He didn't cry, although I believed he had a right to.

"I hope your day was better?" he said, with a laugh.

"Only slightly."

"Barley whining about your brother and what a dick he is?"

"Tye—!"

"A joke, Sara. Joking!" He took a swig of his beer, wiped his mouth, and then took the chair opposite mine at the table. "I've got to find humor in something. This is bad, Sar. Really bad."

"When? Is it effective today?"

"In three weeks."

"Not a lot of notice."

"No," he said.

"Are they giving you severance?"

"Two weeks."

"Two weeks!" I heard the clock ticking in the background; the duplex's electric stove had the loudest ticking clock on earth. "It's high-tech, Tye. They can't do that."

"They can, they *are*."

"I thought they gave real severance packages."

"Apparently not. Not anymore."

83

I felt this heaviness in my belly. I put my face in my hands. "Oh, Jesus."

"I will get a job, Sara."

"I know you will. But I ought to have studied for the bar. I should have done it. We wouldn't be this vulnerable if I had."

He glared at me.

"No, I didn't mean that. It's just, I should – it would be wise." We'd been sitting on the nest egg from the sale of our home in North Carolina; and throwing money away on rent sat uncomfortably with us both. Two incomes would be the only way we could buy, eventually, but would it even be enough?

Tye said nothing, only got onto the computer, his neck and shoulders hunched over like an eagle's. This was the man who loved birds: my birder-husband, looking as if he'd morphed into one, overnight. I lay in bed listening to the ticking of the clock and the clicking of the keyboard as he searched the job listings and shot emails to his work friends on the West Coast. He stayed on for the remainder of the night, while I stared at the long crack in our bedroom ceiling. Moving west, had it been wise? I remembered suddenly our arrival at the airport, the poster with the message, as we passed idly by on the walking escalator toting our luggage and my pregnant belly: YOUR HOME IS NOT AN INVESTMENT. Although everyone treated it as if it were. Perhaps that ought to have been our first clue that the cost of housing was driving every part of this economy.

At the weekend, Tye and I took a walk at the Peace Circle in Sebastopol, where Barley and I had spent the afternoon earlier in the week. The sunlight was glorious; the ocean breeze had kicked in, bringing with it smells of honeysuckle and a faint, tenuous scent of eucalyptus. We were no more than eight or nine miles from the coast.

"We should go birding sometime, don't you think?" I said, staring out toward West County, with its cascade of unbroken hills, valleys tethered by vines. He nodded. Tye took my hand as we walked; Jacob slouched in the pack against my chest, sleeping easy and untroubled. High above a hawk flew and swooped, pivoted and circled again.

The blue sky arcing overhead, wide and unimpeachable, seemed to offer a promise of a kind, as if in response to the precarious moment we now found ourselves in. I wanted to locate some part of this place that might offer solace to us both. The outdoors anywhere here, I had come to find, helped to strengthen my resolve that we could make this work, all of it – in spite of my mother's crisis, in spite of the tilting economy.

"Do you love it here? Any part of you?" I asked, as we approached the blackberry brambles. I was seeking validation that we had not leveraged ourselves beyond repair. I pushed past the brush, sheltering Jacob's head from the brambles as they sprung back.

Tye had sped ahead of me, while I focused on the stone walkway, stepping from one worn slab to the next, the weight of Jacob's pack swinging unevenly as I strode. Before us the playground, its wooden-beam structure towering above a mix of wood chips and dust, lay abandoned by the last family that had vacated it. I spied an empty black-plastic seat and veered toward it.

Tye, still wandering in the opposite direction, spun around once he realized we were no longer behind him. He circled back. Standing above me, he said, "It is beautiful, Sar." I had dropped quietly into the swing with Jacob pressed solidly against me. Staring up at my husband, a small smile had returned to my lips.

85

July 2004

Chapter Seven

Over the next three weeks, Tye spent until late into the night, every night, trying to secure another job. Tye's father had always worked hard, too, despite the alcohol problem. My husband's hours remained the same. He wouldn't slack off; in a way, I respected him for that. But a crisis only made him retreat further from us.

One Saturday morning we drove to the base of Mount Tam, where Priuses and SUVs lined up side-by-side in the hard-packed dirt parking lot. There were just a few cars in the lot; it was early yet and still foggy and the pine trees, jagged and carved from years in the wind, hovered at the edges. Tye got out first to extract our packs from the trunk. I stretched my back, hanging on the car above the door, staring at my old tattered boots. A black, four-wheel drive Subaru pulled in beside us. The door swung open and a tall man with strapping shoulders and curly hair sprang out of the driver's seat. He threw me a brilliant toothy smile, a devilish I-want-to-fuck-you grin. I knew that face, and shuddered when I saw him. The passenger door flew open, the side closest to me, and a tall thin woman, her blonde hair pulled back in a ponytail, emerged, her designer backpack in hand. She lifted her gaze toward the man she'd arrived with, then at me, with a flat, almost unkind expression on her face.

"Don't I know you?" The man called over to me.

Tye slammed the back of the trunk, with our worn daypack in one hand, and the older-style backpack, given to us by Barley, in the other. Tye cleared his throat, confused.

"*Do* you, Sara?"

I paused. "The play group. At the Sebastopol public library that day."

"Right," the man said from across his car. "That's right. The theatre group I told you about." He said to his wife. "Up in Sebastopol."

I'd met him at a library event I attended the day after the Kaiser visit. When I'd told Emily about him, she said, "Hey, if you don't want to eat the chocolate cake, girlfriend, you got to put it out of the house. Don't go back." I hadn't.

"Ah," the woman said, eyeing me up and down. I dropped my gaze instantly, feeling as though I'd brought on his unexpected attention again. I was in my mom jeans, in a pullover sweater; I couldn't have looked less sexy. She straightened, arching her back. Her sweatshirt fell to her neckline, revealing her scoop T-shirt, her taut skin tanned against a thin layer of tasteful silver necklaces. "Beat you to the top," she said, with a wry grin. They slipped on their backpacks, unstrapped their mountain bikes from the back of their shiny Subaru, and pulled on their helmets. As he mounted his bike at the head of the trail, he flashed me one last smile.

Tye was strangely silent as we headed out of the parking lot. But then he said, "That was odd. You know, I want to like these people around here more than I do. But everyone is just so… fey. Don't you think?"

I agreed, and wondered why I'd ever found the man attractive.

We climbed the ascent. The smell of sage was pungent in the damp morning air. It was windy and we put on our windbreakers, Jacob in a knock-off Land's End jacket I'd gotten online in their discount area. We were shopping smart already, with a week to go until Tye's two-week severance

87

kicked in. Tye was walking ahead, Jacob bouncing in the backpack behind him. At nine months he was getting more rambunctious daily. Jacob was tugging on his father's hair, and Tye kept shrugging him off. I loved Jacob's playfulness, but Tye found his mischievousness irksome. To keep him from ungluing at Jacob, I tried to get conversation going, but he didn't answer; he simply shrugged his shoulders, spun around, and continued up the hillside.

I followed after, and for twenty minutes we walked in silence to the top. Then we stopped for lunch. We dropped the backpack and placed our blanket across scrubby patches of grass, wildflowers catching at the edges, and over the hard ground. Now that the sun was out, the ground was dry again. While Tye minded Jacob, tracking him around bushes to ensure he wasn't racing toward any cliffs, I put out our sandwiches and we began to eat. Jacob scrunched his face and started tossing his food across the blanket. Tye tried to stop him, but Jacob began to flick a chunk of bagel with his foot, taunting his dad.

"Jacob, settle, sweetie," I said.

"He's not settling, Sar." He grabbed his son by the arm and shook it slightly. Jacob took the bait, leaned forward against his father's shoulder and with a wry, almost mean grin, yanked his dad's hair.

"Stop that, Jake!" Tye said, and then slapped his hand, hard.

Jacob recoiled and began sobbing instantly.

"Tye, what was that about? You don't slap him." I leaned over to Jacob and pulled him over to me.

Tye's face darkened.

"He's a child – he's an *infant*," I said. "What are we modeling? Not to mention, it's just blessedly unkind." I thought about Tye's father and his harshness toward him, inhaled sharply at the thought of it.

"And what are you doing now, Sara? What kind of modeling is that? I reprimand him and you cut me down?"

"But it's not okay to just hit him."

Jacob stopped crying and was looking from one of us to the other, not fully understanding, but clearly knowing he was the subject of our discussion.

"Were you hit? Did your parents hit you?" I asked. "Mine didn't hit me, I'll tell you that." I set down my tuna sandwich, knocking my apple juice over my pant leg. "Dang." I shook my head. I was tired. It had been another late night. Tye wanted us to start having Jacob "cry it out" – but I didn't want to – and we hadn't resolved the disagreement.

"Occasionally, yes. When I was out of line, not hit. But spank. An idle spank on the bottom."

I sighed. "Jacob is angry at you. He is angry because you are gone a lot."

Tye stopped chewing. "And I *am* gone a lot, Sara. I'm earning a living."

I knew I was fragile: from lack of sleep, from my mother's first appointment yesterday, from what Tye had just done to our son. Sure, it was just a slap. But it was just so unneeded. "I understand that. I do. I don't fault you that. But he's your son, and he looks to you to be there for him, not against him." I picked up my son, tossed him over my shoulder to get him to laugh, and went to the edge of the clearing to stare out across the Bay. Everything seemed thin at that moment: the last of the fog, the stretch of Bay Bridge arching across the solid blue-grey surface of the water. A line of cars, tiny grey objects, floated in a narrow strip across the bridge. Flecks of white marked the caps on the water; and in the distance lay the uneven lines of the Berkeley Hills.

I felt Tye come up behind me. He reached a hand

toward his son, who recoiled. But he kept at his son, tickling first his ear and then his foot. Tye won him back; and Jacob let his father stroke his hair finally.

That afternoon, while Tye was back on the job search, I went down to see Emily. I told him we'd clear out for the afternoon so he could focus. But I felt the need too for a visit with Emily. We hadn't talked in months; she knew about the job loss – I'd sent her an email – but we'd not had a conversation. She was my closest friend. I told her things weren't going well with Tye, but I didn't tell her he'd slapped our son that morning.

"It's the job loss, right?" Emily said.

We'd been sitting the last hour in an alcove in her kitchen, talking about her kids, gone at summer camp for the day. Jacob was asleep in the other room; miraculously, he'd not woken when I transferred the car seat into Emily's living room.

Emily had been in Law School with me but had dropped out, and then moved to the Bay Area ten years earlier. She'd known she didn't want to be a lawyer; she went back into public policy, before taking a few years out to raise her kids. She had a terrific marriage to a man who climbed mountains in his spare time; they ran a bike shop – a successful one – in the Bay Area. They went on exotic trips, and always seemed to be in unison on their decision-making – unlike, I was beginning to feel, my husband and me.

"He's just lost his job. It's got to feel horrid," Emily said. She stared at me over the mug. Emily blinked her eyes slowly; she had a way of gazing so directly at you that had to look away. She'd been brutal in the court room – if effective. The Law just hadn't been for her, a decision she'd made peaceably years ago. She was content to run a business with her husband; it wasn't my choice, but I respected it was hers.

"Yeah. He's handling it okay." But even I could hear my voice going flat.

"How about you, Sara? Are *you* okay?"

"Well," I said, as I let out a light breath.

Emily snapped shut the laptop, where she'd been running numbers for their business all morning. She stood up to rinse vegetables in the colander, in preparation for dinner. The sound of running water caught me by surprise, triggering a memory.

"No, it is not okay. I am having this recurring dream. We're in the duplex and the creek water is rising and Tye's gone to work in Vallejo – where, of course, he won't be going for much longer," I said, with an uncomfortable laugh. "And he leaves the house with his iPod and he can't hear me calling to him. I take Jacob down our lonely road and we go walking and then we're running after him, but he doesn't stop. Does that sound good? I don't think that sounds good."

"You're stressed, he's stressed. It doesn't have to mean anything," she said. She spun around, glanced at the clock; she'd have to do the pick-up run soon.

"No. Maybe it doesn't," I said, because I wanted to believe this to be true.

Emily's phone vibrated; a photo of Tony, her husband, flashed across the screen. He was at the shop; Saturday was their busiest day. Emily met my gaze and, as if knowing what I was thinking, she let his call go to voicemail. I watched as she drew a hand over her face – the exhaustion of three children and a business. She didn't have the time to split hairs, the expression on her face said; either that or she wasn't accustomed to a man who was defecting.

I told Tye about the dream that night. I hadn't planned to. We were lying in bed, side by side, on the futon we said

91

would morph into a bed, though we hadn't bothered to shop for a mattress. The lights were out, the glow of the night-light leaving a yellow halo at the bedroom door, reminding me of the night in Chapel Hill when we'd first slept together. Outside, the leaves streamed down on a breezy fall night, spinning in the streetlight, leaving patterns on the wall of my upstairs apartment. I wanted to return to that place, but I had no idea how to get back there.

I was silent. I lay listening to the rattle of our neighbor's fence, then heard the slam of a front door.

"You okay?" he asked, turning toward me on the futon.

"Yeah, just tired," I said. "A little distracted."

"Want to talk about it?"

"I don't know."

"Tell me, Sar."

He didn't often ask these days. So I said, "Okay, I had an upsetting conversation with Emily today. She asked me how I was doing and I told her" – I paused – "about this recurring dream I'm having."

"And?"

"Do you really want to hear it? I'm probably making too much of it."

He yawned. "Sure, go ahead."

"And?" Tye asked, when I had recounted the dream.

"And what? Don't you think that's pretty apparent?"

"Yeah, I guess." His nose in silhouette rose and fell as he spoke. He was looking straight ahead, not at me.

"What do you think it means?" I asked.

"What do *I* think it means? It's your dream."

"Tye, you've asked me about it!" I let out a half-laugh.

"Well, that you don't know where I am, I suppose."

"Doesn't that bother you?"

"Sar, it's a dream."

"Yes, but it's significant, don't you think?"

His face was still for a moment. I scanned his profile looking for some recognizable reaction. I wanted his reassurance. "Sure, we're in different places, I get that," he said, clearing his throat. "That's part of what's happening, I'm working, you're at home with Jacob."

"But that isn't my point."

"What's your point?"

Tye was tired; this wasn't the moment. But I pressed on: "My point is that I must be worried we're growing apart. Tye, are we growing apart?"

He didn't say anything at first; then, "Sar, it's late."

Maybe he saw no way around it, or it didn't upset him nearly as much as it upset me. Or had parenthood and the commute and our lives in California, like my dad, still working at seventy-two, made him too tired to care?

A good wife would have said it right then: I was worried – scared, in fact. But my fear had paralyzed me; I couldn't find the words or was too afraid to articulate them. Instead I reached over to caress his shoulder, ran my fingers over him and began to stroke him. I wish I could say it came from a place of desire but it was from some desperate animal place in me that wanted to *make* him care, make him re-invest – or make myself re-invest. I ran my lips over him until I found him and took him in my mouth. The shadows of the night-light played across the ceiling, as if in mockery of the moment. Afterward, I pulled myself up to our pillows and lay beside him. He spooned my back, grasped my knee and squeezed it, as if to signal his desire but a limited energy. I wanted him to reach out and reciprocate. I wanted that passion returned.

"I'm sleepy," he whispered. "Are you okay with that?"

I nodded, silent. I was facing the other direction, too numb to feel a thing. Tye may already have retreated, but I was not far behind.

September 2004

Chapter Eight

Tye wasn't the man he thought he was, he was the man other people wanted him to be. For most of his professional life, Tye rarely complained about his lot. In Raleigh at the station, when he developed their first website – riding the first wave of the high-tech world – he seemed to like the work he did. He liked solving problems and delivering goods and being there to save the moment, even if he would never save the company. He'd always gotten good reviews and worked well with others. He didn't ask a lot of the world. He said growing up in Maine was a simpler existence: open space and a pace that never hurried you. His dad had been a high-powered professor, but he was also an alcoholic, and Tye linked these two in his mind, intentionally taking the curves more slowly in his own professional life. But "slow" didn't really exist in the world of IT anywhere in the Bay Area. So I wasn't surprised when Tye opted not to take the position he was offered in Silicon Valley after the Vallejo lay-off. He applied because he wanted to keep his options open, he said, but in the end he decided the Valley was too volatile. A top firm had laid off 5,000 in 2001, then the competition followed with more layoffs still. The chief CEO in the industry, Tye said, didn't hide the cuts at all. So Tye may have been wise in refusing the position offered him in the Valley.

He was out of work for a total of two months. When he came home one night after an interview to tell me, yes, he had gotten an IT job at an ad firm in San Francisco, we were both thrilled. It seemed, at first, an utter victory. But by three weeks in, the job was already intense. He'd put in eighty hours since the previous Saturday, slept at the office on

Monday and Tuesday, and was home by midnight on Wednesday. By the weekends he wanted only to be disappearing. "My socks actually stink, Sara," he said that night, as he pulled them off and fell back on the bed. "I'm ready to go surfing in El Salvador... Do they even surf in El Salvador?" He sighed, surveying our bedroom. Laundry cascaded from the hamper in the corner. We had no artwork up on the walls still, only the stained-glass dove in the bedroom window offering solace to the busy-ness of our lives.

Tye said he would have another nine more months at that pace until things slowed down, until the code was finally ready for migration. But that night, he told me about Pam, his boss, who was just named VP "at twenty-fucking-nine," and who never seemed to stop. "She's got no kids, no family within three thousand miles. No responsibilities other than *this*," Tye said. "She comes up to me and says the client has fifty-four new requirements we've missed. I wanted to say, 'What fucking requirements? What I require right now is something to *drink*.' Jesus. Anyway," he continued, in a rare moment of disclosure, a rare confession about the intensity of the demand, "we know it will require modifications to at least the database calls, maybe more. We're on fixed price, but the mid-level supervisor Reynolds said yes anyway. So she says to me, 'I need your estimate for the additional burn by tomorrow morning, and then you have 'til Monday EOD regardless.' I wanted to say, 'Sorry – no can do.' But I didn't, of course."

I stroked his forehead as he lay beside me, feet hanging off the end of the bed. Pulling at the tufts on the bedspread, he said, "You okay with a move?"

"A move?" The light from the bedside table left a round globe of yellow outlining our bed, where Tye was sprawled; it was impossible to know if we should still be celebrating this new job or simply strapping ourselves in for a horrendous long ride.

"Yes. To Marin maybe? It's a brutal drive from here to the City."

"Sure," I said. "But it's a lot of work and it's shitty timing…"

"How is it shitty timing?" He stared up at me.

I leaned toward him on the bed, as if the closer proximity would help him see it. "Tye, it's a job, and I know we need it. But a move right now, it's a disruption." My mother had been in chemo for three months: six weeks, followed by six weeks' break, and now six more solid weeks. I had driven down every day some weeks. "My mom's starting radiation this week. She needs me. It's not great timing. But yes, I get it. We can do it. But later, please."

He scratched his head, then shrugged the upper half of his face. From where I sat, looking at him upside down, his face looked clownish and I started to laugh.

"What?" he said.

"Nothing," I said.

"What is it?"

"Nothing, really – you just looked funny, that expression you made."

A shadow crossed his face. "Sara, this job is no joke."

"I get that. No job is a joke here. They're all killer, I get that. But if they're going to work you like this they ought to be paying you for killer, don't you think?"

He frowned. "Are you complaining about my pay? I'm just glad to have a *job*."

"I didn't mean that, Tye – ."

"Then what did you mean?"

"I just meant they ask ridiculous things of you. In Silicon Valley, at least they give people stock options for this amount of work."

"We agreed the Valley wasn't a good idea."

"I'm not saying that." I paused, trying to articulate what I was feeling. "I'm saying, is it worth it? We didn't want all this, did we? I mean, the whole thing. What does the money matter, when we have no time?"

"You're the one who wanted to move west," he said, bolting up and swinging his head around to face me.

I let out a slow steady breath. "It's midnight. Do we really want to go here?"

Now I was the one not wanting to talk things out. Tomorrow he would have another long day and it was my mom's first day of radiation. I wasn't going to expend my energy on a fight.

"We are here so you can be with your family," he said. "But we're a family, too." His voice nearly cracked, betraying his emotion. A solitary line across his forehead made something like the shape of a seagull.

I put my face in my hands. A white candle on the bedside table gave off a pungent, almost sickening, vanilla odor. "Yes, we are here to be with my family, but you wanted this move, too. You wanted this opportunity. You wanted to move past the station in Raleigh. It was your want, too. But these hours – well, they are *hard*. They just are. I am single parenting. And I wouldn't mind that because it's a privilege to be home. But my mother is ill, and Ephraim's marriage is falling apart – ."

"What about Larry?"

"What about Larry…?" I mimicked. "You know Larry. He's not in a position."

"He's her son, too."

"Tye, this isn't fair. He's my brother; he's not where Ephraim is. I'd expect more of Ephraim." Ephraim's life had been dependable, until now, but work demands and shuttling kids meant he couldn't take our mother for her treatments. It had fallen to me. Larry had accompanied my mom and me, if only for a treatment or two. I didn't resent him for it, yet.

The wailing began downstairs, and my shoulders lifted. But the cry didn't sustain; Jacob must have fallen asleep again. I sighed in relief; I didn't want the discussion about "crying it out" again. We didn't need to add more to the argument.

In the silence that followed, Tye stood up and began to unbutton his shirt, nearly snapping off the buttons. The thin black curls of his chest hair wound around his shirt's edge as he tried to pull it off. "I think you're prioritizing them. Not us," he said.

I gasped. "You can't mean that, Tye. Am I to let her go through this alone? My dad's out there making a living, like you. He's handling all the work on the home front. Every last bit of it. They have no money for outside help. You know that. Besides, I want to be with her. I want her to make it through this. She's my mother." I stared up at the ceiling, trying not to cry.

He pursed his lips.

"What is it that you're saying, that you feel neglected?" I said. "Or—"

"Well, we haven't slept together in weeks."

"We haven't slept together because you never want to sleep together," I said. "And really, if I had to point the finger, I'd say you're the one neglecting your family. You are *never* here. You never tell them no. Can you not say no?"

"I'm three weeks in," he said, his voice beginning to rise in volume. Behind him on the mantle sat a framed photograph of our wedding, our faces pressed close together, faces appearing to be in rapture. "I can't let up. This is the trial period. They never say that, but it is." He paced at the base of the bed, which he almost never did.

"But even in Vallejo, it was the same."

He snapped his head back, his color rising. "You telling me how to do my job?"

"No, Tye, I'm just..."

"Just what?"

"I'm incredibly tired," I said. "I'm incredibly exhausted. And I want a husband, not an automaton who comes home with absolutely no energy for the rest of us. I told you I could study for the bar. But every time I bring it up—"

"Fuck the bar. Jacob is young, we agreed it was best for you to be here."

"Is this about your parents, Tye?" His mother had stayed home. For Tye, this was the model. Anything less meant failure.

He stopped pacing and then yelled, "Lay off my parents!"

I exhaled quietly. I didn't want to incite him further. But then I couldn't hold back. "Your work defines you, Tye. It's what matters."

"And it didn't to you?" he exclaimed. "You were a god-damned work-a-holic when you were in Raleigh at the PD Office. I never saw you."

"That's not true."

"All during the Susan Holeman case, you were gone. That's wh—"

"That's wh-why? That's, what?"

He paused, dropped his gaze. Outside I heard the screech of an owl, and then the sound of a car traveling swiftly by, trundling along our road. Then a silence that left me feeling utterly chilled.

"Did something happen – there? What happened, Tye?"

Inside your body, when someone has betrayed you, you feel this gap – like air falling away. A distance between what you are hearing and what you are feeling. I felt it in

99

that instant. He didn't even need to say it. "You had an affair."

He looked sidewise toward our window with the dove of peace in the window, lifting his eyes as if paying it homage. His lower lip trembled.

"Why are you telling me this? Why now? Do I need to hear this?" I put my hands to my ears. "Jesus. With who?" But I didn't want to know.

"With Lisa."

"With Lisa! My Law School friend, Lisa?"

He faced me now. "It was once. Only once."

"Does that make it okay? I don't care if it was fifteen times. It happened. Why?"

"Because you were gone." He stood absolutely still, facing me.

"Because I was gone," I said. Then, as it sunk in: "Because I was *gone*?" I felt the breath go out of me as I leapt to my feet, the floorboards squeaking beneath my weight. "So this is why you don't want me to work, because you'll have to have an affair?" I nearly spit out the words. "Fuck you, Tye. That's not a good enough reason. You can tell me I am gone too much. You can *say* that. Jesus, you can just use your *words*." Jacob, not even a year old yet, had begun to speak this past week – and the celebration around "using your words" had become a family joke.

"Don't talk to me like that, like I'm Jacob. Like I'm your *child*."

The sting in his voice hit me. I felt like a solid pane of glass that had shattered. "You are turning this around," I said, quietly, "as if it's about me. As if it's about my betrayal. That is in no way fair. It just isn't." I was in shock. I couldn't cry.

"I'm sleeping downstairs," he said, backing up to the bedroom door, his shadow dancing against the wall behind him, making him seem taller than he was. The shadow was block-like in shape, the softness of his figure lost in the silhouette it etched in the wall.

"Wait, no – I get to kick you out of the bed. I get to do that. You haven't even apologized. Jesus." The tears hadn't begun, but congestion in my nose had. I'd not cleaned the dusty room in weeks. I reached for a tissue on the bedside table. A photo of Jacob mooned over at me. That's when I began to cry.

September 2004

Chapter Nine

It was Barley who joined me at my mother's appointment the next day. She was to pick up my mother and I was to join them at Kaiser after leaving Jacob with the sitter. I was touched she was willing to come out to help. She was, after all, my sister-in-law – my mother's daughter-in-law – and that would not change.

From the beginning of her son's marital crisis, my mother had not blamed Barley for the affair. My father had said, at the first family gathering after the news came out, "Sara, she is not going to stick it to Barley. That is just not who your mother is. Fifty percent of marriages don't make it. That is a fact." It was a barbecue at my parents' home; Barley and Ephraim weren't there as she had a meeting out of town and Ephraim was working, so it was just Tye, Jacob, and myself, with my parents and Larry.

"Even though it's an affair?" I asked my dad as I stood with him at the grill. *Are affairs not unforgivable? Didn't they drive a permanent wedge in the marriage?*

My father was shorter than me and had the proverbial plumber physique: short, slightly bowed in his legs. He was skewering meat over the grill, a straw sunhat on his smooth bald head. Barbecues were my family's favorite kind of gathering; my dad liked to load up at Costco with pre-formed burgers, industrial-sized platters of hot dog buns, and Calistoga drinks stored in plenty of ice in the cooler, tucked against the back side of their stucco home. The paint had begun peeling where the westward sun exposure was most severe. I hadn't recalled their house being in such need of repair.

"Yes, even though it's an affair. She loves Barley. She's

102

not bitter like that, your mother." He slapped the burgers on the grill. When my mother appeared with a plate of deviled eggs, he said. "Hey, we could have gotten a divorce any number of times, couldn't we have, Fern?"

"Divorced? You'd not have divorced me, Ken. I'd have had to throw you out," my mother said, with a laugh, then placed the plate on the picnic table, and went back inside.

When we were alone again, he said, "Nobody's thrilled about it, Sara, but it happens." He leaned over to pick up the lid from the barbecue, came back up slowly, and let out a sigh. It was impossible to separate his tiredness from his sadness in seeing Ephraim's marriage dissolve. They accepted it, I realized as I locked the car and walked toward the massive industrial complex of Kaiser, but no one particularly liked it.

The Richmond Kaiser hospital is set back from the interstate, but the freeway noise is endemic to the region, and the entire area is defined by the ceaseless noise and the endless concrete divides between town and interstate, some with graffiti, some a blank steely grey. The bougainvillea part of the lot was filled up, so I parked in the far corner, where cans were overturned and high cement walls precluded any greenery at all.

On the walk into Kaiser that morning of my mother's first radiation treatment, I overheard two people behind me talking. "I guess they're separating," the woman said. "They've just started the legal proceedings."

"Have they?" The man said. I assumed it was her husband.

"It happened slowly, she told me," the woman said. "It was bit by bit."

"Was there any warning?"

"No, well, she said you almost don't notice it. That's the frightening part."

"So a slow thing, really?"

Just as I turned around, I heard her say, "Yes, she said it's like they became strangers in the same house."

My shoulders stiffened; I found the synchronicity of the conversation unsettling. I was struck too by the tone, their exchange building on one another's comments instead of tearing them down.

They stepped off the curb in unison, entering the lobby moments after I did. The woman glanced over at me. Steely-grey hair with streaks of solid black, in a fitted suit. He was dressed casually in black trousers, an open-collared shirt.

"There," the woman said, "Elaine!" She crossed the room to join her friend, tucked in a seat in a corner of the waiting room, with a scarf wound around her head.

The room was filled with women in scarves of all colors; older women and young-ish women; women my age. At the far end, a husband in a beige linen suit accompanying his wife, presumably, who wore loose linen clothing and a stylish felt hat. At the flat open desk area, Barley stood talking to the receptionist and then turning to my mother as if translating for her. By the time I joined them, they were ready to take a seat. Barley explained that they'd gotten all the paper work in. We parked ourselves in three adjacent plastic chairs, and my mother reached for a *Home & Garden* and began studying it. My mother, ordinarily loquacious, said little. She wore a light sweater over dark grey slacks that hung from her hips; she had lost weight during the chemotherapy treatments and the radiation oncologist had told them it was important she keep her weight up during this next phase. My dad had been on massive cooking binges but my mother's enthusiasm for food had dissipated. She'd always been thin, but now was swiftly becoming rail thin.

She smiled. "You okay, sweetie?" she asked. "Barley's

been a trooper this morning – haven't you, Barley?" She pinched Barley's leg playfully through her dress. Barley smiled back, but like me remained somber.

We were allowed to accompany her into the radiation area, and then a radiation nurse in a full suit of white and a clipboard took her arm and led her away. My mother looked as if she was going off for a club date, not to have her cells zapped. I felt my stomach lurch, watching her walk through the double doors. They let us remain in a nearby waiting room, with no windows, lit solely by harsh interior lighting, and featuring upholstered plastic chairs and a good-sized aquarium in the corner. Appliques on the wall, designed to improve our sense of well-being, offered messages in needlepoint: THINK POSITIVE, one said; another, above the aquarium, said, BE GENTLE TO YOURSELF!

Barley took a seat beside me.

"Are you doing okay?" I asked. I didn't want to be asked the same question.

She turned her head side to side slowly. "Just, I'd say."

"You're kind to come out for this, Barley. I really appreciate it. Did you have to take time off from work today?"

"No, I didn't. I was off anyway. For the move, you know… To finish it up."

This past weekend she'd secured her place; I knew this was coming, but I'd forgotten the timing. "Oh."

She stared straight ahead for a moment.

"It must feel very real now…" I said.

"Yes, actually, this past week was the first time the kids were at Ephraim's for half the week." Her tone went flat. Her necklace had caught in one of her silvery locks, and she couldn't seem to free it.

She turned to face me, her expression visibly pained. "He had them for three days, I cried every single night. I

105

wasn't taking them to school in the mornings. It was surreal." An orderly walked by in the hallway pushing a tray with medical supplies, cotton pads and bed covers, plastic cups and swabs, and below them metal trays that clattered; the clanging reverberated in the hallway. One of the goldfish circled madly at the far end of the tank. "I know that was the arrangement we made," she said, "but I thought I was going to die. I really did. I couldn't believe how much I missed them. It was visceral."

I let out a slow sigh. "It sounds horrible."

Barley bit her lip, then stared up at the flat white ceiling above us. "It is."

After my conversation with Barley at Kaiser, I decided Tye and I should patch it up. People had affairs all the time, and the marriages survived. There wasn't a need to end a marriage over it. He spent a couple of nights sleeping on the sofa; we had yet another fight three days later, and then we both promptly forgot about it. Eventually, we began to sleep together again, if intermittently. Secretly I was upset for a longer time, but I had bigger issues to contend with.

My mother's health situation resolved by October; she called one day, after her follow-up, to tell me that the tumor had shrunk. "It's cleared!" she announced, in a sing-song-y tone on the phone that day. "Well, no sign of it now," my dad said in the background, his voice betraying his skepticism; they'd gone to the appointment together that day. My shoulders dropped to a normal level for the first time in five months.

The only thing that remained, though, was the $40,000 medical bill from oncology – it had to do with outside specialists and second opinions – that had not been picked up by Kaiser because of her shift in plan. The tumor was gone; the bill was not. I set to work to sort out their medical insurance, the gaps in coverage, and to determine once more whether we might be able to plead hardship in their case – or not. Whether they would need to take out a second mortgage on the house to clear the bill, or whether there might be some other route to fiscal health for my parents.

It took another four months to resolve the medical debacle: the bill had to actually arrive in hand for it to be contested; it took a solid two months for it to move through the system; then I proceeded with a letter-writing campaign, attaching tax forms and Social Security statements, and a host of other documentation I have since forgotten, to request charity from the Kaiser Foundation. I did not win the battle; but we got it down to $11,000. Then I marched my mother into the bank where she once worked and which now held her accounts and coerced the manager into letting her have the funds as a personal line of credit. The banks still let you do that sort of thing in 2004. We lurched out of the bank that afternoon for my mother to announce, "Thank *God* you moved back to California!" I was glad she, at least, felt that way.

My parents began to pay it off monthly, but in the meantime I again coerced my mother, this time into resuming their ordinary health care policy – although the cost was already on the rise. Ephraim and I agreed to split the difference. There was no other way to make sure this would never happen again. The $200 a month we were each paying – $400 total on top of the catastrophic rate of $300 per month my parents were already paying – meant that in essence our two families were paying $8400 annually for what would amount to two annual Kaiser visits in a year for my parents. I tried not to think of this social inequity on a daily basis.

That same year, Tye's job at the advertising firm capped off at something like 65 hours a week. He stayed steady on it, and I bit my lip on the hours and kept on with Jacob's care at home, got us packed up and moved to Mill Valley. Things remained at status quo. Until three weeks later – right after I had finally decided we were settled in, in January 2005 – I learned I was pregnant.

Tye came home from work that night at a decent hour, as if by some preternatural sense he knew I had some news. He slipped in the front door at 7:30 pm with a smile plastered on his face. He'd had a haircut, trimmed short; everyone who worked in the City was clean cut in IT. He looked handsome.

"What?" he said, defensively, as he dropped his briefcase.

"It looks great!"

"What?"

"Your cut…" I pulled off my apron, sidled up to him and gave him a kiss on the cheek. He looked surprised. Jacob, well over a year old now, was in the other room throwing Legos about. The sun was low at this time of year, dark by 5:30 pm; but for us an early arrival home was still a victory.

"I'm pregnant," I whispered.

Tye's smile vanished.

"That's good news, right?" I asked.

"Wow. I guess. It's just… we're only now getting settled." He pulled off his tie and tossed it onto the briefcase. The sofas – our sofas – were finally out of storage; my mother's mahogany table she'd given us as a wedding present. Above the mantle hung framed photos of Jacob; my mother's portrait, painted by a Sacramento artist of some repute; a painting by Soti of the Sonoma landscape (no longer in our reach). We loved our Mill Valley bungalow, with its high ceilings and moldings on the stucco walls, painted in pastel colors, and hardwood floors, rental or no. We'd burned through too much of our savings when Tye was out of work those two months to buy, perhaps ever. We'd made this house our home.

"I'm excited, mostly..." he said, in a flat tone. "It's just tough timing." He had five o'clock shadow; the one light cast by the living room lamp made his face darker still.

I walked into the kitchen without a word. The past year and a half had trained me well.

He followed, and slid onto a bar stool at the island in the middle of the kitchen. "Sar, you know what I'm saying?"

"Some people would actually be happy at hearing their wife was pregnant."

He didn't laugh.

"It's never perfect, Tye." I returned to slicing vegetables. Above me, along the rail of pots and pans, hung long strings of garlic – I'd tried to imitate my sister-in-law's kitchen, just as hers had come undone. I reached for the garlic and began mincing it. "So, in that sense, no, I don't know what you're saying. I thought you wanted a second child. I thought we both wanted a second child. Was I wrong?" In the windowsill hung the birdfeeder, which I noticed had gone empty.

October 2007

Chapter Ten

Maybe every marriage has its lynchpin moment, some event that marks the unraveling of the weave of its union, an instance when the fabric gives way. For Ephraim and Barley it was her affair. For Tye and me, it was that incident on the street corner, two years after Mark's birth.

It was Columbus Day and Tye had the day off. We'd walked down to the coffee shop, in the island at the center of Mill Valley. Each side of the café bordered some stretch of sidewalk or patio, with its three edges, each of differing length; my little family, its own lop-sided triangle, gone parallelogram with the addition of our second child.

Downtown Mill Valley is nestled into the hills, its creek beds surrounded by dense foliage, a place where you ought to feel safe and protected. It was early fall, cool that day, the air crisp, the smell of sage – a remnant of the hot summer months – pungent even in town. We were all in heavier-weight clothing, preparing for the change of season.

Mark was in the stroller. Tye was ambling in front of us, staring up at the trees, which in this part of town were not so tall. Jacob was walking ahead of me, frowning, while I pushed the stroller. We were not going to the café he wanted to go to, and he'd gotten into a four-year-old's fury over this harsh reality. Mark was laughing and gurgling. I lit up watching him, then realized my eldest son's frown had everything to do with this, so I countered this as best I could: "Hey, guy, how you doing up there?"

We reached the stop sign. Tye checked for traffic and kept walking. Jacob stepped off the curb right, and because he was ahead of the stroller, I couldn't catch his hand quickly enough. I saw the car approaching and screamed. Tye stopped, full on. The car heading toward Jacob wasn't stopping, and Jacob's face fell apart as he stared right at it. "Get him, Tye. GET *JACOB*," I yelled. Then I was over the stroller and between the car and Jacob, without knowing how I even got there, my parenting instinct embodying me physically the way it does when one smells the possibility of death.

Tires screeched. The scent of burning rubber. The car stopped inches from us. Jacob was terrified, sobbing. I was no longer breathing, the sunlight startling in its sudden brightness. Tye's face had gone pale, in shock from what had nearly happened. He got it: that he hadn't paid attention, that he hadn't been watching. He actually looked contrite.

We were on the other corner now. I waved thanks to the driver, remarkable that in the midst of that moment my attorney brain never stopped working, coupled with a set of manners I'd picked up from living in the South.

Jacob was sobbing loudly still in my arms. "Did you not see that car?" I asked Tye. "Were you not watching your child?"

Tye turned bright red but didn't respond.

I bit back tears. "I don't know where you are, but you are not *here*."

"It's not my fault," he yelled back. "And hey, he's okay."

I laughed, a hard bitter laugh.

"Sara, I'm sorry. Good *God!*" On the corner, within complete earshot of at least a dozen older men, small children in families, couples sat placidly having coffee outside the café. And then, under his breath, "Table it. Now. We'll talk about it when we get home."

He clutched Jacob in his arms, having extracted him

111

from mine. We were fighting over who got to hold the saved child, when no one here, myself included, seemed to see what we clearly weren't saving.

That night at home, after the kids were down, I still wasn't speaking to Tye. The children were particularly tough to put down that evening. Tye was still with Jacob, settling him, and I'd taken a book to bed. I had a massive headache.

I heard the light go out downstairs and then Tye's footsteps falling on the stairs that led up to our bedroom. He put out the light when he reached the room, only my bedside table lamp was still on. He pulled off his clothes in silence.

"Are you not going to say a word?"

"I have apologized, Sara. What the hell else more do you want?"

I shook my head, my hand resting on my clenched jaw. "I just don't get how you don't see this. You don't see that you don't even act as if you are in this family. It's like you are everywhere else, all the time."

"Sara," he said. "I am tired."

"I know you're tired. But it's like you don't even *want* to be here." I was leaning forward, my knees drawn to my chest in self-protection. "It's like you don't want to be with *us*. That is the issue, Tye. Do you not see it?"

He was down to his boxers. He played with an errant chest hair with one finger. He looked at me plaintively, and didn't answer.

"We are here," I said, wiping the tears from my cheeks. "And you are somewhere there." I swept my hand across an imaginary gulf, across the large space between myself and my husband.

The next morning, after Tye went to work, I decided to take my children up to the Library for a kids' event. I strapped

112

the boys in safely, I thought, to the double-stroller and left our home. On the path up the winding hill, beneath the shade of the redwoods, in sight of the English ivy and the ferns, on the steep bank above an unexpectedly dry creek bed running behind the Library, we met Zeke Harris.

PART VI

MILL VALLEY, CALIFORNIA
2008

Four Years Ago

Early January 2008

Chapter Eleven

It was January and the trees were bare; my favorite time of year: clear, crisp, with a shockingly blue sky overhead. The crocuses were poking out by now, and I was waiting for them to come alive. I went walking a lot those days in the neighborhood, when the kids were at preschool and I couldn't take the studying anymore. I walked to the west, circled and looped, as if preparing for a journey greater than the one I was on.

I saw Zeke one day, coming out of his house as I was approaching. Later, I would ask myself did I go that way because I remembered Zeke lived that direction? But at the time, I didn't acknowledge where I was walking or why. It was safer that way.

"Hey," he said, coming up to meet me. "Which way you walking?" He stood there blinking at me – waiting, it seemed, for me to join him.

"I was going down to the park," I said, which was only partially true.

He fell into step beside me, and we began to talk. He told me about the on-going design job in Chicago – no libraries or museums or anything fancy, but a small café and speakeasy that incorporated a rooftop garden, which he liked because he rarely had the chance to do landscape architecture without being a bonafide architect. He'd been down in the Bay Area, too, doing re-models, because no one was building here with the downturn in the economy. "It's the state of the industry. It is what it is," he said, with a wave of his arm. "You have to roll with it."

The air was brisk and lovely and I felt alive. I felt strong and excited about what I was doing, too, and I told him –

because he really wanted to know. "It's a little strange, though, to be studying for a test again after all these years. But what about you? How did you get into building design?"

You could see it – not in his hands so much, but in how he held himself, upright and solid. He looked like a builder.

"I was a contractor," he said, "and I needed to get out."

"My dad had a plumbing business," I said. At college I didn't talk a lot about my dad's business; all my friends in LA had lawyer dads or corporate moms. Though in grad school, in Chapel Hill, at least, there'd been some regular people.

"Oh?"

I told him how my dad wanted something that would work around our schedules after my mom went back to work. He asked about my family, my brothers. He was one of three, two girls and one boy – the opposite of me – and we talked about coming from a large family, about the mayhem and the craziness of it. He'd grown up in Milpitas, in the shadow of San Jose, which became the center of Silicon Valley, with a dad who also worked in the trades, his mom having stayed at home until finances forced her out, too. We talked about growing up in California in the late Sixties and Seventies, both of us out of the fray because we weren't in the hotter spots of the Bay Area. He went to school at San Jose State for a time to study drafting, then dropped out because he didn't see the point.

"I don't know, maybe I could have done more for myself, educationally," he said. "But building was... easy. I got on with different guys, went up to Idaho, traveled around a bit. Learned from some good builders, and then came back home. But I didn't want to go back to the South Bay. That was '89; it was already a rat race by then." He went first to Sonoma County, when everyone was moving

116

up there, then down to Marin because it kept him in proximity to the City, where he could get work more easily.

"Why didn't you become an architect?"

"Didn't see the point. I was getting jobs as a designer, so I mean, why go to the expense, let alone the time? It takes forever." He laughed. "Besides, they're a different breed. I don't know. Lately I've been thinking I need to re-design myself." He narrowed his eyes. "Either architecture or something *completely* different," gesticulating wildly as he said it.

I watched him, curious. Zeke inhabited not just his body but this *place*. His was a distinctly Western spirit. And that attracted me because I felt this myself now, too. The quickening of California, the intensity the place demanded of you compared to Carolina, simply to survive: not just the traffic or the expense, but the frenzy of daily life. All of it required a certain energetic charge. And Zeke had that charge, that energetic drive, too.

We arrived at the park and by force of habit I went directly to the swing set. Only then did it strike me: I might see someone there I knew, one of the neighborhood moms. Would this look odd? Was it strange what we are doing, walking and talking, midday, without kids? But there was no one here I knew, and we sat in the swings after they emptied out and talked some more. We didn't discuss my husband, we didn't discuss my children; we just talked about our lives.

But these were the swings I regularly pushed my children on and the park a centerpiece of our family life.

The thought made me bolt off the swing.

"Well, I should get back," I said, as if reminding myself of the life that required tending to.

He eyed me, curiously. "Really? Things were just beginning to get interesting."

A current ran through me. I offered no response, only turned on my heel to walk home.

On the way back we were both quiet. He'd never said where he was going when I ran into him. Did he join me on purpose? Why had I agreed to come? It was as if I'd stopped thinking at all.

At the walkway to his house, he stopped and asked me, "So will I see you again, Sara?"

We walked every few days after that, and then it became daily. I told myself it was my study break. But I knew it was more than that, and then the guilt began creeping up on me. I was not telling anyone about this, not even Emily. I couldn't bring myself to say it, because it felt too large, and I didn't know what it meant. We were just together. And it felt organic. With each walk, we got to know each other better.

"I read the paper Sunday morning," he said, one time. "Before coffee. Just to wake up." He stared up at the sun, squinting.

Why was he telling me his morning routines? It felt odd to tell him mine. "My dad couldn't even get out of bed without his coffee," I said. "My mom would bring him the cup – he was always up early – in the trades you had to be. Well, you know that." I blushed. "My mom didn't have to be at the bank until 8:30."

He pressed his lips together. "At least they were in the same house."

He told me about his parents' divorce and how hard that had been because of the fighting and the taking sides, and the fact that his dad's work life had been spotty and he hadn't modeled a career track, even as a tradesman. Zeke told me he'd always identified with women, having sisters and his mom. And because he was used to talking with women and advising them, we argued about things. One day, we walked in the hills above my home and I laid out to him my worries about the job search.

"So you think I should be calling these firms?" I said.

"*Of course*, you should call these firms. Why would you even hesitate?"

"Yes, but – I haven't passed the bar yet. What would I do?"

"You're assuming ahead of time that you've got to line it all up. It just doesn't work that way."

I laughed. "I could shuffle papers, do their Xeroxing."

"Xeroxing? Who said anything about fucking Xeroxing? We're talking about *depositions*, isn't that what you did in LA with Trisha?"

"No, not for Trisha – that was in Law School, when I was an intern."

He was already making himself the expert on the topic. Zeke inhabited your world through language, through what he learned in conversation with you. He had a way of taking your story and making it his own. He liked to give advice; more than anything he liked to be listened to. He liked to be heard. But I did listen, because he said things that were useful and reminded me that I wasn't always right. He pushed me toward humility. And he made me think.

"Okay, so taking depositions," I said. "Do you know how *menial* that is after practicing as a public defender? And then I'm going to be taken seriously as a lawyer in that office? You've got to be fucking kidding."

"Menial isn't a dirty word, Sar. It's real people doing real work."

Zeke swore a lot, coming out of the building industry, having shed his designer veneer after that first walk. And I began to pick it up. I liked it because it reminded me we were no longer in Marin, we were in the less hip towns of our past: Albany and Milpitas, where the genteel intelligentsia never wanted to go, and where we never missed them. That was part of what drew me to him: he spoke my tongue, and with every conversation he brought me closer, it seemed, to what I knew to be home.

We'd been walking for several weeks, when Zeke said to me, "There's something you should know." I assumed it had to do with his career or schooling or design. He had told me once that he liked women's feet – not as a fetish but because they grounded women to the earth. He had become a builder for similar reasons: a desire for balance, a love of symmetry, all of which had drawn him to Buddhism, which he discovered while getting licensed for design, and had absorbed Buddhist teachings into his work. He was interested in their place in the design world. He wasn't much for yoga, at least as a steady practice. But he put the principles to practice in his life, daily, moment by moment. I didn't have a spiritual path when Zeke told me this, but I liked that he had one. It helped me to understand how he framed his world – his sense of healthy detachment, his appreciation of things ephemeral. It only made me want to know his world more.

Building for Zeke was synonymous with living. Even if people never appreciated the backbreaking nature of manual work, he did. But he felt stymied by his work, too, and talked about his career a lot. He knew far more than half the architects he worked with, but felt limited by what he hadn't studied, what he didn't yet know. "I've got to pay the bills, though," he said, with tight smile. Further schooling felt virtually impossible.

It was mid-January, mid-morning, the sun was not yet high. A cold front had come through and with it a set of cool days. The sky, visible in strips between the cedars and

120

the redwoods, was a sharp, unflinching blue. We were blocks past the park we'd gone to on our very first walk. The traffic had diminished, the road narrowed. To one side an incline, on the other the steep hillside, pine needles and scrabble beneath our feet. A car door slammed in the distance, the wind whistled in the tops of the trees, the needles and pinecones crunching beneath our feet, when Zeke turned to me and said, "My dad used to beat me." He inhaled sharply, a snake's hiss.

A chill came over me. "When, why – I mean, for what?"

"What is it ever for?" Zeke stared straight ahead, his face immovable, his body stiff. "I was the oldest. I guess I took it for the girls and maybe to make sure he wouldn't hit my mom." He had picked up his pace, and I had to pick up mine to keep up with him. I nearly slipped on the scrabble, stepping over the exposed roots of a row of eucalyptus, its bark peeling off in large sheets like cast-off paper.

"I've heard everything in my interviews, believe me," I said. "Hair-raising stuff. You won't shock me."

He was five when it began, he said, but things didn't get really bad until his teenage years, when his parents divorced. He spoke about the paddles as a kid and then harder things: a book thrown across the room, the back end of a knife used on the flat of his back, things that would terrify a child. His voice grew thin and strained. And when he talked about the knife against his back his voice wobbled.

I felt sick at the thought of it. Instinctively, I reached out to touch him, but he was too far ahead and out of reach. "Did you ever do any counseling? – as an adult," I asked. "To help you get over it."

He smirked. "I didn't have that kind of money, Sar. I had an uncle who intervened and talked with me a lot and that helped. In my twenties, I took up yoga and tai chi and tried to find a way to manage my anger. I guess that's when I became a Buddhist."

"I thought that was about the building."

"That's about putting the practice to work, that's different. That's the expression of it, Sara. Not the reason for it. It's our reasons – our motivations – that matter."

I wondered obliquely what his motivations were in walking with me.

It was cold in the shade. I pulled the scarf tighter around my neck. "How did it affect you?" I had found in my work as a PD that victims eventually became perpetrators. If we got involved, would Zeke beat my boys because he was beaten?

"How did it affect me?" He laughed bitterly. "I wouldn't let people hug me for a long time. It made it hard to get close to people. And I learned to read people *really* well," he said, wincing. "For protection." Zeke held a tiny twig in his hand, and as he walked he snapped it cleanly in two. I watched, unnerved, as he tossed the twigs aside.

We turned a sharp corner in the road, a car whizzed by. Zeke zipped up his jacket, his gaze intent on something directly in his sight line. He paused, blinked, narrowing his eyes. He had a way of looking right through things to their essential structure.

"And in relationship?" I said. "How did it affect your relationships?"

"I don't let people in easily." He shot me a bitter smile. "But maybe you've figured that out."

I paused. "When was your last relationship?" We had not spoken about our relationships up until this point. Mine was obvious. His was not.

"Two years ago," he said.

"How long did it last?"

"Two months. I ended it. She wouldn't let me touch her," he said. "She had issues, I guess you could say."

I said nothing. I kicked at the scrabble at our feet. What Zeke wanted, I realized when we emerged from the trees, wasn't the sun on his skin or the ideal career. He didn't want to get ahead, much as he spoke of these things. What Zeke wanted was to be loved. At least, that is what I believed at the time.

That night, as I set about making supper for my family, peeling carrots and spinning lettuce. I cut the onions and garlic, and then ran the water to keep my eyes from smarting. I washed my hands, lost in thought, and when Tye put his hand on my shoulder, I started.

"Okay day?" he asked.

I threw my husband a wan smile, nodded, and then looked away.

January 2008

Chapter Twelve

Zeke Harris didn't come from money; he hadn't grown up in poverty, but he hadn't grown up in plenty. And what he did have now, he'd worked for. This changes a man – or a woman, for that matter. It makes them cognizant of where they stand in the world; it makes them hungry and hard working. It can teach a deep sense of humility. It can also foster a false sense of pride. It would take me a long time to determine where Zeke stood on that continuum.

Lots of people assumed Zeke was Jewish because of his name. He did have a Jewish grandfather – Zeke's namesake – who had been a poultry farmer in Petaluma and part of the radical Jewish community there in the 1920s. But Zeke's dad broke from his father's world and stopped practicing Judaism, and the Gentiles marrying into the family diluted what Jewish culture Zeke had inherited. There was one quality he did inherit, though. Chutzpah. He had audacity, a kind of impertinence, as the term was traditionally defined. He also had zest for life. He enjoyed the feel of wind on his skin. In summertime, he shed his clothes readily. Not to tan, but to feel more alive.

For a long time I thought this meant Zeke was merely a sensualist, that everything he did was about building his comfort zone, his career, his place in the world. He seemed at first like a man who cared more about what he achieved than about who he was or how he treated other people. I wondered about his moral code and what he believed in, what he stood for. But was I looking at my own? Was *I* slipping into being a sensualist: was I spending time with this man simply because being with him made me feel good? I must have crossed some line with this question that last day we walked, because that's when everything began to turn.

That day we had a fluke warm spell: the temperature soared to sixty-five degrees, warm for January, even in Northern California. We were up the hillside, a mile or two from my home, and we'd stopped on the side of the road for me to take off my sweatshirt. He watched me, my shoulders, my T-shirt, my narrow hips, taking me in. Then he stripped down to his T-shirt, exposing his stomach briefly and one of his shoulders.

Was this Zeke, shedding layers to get closer to the sun? Surely he knew the effect this would have on me. Seeing him undress left me breathless.

Some poet said that we fall in love piece by piece. I was no longer aware of which piece we were on each time we walked, what part I was surrendering, without even knowing it. We'd been walking daily for weeks now. We didn't hold hands. We talked, we laughed, we joked, we harassed each other. But we never touched.

He stopped beneath a massive redwood tree. "What are we doing?" he said.

"Doing?"

A frown fluttered across his face. He pulled my arm to stop me. "Yes, what are we doing?"

High above us, the branches of the redwoods waved in the breeze, winking at me through sunlight.

"I mean, here. Walking, talking. *Us.*"

I froze, unable to answer.

His hand was on my skin, his hand firm against my bicep. He didn't let go of my arm but pulled me closer. As long as we hadn't touched, I could claim we were simply friends. He had just crossed that boundary.

A car whizzed by, swerving to where we stood on the side of the road. Zeke pushed me hard, instinctively, from the road toward safety. "Jesus," he said, loudly, immediately angry. "That was close. Too close. Son of a bitch."

I was scared suddenly, but not because of the car or Zeke's harsh response.

"Are you okay?" he said.

I nodded. But my chest was tight.

He paused. "I like you," he said.

"I know," I said.

"You like me," he said.

I wasn't sure it was a question but I answered it. "Yes."

"A lot?" He stepped toward me.

"Yes," I said. He was so close to me now I could smell him, a sweet musky smell, so unlike my husband's. But even I heard the hesitation in my voice.

"We shouldn't have come here," he said.

"No," I said. "I mean, yes. I wanted to come here. To be here, with you."

He surveyed me, waiting, and dropped his hand.

"I just don't know what to do about what I feel," I said. But it wasn't enough.

The risk – what I was risking here – he didn't seem to understand. The wind cut across each piece of my clothing, undoing me. I wanted him to touch me again. But now he wouldn't. He smelled my fear. He knew I couldn't, wouldn't, move forward.

He flashed me a hard, bitter smile, but said nothing, and we walked back in silence.

I hadn't told anyone about these walks I took with Zeke. And when we stopped walking – the very next day, in fact – I had no one to tell that they'd stopped. I hid in coffee, I hid in my books, I hid by driving and crying. In my head, I said what I would have said if those trees, waving above, hadn't made me think of Mark's birth, and what I owed him – my boys, if not my husband. I owed it to them not to blow it, if kissing Zeke meant blowing it. I owed it to them to be true to something, even if I couldn't be true to *someone*. Not even myself.

At night I lay in bed with Tye and tried not to think about Zeke. I focused on the boys over the next few weeks and when they were sleeping studied late into the night. Tye was working long hours, too, which meant I was mostly asleep when he came home, and didn't have to face him directly – in bed at least. Zeke and I didn't speak for weeks. I kept going over what had happened, and then one morning I remembered our talk about the abuse: when Zeke pulled me toward him and I resisted, something in him had snapped. Everything in me was saying no, but he wasn't going a step closer to me until that changed. Until everything in me said yes.

One afternoon I called Zeke. He told me he was under deadline on a project and couldn't talk for long. But I knew it was a guise. It was daytime, and the kids were at preschool. It was the hour we'd have gone walking, if we were still walking. I leaned across the counter of the island in my kitchen. I had propped myself up by the elbows, the cell cradled to my ear. My heart was beating harder than I expected, somewhere between my chest and stomach. Why was I calling? I didn't know, and he figured this out almost instantly.

"Sar, what's up?"

"I called to say hello, that's all."

"And?"

For a moment I was pissed. I didn't invite this, I told myself – or had I? "I miss our walks," I said, finally.

"I'm in the car," he said. "Hang on. I try not to talk while I'm driving." He was pulling over, his tone softening.

I plucked at the plant on my counter, pinching leaves back, trying to maintain some kind of focus. I didn't know what to say to him. Then he began talking: about the job he was on, about what a "disaster" the team was he was working with. He made me laugh describing one of the architects, and I remembered all that I liked in him. I felt a wave of relief.

He stopped, and said, "How's it going for you?" He always wanted to know how I was. He wanted to know if I was still studying for the bar. I told him I was.

"Good," he said. I smiled. He had always supported my career. Then there was a long silence.

"Sar, what are you doing?"

"What am I *doing*? As in today? In my life?" I didn't know where he was going with this line of questioning. But then again I didn't know where *I* was going, which was the heart of the matter, wasn't it?

"You know what I mean. I'm not going to tell you what to do, Sara." I heard car sounds in the background, honking. His cell dropped out for a moment. "I'm not going to have an affair with you – you know that. You're *married*. I have a moral code."

"I know, Zeke."

We were both silent. And then he said, "I want for you what *you* want."

What the hell did that mean? I suppose I should have asked him that, that it might have made certain things clearer. Instead, I said, "Can I ask you something?"

"Ask away."

"How do you feel about me?"

He paused. "I'm not answering that. I'm not going to fuel this."

I let out a deflated sigh. More sounds of cars whizzing against his silence. I groaned.

"You okay?" he said, after a moment.

"I think so. I'm just—" I felt myself unmoored.

"Just?" He always made a big deal about the word, how misused it was.

"Okay, I'm in a really bad place in my life right now, Zeke." It was February and daffodils and crocuses had sprouted everywhere in the yard, their cheerfulness countering the reality of my situation. Above them the oak tree was nearly in bud.

"You've got to figure it out. That's your job. What do you want?"

"What do I *want*? Since when am I allowed my wants? I'm married. I have a family. I'm not even certain my wants get to enter into the picture."

"That's bullshit and you know it."

"Zeke!"

"I mean it. What do you want?"

I straightened and then stared up at the ceiling. "I want a good marriage."

"A good marriage," he said, as if this was a ridiculous goal. "You *make* a good marriage. Is this the marriage you want, Sara? Is Tye the man you want to be married to?"

He gasped into my silence. "Are you going to live a lie or you going to live the truth? Which is it going to be?"

I couldn't believe he was pushing me like this.

"I gotta go," he said. "I've got a call coming in."

"Zeke!"

"You know where to find me, but I'm not sorting this out for you. I don't want the blood on my hands."

"*Jesus*, Zeke! You're not making this easy."

"I can't. It's too big. You have to figure it out."

We hung up. I pivoted and leaned hard against the island until the edge of the counter dug into my back. I wanted to feel that pain. Was it my penance? I squeezed my eyes shut tight, then opened them, taking in my surroundings: the kitchen counter with unwashed pots and pans; my orchids, drooping from lack of attention. My household, coming undone.

March 2008

Chapter Thirteen

My conversations with Zeke had put the "third child" question on my home agenda. It should have been obvious that it made no sense at this juncture, given where things were, but that didn't change my desire. Perhaps I needed to hold onto what I believed actually worked in the marriage: my role as mother. But would another child stem the inevitable?

One Sunday morning, while the boys were sleeping and Tye and I were still upstairs in the bedroom, I blurted out, "We could have a third, you know, we could do it."

"No, Sar, we could not," he said, looking up from the computer resolutely. "We can barely keep up with Mark and Jacob."

"I know it's work. Parenting's work. But I'm the doing the work."

"I'm not doing it, Sar. Period." He pushed back his chair and got to his feet and, as if to make the point, began pulling up our clothes, scattered around the bedroom. The house was a mess; how could we accommodate a third?

It was visceral, this desire: holding an infant, the weight in your arms, the steady pressure against your chest, your heart. The smell of my boys, how it lingered, even after I left their bedroom. Their compact little selves, the shape of a thigh, the turn of cheek, hair sprouted like straw. I stroked an ear, watched my son climb from my lap. *Too much work, not enough money, who has the time?* There was no logic to it.

I didn't convince Tye; that should be obvious. Then three days later, he stepped across the front door, tossed his jacket on the coat rack beside the door – where it landed like defeat, clinging to the wooden peg – and told me he was being laid off.

That night, after putting the boys down, I returned to the kitchen to find Tye picking at the last of his meal. I slumped down in the chair beside him. The smell of coffee permeated the room; he would be on the computer late starting the search.

"Are you not completely ripped about this, Tye? Honestly. You are a hard worker. I am dumbfounded. I want to know how can they lay off the tech person? I mean, Jesus, they can't run a business without one."

"Sar, it's a merger. They've new people coming in to fill the positions; it's all out of our hands."

"Since when do ad agencies merge?" I asked, completely indignant.

"Everything merges, especially here." He pushed back his plate and said nothing.

As I cleared the table, we talked about the economy and the fact that the Dow was at half its value from fourteen months ago. It looked like Obama might get in and everyone we knew was ecstatic; even I was working on the campaign, and I'd never gone door to door for anyone. The job loss in California in the past year and a half had been nothing short of astounding. Silicon Valley jobs were tanking on every side. The price of gas was going down, but nothing else seemed to change. Everyone here not in the $100,000 set struggled to survive. I wouldn't last a day on my own.

"It's a good thing I'm taking the California bar," I said.

"But you're months away from taking it, right?"

"I can step it up." I leaned against the island in the kitchen of our rented home, the boys' empty glasses and half-eaten food still on their plates, and briefly landed on some small island of gratitude that we hadn't bought. We'd have been sunk by now.

I crossed the kitchen and stood above my husband. He smelled of sweat, the sweet scent of laundry detergent, and the faint odor of smoke from the office – the blend of home and work that shaped his world. I tried to massage his shoulders, but they were hard, the hardness everyone felt here.

The job search began. I began to wonder if I could sign on with a law firm prior to taking the bar, whether I could get something provisional. I was finding this process harder in my own mind, bucking up to take the bar and finding a job, having sailed right through the job search after I passed it in North Carolina. In Law School the recruiters are all over campus and you've got the job even before you're finished, or you're hired by the firm you did the internship with over summer. It was easy by comparison. Now it was a lateral move. The five years out would cost me. Tye was interviewing now, but he was having difficulty keeping his focus, between the final weeks of work and the new applications, which he spun out slowly. I made phone lists, people I would call once I was closer to taking the bar. Then Tye's steps slowed down, things lingered; applications didn't go out, the phone stopped ringing. And I began to panic.

I called Emily one morning to tell her what was going on.

"I just can't believe that he's not *on* this, Em," I said.

She paused. "Did you not know this about him? Did you not see this when you married him?"

"See what?"

"That he's not that – assertive."

I spent a long time thinking before I responded. He had shown assertiveness when we first moved to California. That had all but vanished this time, I told Emily. I couldn't understand it.

"Are you there?" she said, to my silence.

"Yes, I'm here."

"He's probably discouraged. That could be it. How could he not be? Think of it."

"I don't know. Maybe it's the place."

"We're different people in different places, Sar," she said. "Well, some of us are."

I didn't respond. I wanted to champion my husband and rise to his defense, but my worry, with two small boys, trumped all.

My mother wasn't hard pressed for a response, when I told her Tye had lost his job again. What I didn't tell her is that we'd known for a year that the company was in trouble. I went to see her several days after we got the news. I sat at her kitchen table while she unloaded the dishwasher, stacked her dishes, and slid them neatly into her cupboard. My mother's kitchen had changed surprisingly little over the years. Our family always ate at the kitchen table. We weren't dining room people, and in this part of Albany – in the lower foothills – most houses weren't big enough to house one anyway. The oilskin tablecloth was still on the table, hard to believe because my parents weren't eighty – or whatever age it is that people simply throw nothing away, or conversely throw everything away. It was the table at which she'd raised her children. She told me once she loved the notches we made in the table-top, because years from now, when we were gone, this would be what remained, marking our presence.

"I think you should do what you want," she said. "If that's stay home, stay home. If it's go back, pick up the pace on the studying and take the bar."

"But is that fair to Tye? For me to stay home?"

"What does Tye want?"

"What does Tye ever want? He's overwhelmed at the

134

thought of adding childcare to the mix and juggling our schedules."

"Is that what he said?"

"In a manner of speaking. Tye doesn't usually say much of anything."

She looked at me blankly.

"Okay, that was unfair. He's tired."

"And he's just lost his job, Sara. Can you even afford to help out on the insurance still? I'm not sure that's so wise." She scratched her head, and then got up to wash the pans. She moved slowly, seemed tired, and I wondered briefly if her health was okay.

"We're not broke yet," I said, with a laugh. "What about you and Dad? You guys ever deal with this kind of thing? You know, everyone overworked and overstressed and feeling like you're going it alone. What about when you went back to work?"

My mom was silent. I hadn't ever really asked about their relationship. The water ran steadily as she scrubbed the frying pan from breakfast. "Oh, I don't know, Sar. I guess when I had to go back we struggled a bit." She shut off the faucet and looked away, her gaze focusing on something outside the kitchen window. "But there was never any question we were on the same team."

If she was trying to make me feel better, that particular comment didn't help. Besides, was it even true? We'd heard fighting, and one time Ephraim noticed a footprint on my parents' door. But no one had explained the reasons behind those fights.

"Why?" she asked. "Are you worried? Do you feel you're struggling?" She had intuited, I suppose, that my silence meant something.

"Well, we're not doing great—" I could feel my heat rising. "I mean, he's lost his job. We're reeling, Mom."

"Hardship is a part of marriage. There is no escaping it, Sara. Honestly."

I stood up and began to pace. She set down her dish towel and watched as I circled her kitchen. I stopped briefly to gaze out the back window, turning away from my mother. Rays of sunlight fell in stripes across the patch of lawn in the backyard, forming a nonsensical pattern.

"I don't know, he's not responding well. I don't know what to do." Mark was napping; our time to talk was limited and I felt the pressure of this. "I ought to have married Josef." I blurted out the words almost randomly, as if an afterthought.

"Sara, what are you saying?" She looked at me in complete shock.

"What do you think I'm saying? That man could stand up to me, we could fight."

"You and Tye can't fight?"

"He retreats. He... vanishes."

She set down the dish towel. "Josef, now he was solid." I knew my mother had always liked Josef, but the reminder at this moment did not comfort me.

Mark began squawking in the other room and I brought him out to the kitchen. I rubbed his back as he woke and stared out through the picture window I'd taken out years ago by accident.

"I stayed home for as long as I could," my mother said, returning to our prior conversation, "and then I went back because we needed me to. It might be your moment. Is there a reason why you're resisting? You're not usually this indecisive." She frowned.

I sat in silence, nursing Mark at the table, while my mother resumed her dishes. I assumed it was my marriage – or my confusion about Zeke – that was holding me back. My mother returned to work when I was six; I remembered coming home from school to an empty house. Coming back to California, I'd assumed she'd be our care provider, easing my return to work – but the distance to the North Bay precluded this, and Ephraim's proximity, coupled with his crisis, meant his kids' needs predominated.

Still, the dual conversations left me unsettled. On one hand, the Josef story; on the other, the issue I had brought to her, the Work Question. It struck me now the particular way she had abandoned that vital strand for my surface question.

"And if Tye can't get work?" I asked finally.

"Then you deal with it. In the end, you have to decide where it is you want to be, Sar, and who you want to be with, no?"

She meant, of course, my son, though the new double meaning of my mother's words were not lost on me.

Later that night, when Jacob was asleep and Tye was on the computer, I called Ephraim to tell him the news about Tye. He was the one I'd always gone to when things got rough, before we moved back to California. I was closer to Larry, but felt Ephraim, having children, would get the enormity of the situation. He reminded me of the time our father lost his job.

"I was maybe twelve, you would have been six," he said. "You might not remember this but he and Mom were at the kitchen table, and she said, 'You're going to find a job. You will make it happen. But you need to remember the family. We need you. You've got to find a way to make the choice that works for everyone.' "

I did remember it. I stepped onto the back porch, out of earshot of my husband. It was still light outside, the days growing longer before it began getting dark. "That's when dad went into business for himself in plumbing, right?"

"Yeah, he figured out what he needed to do for his family." Silence. This must have grated on him, surely, because of Barley.

"Of course, he went into plumbing *because* he'd lost his job. I can't believe she didn't mention it and I was just down there."

"You know Mom," he said. "She doesn't remember half this stuff. Her mind is on other things. Or she chooses not to remember."

I plucked at the African violets in pots on the back patio as Ephraim talked about a complication with his partnership at the firm – "and financial matters are riding on it" – and told me the status of things with Barley. Inevitably my attention strayed, as I didn't like this topic. I knew about my dad's dad, who had been "a disaster," my mother once said. "He just couldn't deliver the goods. So your father's had a hard time of it."

But my own father never hit an out-and-out depression. His job loss was brief. He found his trade in plumbing and stepped up to the plate. He came home tired, but even as a kid I never felt he wasn't showing up.

The next day, Tye went to work and after taking the boys to preschool, I got in the car and drove, which is what I did when I couldn't focus on studying for the bar. That day I drove to West Marin, wending my way toward the coast. The hills were a deep, emerald green. This year's drought was over. It was our seventh season, and we had grown accustomed to the rain. Gulls cast overhead, weaving above the road. As I drove through barren hills toward a bank of steady fog, I thought again about how we had landed here. When we moved west, I had believed my tenacity could stretch to my husband; I thought my locomotion would carry his slower, more Southern pace. But it couldn't. Tye was paralyzed, while I couldn't stop my forward momentum, wherever it might lead. I could no longer separate myself from the place where I was from.

Tye wasn't someone who opened up easily when things were hard, and the impending lay-off was definitely hard. He kept to himself, his face still and unresponsive as a stone. Like the smooth stones we found on that river my brothers and I used to walk near Davis, when we visited my mother's family in Sacramento. It was a dry river with long flat rocks – shale – that you could throw and keep throwing. This was the land where you could do anything, reinvent yourself again and again. But did you even recognize yourself when you were finished?

Tye's making over was an internal process. It took the form of a slow chiseling of self, the way waves break down rocks. He woke early to get on the computer to search for jobs. He pattered into Jacob's room to wake him and say good morning. He kissed my forehead after coffee before driving to work. He left home early, arrived home late. His days were relentless. For anyone it would have felt like a grind, but for Tye, who preferred to be out on marshland watching birds, it was grinding and it ground him down.

On weekends he tried to do house projects. He was into fixing things. It showed perseverance; and he did have perseverance, even if the direction he channeled those efforts into was sometimes counterproductive. Like making a seesaw for Mark who, of course, was years away from using it. But it was his form of dedication as a parent.

One day he was outside nailing an errant section of the fence, the wood rotting where it met the soil. Tye was to be watching Mark, while I took a hot bath. Mark was wailing because he'd dropped another toy off the deck's edge, and

I'd come out to see what was up, my hand shading my eyes from the relentless sun.

"Jeez," Tye sputtered, dropped his hammer on the lawn and began picking up the toys. He tossed them across the deck and into the basket. Half went in, the other half fell off the other side of the deck, and he went to retrieve them, blowing his work rhythm.

I watched, trying to figure out what was going on.

He lifted his face, red from gathering toys. "Sar, it's not your problem."

"Okay, it's just every time I ask you to watch him it's this monumental task."

"Let it go. This is how I do it, so let me do it."

"Okay, so you're not going to parent the way I do. I get that. It's just that you seem so irritated by him, by having to attend to him at all."

"Sar, I've heard you. Drop it," he said. Then he picked up his hammer and went back to work. I dropped onto the deck in my light cotton shift and sat beside Mark. He blinked in the sunshine. I righted his cap, wiped the spit up from his mouth, and watched my husband, who turned his back on us both.

Tye began banging on the fence and the hollow sounds reverberated against the backside of the house, creating a solitary echo. He dipped down to pick up another nail, and this time with three solid hits nailed it into the fence. And then, complete silence: no hammering, no traffic; even Mark had settled, rotating a top peaceably on the surface of the patio. I could hear its whirring sound. Tye's dad, he told me once, was known for his stony silences when he wasn't drinking. Tye wasn't a heavy drinker, so I'd never made much of that family lineage, but Tye's silence sent a chill up my spine. I struggled to my feet and then left the two of them and went inside to take my bath.

I suppose that's when my anger began, quietly and not for any dramatic reason. I knew how hard Tye was working. I knew he'd just lost his job. I knew he wanted to be a good parent; it wasn't that at all. It was the absence in his presence.

Tye was sitting across from me in the breakfast nook the next morning. In the sunlight, the flecks of grey were prominent in his hair, the creases in his forehead like the line drawings Jacob made depicting birds in the sky.

"We didn't use to talk to each other this way," I said.

He inhaled sharply, looked straight past me out the window, his gaze unbroken.

"Dad?" Jacob called out from the other room.

Tye didn't respond, and for the first time I realized, with no small degree of shock, that my husband was depressed.

June 2008

Chapter Fourteen

Tye secured an interview or two early in June and came home in better spirits. We'd made love the night before, more passionately than we had in some time – although I credited the alcohol for it and throughout Zeke came to mind more than I cared to admit. As Tye brushed past me the next morning, and looked me in the face, I saw for an instant an expression of vulnerability in his face. Outside a cardinal landed on the windowsill, a sharp, reddish orange, tapping its black beak on the wooden ledge. Tye blinked, turned to watch it, and I shuddered, as if knowing precisely what lay ahead.

He smiled, turned to me, and said, "God, I need to go birding."

"Yes," I stroked his cheek, sadly.

Mark raced into the room, right for my knees. I nearly buckled and went down.

"You okay?" Tye laughed, clutching me by the arm.

I nodded, then swept Mark up into my arms and held him close. I was afraid of losing what we had, and what if we didn't have it anymore?

Tye found a birding weekend online a few weeks later and he wanted to go. I told him he should go alone; I could take the boys to Train Town in Sonoma. But whether from guilt or lack of forethought, he insisted we join him, and I agreed.

We traveled to Point Reyes Peninsula, just north and west of where we lived. The expedition was to begin at White House Pool Park, a special event sponsored by a local birding environmental organization. We pulled into a lot packed with Priuses and Harley-Davidsons, as the coast of California drew all kinds. The summer fog had burned off early, the sky was shockingly blue.

"Great day," Tye said, as he rolled out of the car, weary from a long workweek.

"Yeah."

"It's really blue out," said Jacob, staring out at the marsh. "The air is really blue."

"You mean the sky?" I laughed and ran my fingers through my son's hair. I'd had moments of genuine happiness that morning, the first lift I'd felt in months. The boys were hushed, unusually so. I slathered their faces with sunscreen, put on their caps with long bills for sun protection, and drew on my own sunhat. Tye threw me a lop-sided grin. We put Mark in a backpack; Jacob was old enough to be on foot.

"Good idea." Tye put the pack on my back. "Thanks for pushing me on this."

We'd arrived late, of course, and so trailed behind the other straggling birders. There hadn't been adequate parking in that lot, and since we were all on our most environmentally sound, best behavior, some had carpooled from the Dance Palace – the truly organized people who had arrived on time. We straggler birders kept our cars at the Lodge. To reach White House Pool Park, we had to traipse along the two-lane highway and then a secondary road for about 500 yards, beneath the willows and the cypress, but we were on the road, at least, and not brushing up against private property. That was one of the golden rules of birding, Tye explained: don't cross over onto private land. Now the boys and I were practicing the other golden rule – the birders' desire for quiet, Tye said – even while the cars raced by us toward the Peninsula or back to Marin. Quiet seemed a good beginning. But most fundamental of all, it turned out – something I'd have realized in North Carolina, if I'd gone birding with him then – was that for birders the well-being of the bird always comes first.

At the marsh, the birders huddled with the guide, who discussed what they were most likely to see and identified the bird songs all around us. He pointed out two scrub jays, squawking at one another as they flew by. "They're having a disagreement," he said. "It could be love or aggression. It's hard sometimes to tell the difference." He wheeled around, and the flock of birders all around him followed suit, as he arched both hands around his ears to identify the next call.

I looked on as if these were groupies for some major rock band I knew nothing about. "So do you want us to hang back here?" I asked Tye.

Tye nodded, started to join the group, then doubled-back. "It's really important the boys stay quiet."

"I know."

"Birders are fanatical."

I smiled knowingly.

By mid-morning the birders stopped to snack. I'd kept the boys a good quarter of a mile from everyone, but now we joined the others. There were men in heavy-framed glasses and grey beards, in REI-style dungarees and canvas sun hats, and women in their fifties who wore heavy jeans and button down shirts. I was the only one below forty, along with Tye and our two boys. Everyone was getting sun burned. Binoculars – the "bins" – hung around each birder's neck, both the shaven and the unshaven ones. Smiles were brazen, everybody was feeling good.

Then Mark began running. Jacob knew to keep close by, but Mark had no sense of where we were and what this was about. The marsh dropped off quickly at the edge, and even if it wasn't deep water, it was deep enough to drown.

"Tye," I said, in a clipped but intentionally quiet tone. "Get Mark."

Tye snatched Mark by his shirt, just before he was to topple off an edge.

"Nicely done," I said, when he brought Mark to me. "Thank God!" I said, and smiled in relief and then chastised our son.

Tye nodded swiftly and turned back to join the group. But then, moments later, Mark began to scream.

"Oh, Jesus, Sara, stop him."

"Tye, I don't know what it is."

I scooped him up and held him. He was shaking his legs vigorously, like a KitchenAid blender, and I started to laugh. My husband glared at me. Right then I discovered, in horror, that my son had been stung by a bee.

"It's a sting!"

Tye's jaw dropped, as if to respond, but then he looked toward the group, now fleeing from our screaming son.

"They're starting up again. I will lose them if I don't go. Can you not handle this, Sar?"

"Tye, it's a sting – he could have a serious reaction. We have no way of knowing!" It was Mark's first, so impossible to know how he would react physically.

The women threw me apologetic stares as they vanished around a clump of bushes. But no one came back to help, including Tye.

"Tye!" I called out. But he'd already turned the bend in the marsh.

From beneath his cap, Mark squinted, watching his father go. Then, staring at the red splotch on his arm, he began to get agitated, trying not to cry. I fought back tears too, but not for the same reasons. And because I had brought no first aid kit, I took our son back to bird expedition headquarters at the Dance Palace, where we waited for Tye to join us. I didn't bother to ring or text him; I wanted him to figure it out.

They'd seen a hooded warbler, Tye announced, as we loaded the kids in the car. It was an Eastern warbler, rarely found in this area. Sometimes a hooded warbler thinks he'll attract a mate out here, Tye explained, but he's in the wrong part of the country. The rarest birds are sighted in the fall out on the Point, birds born in northern grounds, their internal compasses so out of whack that when they migrate they fly in the wrong direction. I didn't miss the irony of this, but Tye did. "It's a little golden jewel of a bird," he said, coming back to the warbler. "It's got this black hood pulled over its head and through the bins you can see its bright yellow face framed in black. *Sweet!*" Everyone was thrilled, he said. Someone in the group had once seen a red-winged blackbird riding on the back of a red-tailed hawk, teasing or harassing it. "It isn't just about sighting the birds," Tye said, with a triumphant smile. "It's knowing the bird you're looking at."

Driving home from the marsh, we were both silent, the boys conked out in back. I stared at the black tarmac road before us and knew precisely what I was looking at.

July 2008

Chapter Fifteen

Summertime in Mill Valley is glorious: the morning fog rolls out leaving a rich deep blue sky. The sun overhead is strong. The foliage, even in summer, remains lush, when the rest of the state goes quickly barren. Everything beckons you outside. With the boys home, I had set aside studying for the bar. It had gone in fits and starts for months anyway, ever since Zeke and I had stopped walking. My direction had begun to falter back last fall when Tye made that comment about Raleigh and my work life; it hadn't helped my confidence level any, and the effort involved began to feel Herculean. Oh, I'd kept it up for a few weeks, as if to convince myself that I had some direction. But in truth I had none; hitting the wall with Zeke in January had brought it to a halt. I'd begun studying again after Tye lost his job, but still hadn't regained my momentum.

Stopping the walks with Zeke was my doing: I was the one afraid to open that door and he wasn't going to feign friendship when he didn't feel it. I thought about him all the time – especially since the birding incident last month, when everything I'd once felt for Tye had gone underground and I had gone mute.

I'd seen Zeke's Ecodesigns sign for several weeks now when I drove across town, but I hadn't had the courage to go back to see if he was actually there, until today. I had no plan. I was completely winging it.

The house under construction was on the other side of East Blithedale past Tam High. It was out of the way, and it wasn't as though I had any obvious reason to be there. I slowed down, saw his car, and then almost sped away. He stepped out the front door, which was in the process of being re-framed. I pulled over onto the street. He had his shades on so I couldn't see the expression on his face, but I saw his footsteps falter as he came down the front steps; he was usually so even-keeled and strong on his feet. He walked over directly to my car. My breath caught in my throat.

"Hi, Sara." He took off his sunglasses, holding back a small smile.

I smiled back and felt the color rise in my face. "How are you?"

He scratched his cheek. "Okay, I guess."

"Big project?"

"Not big enough," he said, with a laugh.

"Are you still travelling to Chicago?"

"Occasionally. Are you going to sit in your car the whole time?"

"Uh, no." I paused, feeling embarrassed. "Want to go for coffee?" I scrunched up my nose, afraid he would say no.

"Sure." He opened up the door, threw his shoulder bag onto the floor, and dropped into the seat.

I felt too stunned to speak. My whole body relaxed having him in the car beside me. It felt so natural, so inevitable, the relief palpable.

Then with his foot he shoved aside the kids' toys on the floor of the car. "Their crap's everywhere, isn't it?"

I blanched. Could he really deal with kids? But what was I thinking: that we were going for coffee, or that he was the future stepfather of my children?

"Are you actually going to drive?" He threw me a grin.

"Yes." I laughed. His humor re-engaged me, instantly. "Where do we go?"

"You're the one behind the wheel, you decide."

148

I drove us to a café tucked into a mall between Tam High and the interstate. The sky was cornflower blue, purple flox lining the road, spilling over the pavement. The car windows were open, he'd cracked the skylight to increase the ventilation, and the wind was caressing my hair. He grinned broadly. The day felt wide open – like summertime should be, like a summer day I might have had in college – and the depression I'd felt the past few months began lifting. His presence in my car filled me with incredible joy. My boys were at a friend's. I'd not engineered this entirely, but I had wanted this to happen. I wanted us to be *here*, and I felt almost victorious that we were here together.

We stepped out of the car, slammed our doors in unison and took the stairs in stride, mine as energetic as his. We ordered coffee and found a seat outside. It was all so easy, too easy, to be around him, to be talking and laughing again, to feel so alive.

"Let's sit over here." He motioned to the table at the far side of the deck. "It's further from the road." We sat beside college-aged girls, on and off their phones, and an elderly couple, finishing their meal. Teenagers filed in and out of the door, the young women glancing at Zeke. We ordered. He noticed the table rocked and pulled out some papers from his bag, scanned them almost irritably, then folded them neatly into a small square and shoved them under the errant table leg. He lifted his head and smiled at me, triumphant. Then he lowered his gaze to the table, looked at my ring finger, and blinked.

"How's the family?" He threw me a bitter smile.

I set my left hand on my lap, almost instinctively. "Fine."

He crossed his arms. I'd seen that defensive posture before. "Where are the boys? Shouldn't you get back to them?" His mouth twitched. Then he took a sip of coffee, sat back in his seat and watched a young family walk in beside us, watched them as if they were zoo animals, showing the wide crevice between his life and mine. What had I been thinking? That he would really feel something for me, that he might actually love me? Was I blithely assuming he would open himself up, welcome us into his life? He was thirty-seven, a year younger than me, with a lifetime of living that didn't precisely parallel mine.

I explained they were with a friend so I could run some errands.

"So… were you looking for me when you came by?"

I stifled an uncomfortable laugh. "Why? Is that not okay?"

"Well, I'm not sure what to make of it."

"I wanted to know how you are."

"How are *you*? Isn't that the real question?" He took another sip, then dropped his gaze to the metal tabletop and began tracing its pattern with his finger. He looked up. "How are you, Sara?" He asked, and I softened.

I told him I'd been studying but I had lost steam on the bar, that Tye had been so non-supportive of the idea.

"When has he ever been supportive of you, Sara?"

I said nothing, only looked away. He knew how to go for the jugular. "Tye thought I should stay home with the kids, that is until he lost his job for a second time."

"A second time? Sweet, Jesus. Unbelievable." He shook his head and sipped his coffee. "So are you?… Are you studying?"

"Trying." I felt my own depression settling back over me. What would really come of this visit with Zeke, what had I been thinking?

"Are you insane? You've got to be kidding. It's what you *want*. Not to mention need."

150

"Yes, but I want to be home, too."

"Nah, I don't really buy that. Not at this point. I think you're scared."

"What do you mean scared?" I nearly spat out my coffee.

"To go back out there, to put yourself on the line. To have *cojones*." He threw me a playful smile. "You know you have capacity, why aren't you using it? It was a court case, wasn't t?"

In the months, no, years, I'd been trying to get my life mobilized no one had asked this of me – not even Trish.

"The Susan Holeman case?" I said.

"Yes, the Susan *fucking* Holeman case!"

I laughed. I hadn't thought to call it that.

"What was it, anyway?" he asked.

"The case? Pretty straight forward. An African American woman was charged with assault for fighting back against her white boyfriend – domestic abuse, basically. I had to put her children up on the stand." I paused. "And they helped incriminate her."

"Look. You fucked up. It's that simple."

"What do you mean I fucked up? Okay, so when you don't win you feel like your presentation of the case was somehow deficient."

"You made a bad choice, you made a bad *call* – a woman went to prison."

"Yes, she went to prison – and I could have stopped it, Zeke. Do you not see that?"

"Sar, she got into a fucking brawl in the mess hall. Nine months later. You don't think that was a step *she* took? You couldn't have predicted that."

I started to laugh, every part of me lifting. I scratched my head. Zeke had always pushed me like this. It was what I liked in him, what I liked in us.

151

Then we began to joke about my job search and the possibilities; the menial jobs I was looking at as a stop-gap measure. "It's a job, any job. *Jesus*," he said, "Get over it." Everything we'd talked about on our walks on the hillside.

But then it was over, as swiftly as it had begun. He had to go back. He'd steered clear of any serious conversation after asking about the family. I couldn't tell where his mind was – I had no idea. When I stopped the car, he turned his head to size up the house and talked about the job and the men working on it, how the homeowners were *a disaster*. "She has no idea what she wants and keeps deferring to him, and he's never there half the time anyway. You know, the usual." He couched a grin, and I winced.

He raised a brow as he let himself out the passenger door.

"Want this?" I pointed to his bag. He reached his arm through the open window to the passenger seat to retrieve it, brushing my hand. He looked at me steadily.

"You can call me if you get on the other side of this. But I don't know where I'll be by then. You know that, right?" He threw me a playful glance as he stepped away from the car. Then he turned and walked back through the framed door into his world and away from mine.

I was messed up for weeks after that and I didn't tell anyone. I couldn't make heads or tails of anything he'd said, it all felt so contradictory. So I played it over, every single frame of it, in my head – while I washed dishes and prepared for the start of school, while I watched the leaves turn from green to yellow and red, and focused on the pavement, the leaves falling beneath my feet, wondering when it, or I, would fall apart.

December 2008

Chapter Sixteen

Under the guise of Christmas shopping on Fourth Street in Berkeley, I went to see Ephraim. He had gotten a flat around the corner, so he could walk to work. My brother had made partner, just as he'd lost his partner. The irony of this was lost on none of us.

Today I was traveling solo. A friend was watching my boys; we were swapping play dates to shop during the Christmas season, so I had to make the trip to the East Bay do double-duty. Ephraim met me out front; this was a gated part of town he now lived in, a handful of homeowners, fencing themselves off for safety reasons. This was once the industrial part of Berkeley; former warehouses converted into upscale stores now inhabited the far end of Ephraim's block. But the immediate structures around his home were working warehouses. Some housed inventory for local retail firms; others were converted into artists' studios, where graffiti stretched across aluminum siding, but the remainder were condos with high gates, like Ephraim's. Ephraim liked his new neighborhood and, after taking out a second mortgage on their home, had bought his flat. It seemed unwise in this economy, but he was my eldest brother, so I didn't speak out. Barley was still in the house on the hill with the kids. Ephraim got them three weekends out of four and, on the days she worked, ran them around midweek to their activities. Today he was working from home and met me at the gate looking lighter of spirit, his curly hair shorter and trim and nicely shaped. He seemed more like the Ephraim I knew.

"Let's go get coffee," he said, after I pecked him on the cheek.

153

Ephraim was thin at the waist and broad at the shoulders, and as we walked he turned his torso to take in all the buildings. Remodels were rife in this part of town, and he frequently stopped to examine a new structure and then explained what they'd done.

"I have some news for you," he said, striding ahead. The block above us was REI. I remembered when it had opened and Ephraim and I went to get his equipment for traveling to Asia; before that it had been a drugstore, when San Pablo was a sleepy street. "Barley wants to get back together," he said, over the din of traffic.

A wave washed over me: shock, excitement, fear that he'd get hurt again. "Are you serious? What, her relationship didn't work out?"

"Sara, have you heard yourself lately?" He shook his head, staring straight ahead. "Jesus, poor Tye! Is that how you treat him?"

His words stung and I said nothing for a moment. "I'm sorry," I said, but he didn't apologize. Ephraim rarely did. "Listen, I'm in a really bad place right now..." I said, finally, because I knew I needed to set aside my own crap. "What I meant to say was, what spurred it? Did her relationship not work out? And do you feel okay about it? It's a lot of water under the bridge, Eph. I'm concerned, okay – that's what that's about."

"No, it didn't work out. When do those rebound relationships actually work?" He looked at me pointedly. "They never work," he said, and began walking more swiftly. I had to do a quick clip to keep up with him. I wanted to regain our brother-sister moment. "And, yes, I do actually. I do feel good about it. Look, I don't want to hear any critique of her, okay? No one knows what really happens in someone else's marriage."

The shift had occurred a couple of weeks ago, he said,

154

but they'd been in counseling for the past six months. They both felt it wasn't good for the kids, especially Traci. "I know it's odd to re-marry the person I've divorced – I don't mean tomorrow but eventually. I'm going to rent out the flat – I won't sell it, I'm not going to be rash – but we're moving back in together." Then he stared straight ahead. A truck careened past us hitting a pothole in the road. "We've gone through a lot. You're not in deep enough yet, Sara. You don't know how much there is to go through. It gets harder."

We arrived at Peet's Coffee, the center of Fourth Street, Berkeley's latest gourmet ghetto about two miles from the university near the interstate. The fog had burned off and the morning light refracted off the low cement wall that enclosed the area. Several restaurants already had tables out, anticipating the lunch crowd that would come out to its favored foodie spots. We queued up behind a middle-aged, mixed-race couple, arms draped over one another; she wore a cape and he a Fedora. An older woman in a long embroidered dress stood behind us, and I thought I might have known her, the mother of a friend from high school. There were two sporty-looking twenty-year-olds with backpacks that looked to be students at check-out, haggling with the attendant. Ephraim insisted on treating me to coffee, because he knew I carried little cash on me and that we struggled to get by, now that we were helping out my parents. I accepted the offer.

We collected our coffee at the next queue. Outside Peet's, we found a bench in the sun on the concrete patio where everyone congregated in this part of town, patrons perching casually along the top of the low concrete wall surrounding the coffee shop. A man in a tweed jacket and beret sat cross-legged beside a woman with grey-streaked hair pulled back tightly in a bun; she wore a button-up

155

cashmere sweater and multiple rings on her fingers – Berkeley's gentile intelligentsia, arguing about Proust. I sipped my coffee while Ephraim talked and watched as an elderly white man with a grizzly beard, holding a tattered bag, jaywalked unevenly across the road. An approaching car slammed on its brakes, then honked. The man in the silver-grey Lexus – young, clean-cut – yelled at the old man out the window. The man shook his fist and screamed back, a harsh, blood-curdling scream that made plain he was unbalanced. Everyone turned to stare. He stopped curbside, teetered on its edge and turned back to the car, muttering to himself.

"You don't see a lot of homeless down here. They're usually on Telegraph or Shattuck Ave," Ephraim said.

"You see a lot in Marin now," I said. "We were just beginning to see homelessness in Sonoma County before the move. But it's much worse now." We'd seen relatively little in the Bay Area when I was growing up.

"Barley says everyone has double the case load they had a few years back," he said, and shook his head. "It's not good." The California budget deficit, with cuts in every sector, remained unaddressed; the Assembly had been in stalemate for months that year. Everyone was depressed about the economy.

I suddenly felt tired. "Anyway, sounds like you know what you're doing, Eph." I wanted to sound enthusiastic, even if I wasn't.

He nodded. "I didn't think we'd get to this, but we have. I can't believe what it takes to make a marriage work, Sara."

"What's changed? How did it shift?" He was the architect; I figured he knew something about structure that I didn't.

"I don't know. We missed each other." His eyes filled. They say the real question is whether you actually miss the marriage. "I guess we couldn't let it go."

156

I didn't, in the end, talk with Ephraim about what was going on in my marriage. He needed to talk about Barley. How could I tell him my marriage was falling apart, when everything in his life was rotating around the marriage he thought he had rebuilt?

December 2008

Chapter Seventeen

My boys were waiting at the front door, dressed in matching checked shirts and new black cords. Mark's pants were on the large side because he had such squat legs still. Jacob's shirt wouldn't stay tucked in and kept lifting at his skinny waist. Their sandy hair fell across their foreheads in exactly the same way, and watching them from behind, I felt my first sense of joy at the prospect of this family gathering. Showing off my kids was quite possibly the most pleasurable experience I had in those days, and I couldn't decide if that was a good or a bad thing – whether it indicated I was an exceptional parent, or simply that I had no life of my own. But I stood beside them now, stroking the top of Mark's head. He still let me do that since he was not yet four, while Jacob would have none of it now that he was en route to six. I wasn't sure where Tye was. I never seemed to know. Either I was no longer paying attention or he had – as I was experiencing him in those days – simply vanished.

My brother Larry arrived first with Fran and I took their coats, and she'd brought a hostess gift, which struck me as sweetly old-fashioned.

"Sparkling cider!" I said, with a laugh, figuring this meant she wasn't much of a drinker. "Great." I gave her an awkward hug. We were all now assuming she was part of the family, though Larry had not said anything more. She beamed, the kids jumping around because Larry had brought them something. I threw my brother a smile. Tye was still elsewhere, so I dropped their gifts on the counter in the kitchen, and raced upstairs.

He was at the computer, reading *Valleywag*, the Silicon

Valley gossip rag, his strong shoulders humped over in the chair. The room was a mess: his towel draped on the floor and clothing littered everywhere, his and mine.

"We're having a Christmas party, Tye. Why are you not downstairs?"

"You want me to follow up on jobs, so that's what I'm doing. I'm getting the skinny." His voice was terse.

"Yeah, but like – now?"

He looked at me flatly.

"Honest to God, I don't know where you are most of the time, Tye."

"You know, a small bit of compassion, Sar, would go a long way."

"Compassion? A small amount of *paying attention* to what's going on around you would go a long way." I got what he was saying but this wasn't the time.

He shook his head, instead of telling me how he felt. But was I telling him how I felt? I wasn't, for instance, telling him that the job really wasn't the issue, that this was the one track I could run down safely, that it was simply a smokescreen for the fact that I was in love, or believed I was, with someone else.

"What?" I said, defensively, to his silence.

"Sara, what has gotten into you?"

I paused to gather myself. I hadn't slept well lately; Mark had been up sick two nights in a row the preceding nights. "Tye, we are having a Christmas party and you're up here hiding, and you've lost your job. Any number of these is likely to be upsetting."

"And whose problem is the damn Christmas party, anyway? You're the one who took that on." He stared at me, blinking.

I had decided we should host our annual family gathering, reasoning that if we played the happy family

159

we'd actually become one. A pull-yourself-up-by-your-bootstraps approach to our crisis. Tye had lost his job. What on earth was I thinking?

"Don't go there," I said, because I wasn't willing to concede this.

"Why not?" Tye didn't often get angry, not directly. He'd learned silence and subterfuge as a result of his dad's yelling. He dropped his hand from the keyboard and I noticed the scar on his thumb from the accident he had building the playhouse for the boys. A stark reminder of the relationship he had with them – the one I was thinking of disrupting – and the myriad small ways that he had tried. Knowing how hard he had tried only upset me even more.

"Why *not?*" I knew I wasn't being rational, that something in me had snapped.

He tried to grab my arm to quiet me. "Because now is not the time." I pulled my arm away. "Tye, this is my family. And as for the job, I urged you to start looking when the company showed signs of trouble, and you didn't. You wouldn't listen. I offered to go back to work then, and you declined. And now I try to talk with you about where things are, and you don't respond. You just can't see what's happening here."

My voice cracked, and before I completely lost it, I slammed the door and walked out.

I guess that was my own kind of vanishing.

If I thought things were going to get better tonight, it turned out not to be the case, because Barley had indeed come, and everyone was on tenterhooks as a result. My mom and dad arrived, and I gave them pecks on the cheek. They hung up their coats and milled about the living room, my dad snacking on the hors d'oeuvres and my mom handing their gifts to the boys – one for tonight, one for Christmas Day.

Jacob was ecstatic, and then had to hold back Mark from opening the gift, because his younger brother was still getting the rhythm of things and gift protocol was not yet in his lexicon.

But they were our guests of honor: Ephraim was smiling, the kids – for a change – seemed relaxed and happy, even Traci, and the twins, Aiden and Eliot, fell into playing with Jacob. Barley looked lovely, if tense, in a silver cotton dress to match her silver locks. She had gotten December sun – only Barley could manage that – her skin as olive as ever. Watching her, I decided that she'd had every bit of her cake and devoured it, too, and I immediately felt my blood pressure rise.

"Hey, Barley. Hey, Eph," I said, and lavished a warm smile on my brother. In truth, my upset had little to do with them at all, even Barley. Barley, at least, was trying to make it through her marital crisis.

Jacob and Aiden began squabbling over a toy underneath the tree. My boys got to open a gift on Christmas Eve, and Jacob wasn't one to share easily.

"Eph, stop him will you?" Barley said from across the room.

Ephraim, who was taller than my husband and larger of build, loped across the living room floor and grabbed Aiden by the arm more than a little harshly. "Cut it out, buddy. That's Jacob's gift."

My mother started. She believed strongly in not being physically rough with kids. "Ephraim, let him be."

Barley bristled. Much as she loved my mother, she never liked her interventions.

Ephraim dropped his son's arm and then, to his credit – because he'd always been a loyal husband – wheeled back around. "Okay, Mom. We're on it, we know."

Barley smiled. Ephraim had always stood up for her in

this kind of way. With a husband like that, I wondered, why have an affair?

I knew I had an attitude at my own party. In the kitchen, my mother pulled me aside.

"Sar, what is going on with you?"

"I'm just having a very bad day, Mom," I said, sipping mulled wine – a mistake, since I hardly ever drank. I was near tears.

My mother set the glass aside, put her hand over mine on the counter, and said, "You're going to need to get a grip, sweetie. It's setting a bad tone for the party."

I shook my head, remembering this part of my mother. I'd forgotten she had this capacity: mulled wine out of drinking daughter's hands, dirt swept under the proverbial rug. She straightened the top of my sweater, as if to make me into someone more wholesome than I was. I pulled away.

"Mom, you don't know what I'm up against. Tye just isn't delivering the goods."

She knew he'd been laid off, but she didn't know about everything else.

"Honey, he'll find work."

"In this economy? Mom, he knew for a year – a *year* – that the company was in trouble. And he did nothing. Nothing."

Her mouth twitched. "Are you taking the bar, for sure?"

"I am taking the bar, but not until March. That's three months away, at... about $5,000 a month. You do the math," I said, and then turned to check the turkey in the oven.

"You'll pass the bar; you'll get a job, Sar. It will work out."

She rubbed me on the shoulder, as I pivoted to pull out the bird, the stuffing slightly over-browned, the skin taut

162

and hard from inadequate basting. I shook my head. I'd become someone who judged myself on Christmas dinner, when once I used to *put* people before judges. Without question, something was wrong.

At the Christmas dinner, everything was fine until I noticed the cranberry sauce – which Tye had taken on – was missing.

Tye was at the foot of the table, opposite me.

"Tye, where is the cranberry sauce?" I asked. My tone was not especially vexed.

"What about it? I thought you were on that?"

My mother looked up at me. Fran smiled politely. Barley, knife in hand, stopped, poised and watching.

"Ahh, I thought you were making it."

He pushed back his chair swiftly, with obvious irritation. "No, I didn't make it, Sara," he said, his tone snide. "Do you see it on the table? No. Well, I'll just get a can. We can do the canned jelly, right? It's not such a big deal, is it?"

I pursed my lips but said nothing. My parents stared at the table, Larry looked out the window, and Ephraim caught my eye, but then I had to look away. The fixings on the table, a table dressed for celebration and joy and togetherness. He was right. The cranberry sauce didn't matter. But the meal did. It was, after all, a Christmas dinner, a meal designed to express every bit of our love for one another.

The kids had gone down. Everyone was sitting in small groups, clumped in the kitchen or the living room. Barley and Fran, who was a teacher, had spent forty-five minutes discussing the school system in the Bay Area, which I actually knew something about. But then we got on the topic of the senator who had been caught on tax fraud. Larry was saying something about how everyone cheated on their taxes, why was this any different?

163

Fran, to her credit – and I instantly liked her for this – piped up, "Wait a minute. He's a senator. It isn't small."

Larry turned his chin, as if to deflect her criticism. "Yeah, you got a point."

"It's the honesty question. He was blatantly dishonest. What, they 'forgot about the issue'? That's what they said. Are they kidding?" Fran went on.

"Absolutely," my mother said. "He was dishonest."

Barley shifted in her chair. Ephraim scratched his head. I was sitting closer to the Christmas tree, near the stereo, because I was changing out our CDs for the evening's music.

"Though I'm not sure it's as bad as that presidential candidate," Fran said, to complete silence in the room. Larry cleared his throat. He wasn't seated beside her, and kept tossing his head in an attempt to flag her. Surely she must know Ephraim and Barley's story? But maybe Larry wasn't on this; maybe he hadn't shared it out of privacy, for his brother's sake.

Ephraim's face went pale. My mother's expression nearly undid me. She stared at her coffee cup, her face pinched in a way that added years to it.

"Why did he go public with it?" Fran said. "I mean, his wife was ill. It was bad enough that he did it."

Barley paused. Fran was wrong on this point. "No, he didn't go public. He told the truth bit by bit. His wife urged him to come clean, at least that's what I've read. Maybe he thought he was doing the right thing. That it was best to be honest." I stood up at that moment and promptly left the room, under the guise of changing yet another CD.

A year ago I would have joined in with vigor – on the discussion about the politician, on the topic of honesty and compassion within a marriage – but tonight I was somewhere outside my own body, looking in the window at this festive event, holly sprigs everywhere, chipper little potted Christmas trees with silver balls and golden bells.

The conversation turned another, less stressful direction. My father jumped in – my mother simply too nonplussed to have an adequate response – and began talking about Obama. Moments later, Barley cornered me, coffee cup in hand.

"Can you believe it?" she said, leaning against the wall beside the Christmas tree. "It was just the strangest thing. It's like once we actually got divorced, we couldn't go through with it." She looked up at me brightly.

I didn't know what to say; I'd had too much to drink by then and didn't trust myself to say anything remotely kind.

"We just knew we needed to get back in to the see counselor. And look where we are?" She smiled, her face smooth and relaxed.

I was upset not because she'd left my brother and had an affair, but because she, unlike me, had managed to put her marriage back together. Beside me the Christmas lights flashed in regular patterns. Then the chaser lights came on and blurred before my sight.

"Are you okay?" Barley asked.

I paused. "I am happy for you, Barley. I really am." I pinched my mouth shut, nodded, and said nothing more. I wanted to say, "How could you?" about the affair – that was what had started everything. But saying that meant I would have to ask it of myself. Instead, I stood up, excused myself, and walked directly to our back door. I needed air, badly. To my chagrin, Barley followed me out there.

"Sar, you're upset. Are you upset… that I'm here? That I said what I did?"

I couldn't speak, only shook my head.

"Are you guys struggling?" she asked, through the dark.

165

Her eyes shone in the streetlight. Her olive skin glowed in the light.

My mouth tightened. I deflected, again.

Barley had a way of laying things out plain, so plain that it tended to make me angry. I wasn't proud of this, any more than I was proud of the rest of it.

"Like I said, it does get harder—"

"I don't want to hear that, Barl. How do you know what this is for me?"

Barley stepped closer over the tile slates that paved our yard, as if to shorten the gap between us. She dropped her voice. "There's someone else, Sar. Isn't there?"

I turned to her, and before I could say anything, I simply nodded.

Her face grew dark.

I needed her to be an ally, because everyone, most especially my own mother, had left me by the wayside. Some part of me had split inside; I was severed. Barley alone, I supposed, could recognize this.

When we returned inside, she searched out her husband. Their eyes met, they smiled. I looked around for mine. He was sitting opposite my dad, mug in hand, elbows on his knees, exchanging pleasantries. The last Christmas CD had stopped. There was silence in the room for the first time that evening; for once I didn't get up to change it. I was drinking coffee, having laid off the mulled wine. Then my mom offered me a slow, curious smile and held my gaze. I tried to smile back, tried to find the one thing I could be grateful for that night: my mother was alive, four years after the treatment.

Then Barley turned to me and said, as if in afterthought, "Honestly, Sar," her voice dropping to a low, dark whisper, when she joined me on the sofa. "I don't know what I was thinking. I thought it was love I felt for that guy, but really, it wasn't."

I froze. Some part of me floated to the ceiling and vanished. I saw Zeke's face: not his jocular grin at the coffee shop, where his defenses were up, but the anger, the injured expression in his eyes up on the hillside. And I no longer knew what was true: what my sister-in-law had just told me, or what I felt when I went walking with Zeke, the breeze catching at me, the branches winking and stealing the moment.

PART VII

MILL VALLEY, CALIFORNIA
2009

Three Years Ago

May 2009

Chapter Eighteen

I'd like to say – to my mother or anyone – that I didn't fall in love with someone else, that Zeke wasn't the reason I dissolved my marriage. But that would be patently untrue. He wasn't the only reason; he wasn't even the greatest reason. That I could stand by.

My mom told me two things that year that helped immensely; she said, "Don't melt down," and "Take it one day at a time." I didn't melt down the night of our Christmas party. Or the following March, when I took the bar. I melted down the day I went to Zeke's house and knocked on his door.

He was home – as I had hoped he'd be.

When he opened the door and saw me, his brow shot up. "Sara."

"Can I come in?"

He nodded and stepped back. He was barefoot on clean, off-white carpet. I slipped off my shoes and stepped inside. He wore a blue-and-white checked cotton shirt over jeans. His hair was disheveled like he'd just gotten out of the shower.

"Do you have a moment to talk?" We hadn't talked since I'd seen him last summer.

"Do we have something to talk about?"

"I think so." I faltered here.

"Want anything?" He went to get himself a cup of coffee.

"No, thanks," I said. I didn't trust myself holding a mug right now.

His living room was sparse but inviting, with simple furnishings: a leather-strap seat by the fireplace, and a long low sofa in a tan, textured cover. On the ottoman were design books – Asian art gardens and homemade houses. In the far corner of the room, facing the back garden was a table with cubbyholes that stretched along the wall above it, filled with items stacked by type. He was organized in a functional, practical way.

He watched me scanning his living room.

"I never got to see the inside of your home before," I said.

"No." His response was terse, the closed expression on his face all too reminiscent. "What's going on, Sara?"

"Can I sit down?"

He nodded.

"I took the bar," I said.

"Did you pass?"

"Yes."

"Good." He was standing, not sitting beside me. "Do I get credit for it?"

He smiled.

"Sure, if you want." I laughed, nearly relaxed. "Are you going to take a seat?"

His mouth twitched. He dropped onto the sofa opposite me, placed one foot beneath his thigh in a half-lotus position. I looked around the room at the place this man inhabited, looking for signs of who he was, of his world.

"Get a job yet?"

"Nope. That's next."

He smiled.

"I'm leaving my husband," I said. "I've left him." I couldn't look at him. I studied the fireplace, which had ashes and charred wood as though it was used not long ago.

"I'm seeing someone," he said, crossing his arms.

"You're *seeing* someone?"

"Yes." He let out a long sigh, and then smiled.

"Is it serious? How long have you been seeing her?"

"Not long. I don't know. I don't know how I feel about her."

"You don't know how you feel about her? Well, that's not a good thing, is it?" I was suddenly angry: angry at myself, angry at him, already moralizing and self-righteous. Being near him was hard enough, being near and not being able to touch him harder still.

I stood up, and without either of us in shoes I was nearly his height.

"I guess I should go then."

"Wait."

"Wait, why? For you to string me along?" I turned to look him in the eye. "Do you know what kind of courage it took for me to come down here to talk to you? Do you have any idea what this past nine months has been like in my life? You have no idea."

I marched toward his door. Then he grabbed my arm just as he had up on the hill, and now there was only the breeze of my movement, the thin space between us, keeping me from him, and he pulled me toward him, put one hand around the back of my neck and it tingled. He kissed me and I kissed him back. Whether it was an error didn't even register in my mind. I was already there. I had been there for a long time.

We didn't sleep together. And he didn't leave his girlfriend. It's important that this be known, at least by the people that matter. I'm an attorney – as well as a mom – and it's who I am in this world, I'd like to say. But I lost this case too. I thought I'd re-engage him, then piously wait until the papers were filed. But it didn't go that way. Not at all.

After the kiss, he pulled away. He examined my face closely, and I saw warmth, then a flash in his eyes, a distanced expression, the ripple of a frown across his forehead.

"You're not leaving her, are you?"

171

He shook his head.

I felt myself go cold. Then I smiled at him, bitterly. "You were never going to get involved with me, were you? This was a fucking game for you, wasn't it?"

"You have a family. You have your own kids. I want my own."

I let out a shocked gasp. "You knew that all along, Zeke, and you *liked* my boys. You talked about them all the time." My voice cracked. I turned around to stare at his living room, at the fire he had shared with someone else. I saw its simplicity, what might have been his relative poverty. I glanced at his coffee cup, a small ceramic island on the end table, and felt nauseous. "The whole thing is a smokescreen. You didn't want to be hurt. How long have you been with her?"

"What does it matter, Sara?"

"It matters to me, Zeke." I stepped closer to him. I wasn't going to let him intimidate me. "Tell me. Two months, three months? I have a right to know."

"Four months."

It was a record for him; I knew that. "Whatever you have with her," I said, through near tears, "it won't last."

Then I left through his open door, swept past the tangle of forget-me-nots in his yard, and slammed the gate behind me.

I called Emily that night, after the boys were down. She knew everything now, of course. Except this. I told her what had happened, my voice thick from crying.

"He's chicken shit," she said. "He is. A man like this, he'll marry some woman in a fever and it will evaporate in six weeks. He's not capable of love, Sara. This isn't you."

I pressed my lips together in silence. "What did he even want from me?"

"He wanted to be seen, visible. I think it's a self-esteem issue: you reflected him. Your love *made* him visible."

"To the world, maybe. Or to himself?"

"Both, I'd say. But most definitely to himself," she said, with a laugh. She paused. "Are you okay? This doesn't change anything does it?"

Emily had understood my reasons. She would never counter my actions, if anything she wanted assurance I wasn't backing down.

"No," I said. And we hung up.

In the living room were the remnants of our day: the boy's Legos strewn across the wood floor; a pile of my files from the job search, partially written applications and papers from the attorney, on the armoire I'd converted into a desk area, the center of my job search. A light was on, the light I left on nightly for Tye, who would arrive past midnight, then pull out the sofa bed to make a bed of his own, and remake it before our children woke up and stumbled through the living room to find him gone.

The next day, my mom called to deliver the news.

It was 6:30 at night, and I was trying to get dinner on. The boys were watching a video in the playroom, and Tye would be home any minute. He had called from work to say he was arriving early tonight. I was surrounded by dishes on the counter; at least they were stacked today, even if I couldn't load them before leaving for work this morning. I'd taken an admin job at a local nonprofit, just to keep up on my end of the rent. These days I inhabited a different kitchen: surrounded still by pots and pans hanging above the island, long ropes of garlic between them, and potted plants on the window sill, but now they were cactuses, no longer orchids. I considered it a good day when my counter was clean and the sink basin spotless, but it didn't happen very often. I didn't care much anymore. I was growing my boys now, and that much I could manage.

My mom knew better than to call at the dinner hour, so it had to be important. "It's Ephraim," she said. "He's moving out again." Long sigh.

No one really believed they would make it, least of all me. But I didn't say this. Instead I inhaled sharply. "How is he doing? How are the kids?"

"Traci's doing okay, strangely. I think she knew this wasn't going to work. Frankly, I think Barley was the only one who really thought this had a prayer."

I was glad she said it. I still said nothing. I was not, ordinarily, gracious, but something in seeing Zeke yesterday had shifted things. I had cried late into the night, but I was relaxed, almost at peace. I was moving forward, if in some new, undeclared way.

"What about Ephraim?" I asked.

"It's clear now. He knows it will never work."

"Ahh. I guess that's something," I said, filling the pot with water. I couldn't decide if I should say anything about Tye and me. "Mom, I have something to tell you." I put the pot to boil on the burner, and then slipped out the back door to be out of earshot of the boys. "Tye and I are in counseling." We'd been seeing someone since Christmas, weekly. It had not made an appreciable difference.

Another sharp inhale, this time hers. "I figured," she said, quietly.

"What do you mean, you figured?"

"You're very different, Sar. Surely you know this."

"And you tell me this *now*? Years into our marriage." I paused. "Would it not have been helpful to share how you felt back then, *before* we got married?"

There was a long silence. I felt awful. She'd been ill and wasn't now – it was in remission – but that didn't change the feelings, which I could not bear to admit.

I squinted at the magnolia in our back yard, white

174

blossoms everywhere, weeping from the branches. The scent was lovely, and I tried to breathe it in, slowly.

"I'm sorry to hear it," she hastened to say, but I knew it was an afterthought, and it wasn't what she really felt. She wasn't sorry at all – except for my kids.

When we got off the phone, I came back inside to finish making supper. I sliced tomatoes, diced cucumbers, and minced green onions. I spun the lettuce, pulled a large salad bowl out from the open shelving under the island, and began tearing the lettuce into it. Did she blame herself? I wanted to know, because I'm a mother and I needed to discern what part we own when our children's relationships don't survive – when our children's marriages don't survive. Two of her children's marriages were dissolving, and we were her golden ones. Did she wonder about our dad, about her own choice? I threw in the veggies, reached for some goat cheese in the fridge and broke it into small pieces, the smallest of actions defining our lives. I thought of Ephraim tearing the blades of grass as we spoke that day at their home in Berkeley, the clean even strips as he broke down his understanding. Had I chosen a man like my father? I decided finally it wasn't so, because my father had made good for his family; he'd changed his work to meet my mother's needs. But she didn't choose a strong man, nor had I. I was afraid of choosing strength, of facing up to my right match. I didn't break it down, blade by blade; and I ought to have. And this part I knew to be my own shortcoming.

Tye walked in the door that night looking nothing short of desultory.

"You okay?" I offered.

"No, I'm not okay."

I blinked. This wasn't like him. He threw his coat on the sofa, not on the peg beside the door, and glared at me. "I got a phone call today at work."

My back stiffened. "And? Who was it from?" I tried to sound even.

"Beckett." Beckett was Tye's only real friend within about 3,000 miles, an old friend from college who happened to move into the neighborhood a year ago.

I frowned. "He called you at work? What about?"

"Because he said he saw you going down to that guy's house yesterday. That neighbor." His face was crimson.

I froze, then immediately thought of the boys. "Shhh. Come outside."

We stepped out the back door, the noodles were long since done, but I couldn't stop for them now. I was trying to breathe and think and figure out what to say. Had Barley said anything? That was impossible: she would never have betrayed me like that.

As the door closed behind us, we were enveloped in the smell of magnolia and he said to me, "Are you having an affair?"

"No," I said, distinctly. "I am not." I was a lawyer. I was not going to incriminate myself. Besides, it was most definitely not true. I almost laughed, given the irony of it.

"Then what's happening? Is this what's really going on? Is this why we're in counseling?" His face was dark, though it was still light out at this hour. The creases beside his eyes were quivering.

I felt sick to my stomach. "Yes, I have met someone, but no, I'm not having an affair."

He was silent, his entire face trembling.

I knew this was wrong, that I had behaved wrongly. Not him. Where there was a window between Zeke and me, there should have been a wall – as anyone who's married will tell you. Still, I knew how to fight my case and so I held my ground.

"You know if we divorce, this could fuck you up bad," he said, some part of him still believing this wasn't over. "I could use this, you know that, don't you?"

I did know this. It was quite possibly why I'd said nothing to date. But it was also true that I didn't, frankly, think it was totally germane.

"It's easy to think this is about someone else, Tye. It isn't. I'm friends with Zeke. I care about him. But I'm not having an affair. Besides, he has a girlfriend." I snorted in shock and irritation, even saying the words. "Our problems began long before I met him."

Tye searched my face. Some part of him knew this was half-truth. And it was. I hadn't been having an affair with Zeke, during the past year a half, but I might as well have been. I had already left this marriage, and now he knew it.

We were both very quiet. And then I said, "It's time to go inside; I have to feed the boys."

"You okay?" my mother asked, when I came to the front door a week or more later. She had come to watch the boys so I could walk with Emily at the coast.

"Barely."

The sun was shining through the glass sidelights, the light altogether too bright for me, given the previous night's rough sleep. Every night was a rough night. Most nights Tye barely spoke to me.

"You don't look it."

She followed me into the kitchen, saw the shape the counter and floor were in. I told her about the incident last night in the kitchen, when I'd swept my arm across the kitchen island in a moment of rage. I wasn't proud of it. I saw it as a symptom of the stress of the past six years in

177

California, but it didn't change what happened. She dropped her purse on one of the chairs. "Oh, Sar," she said.

I told her that Emily and I would be going to Bodega Head and that I had the cell with me. I walked toward the door.

"Sar, stop a minute, please," she said. I knew what she was going to say, even before she said it.

"Tye told me there's someone else."

I cringed, my back to her. My hand slipped from the door handle. I pivoted, turned to face her. "Yes, I cared about someone," I said. "But it wasn't an affair."

My mother stood close to me by the front door. I dropped my pack on the sofa and waited as she approached. I put my face in my hands but I didn't cry. I was not hiding, only trying to find my resolve.

"Has he been in the picture for a while?" she asked.

I didn't say anything.

"I'm sorry. I guess it's not my business." Her voice was low and uneven.

"No, *I'm* sorry." I raised my face from my hands. "I was going to tell you, I really was. Once I knew where things stood with Tye." She watched me carefully.

"It's not what took my marriage down, Mom. Tye and I took it down. We both did." I saw this now. I couldn't blame him, though I'd wanted to. We weren't entirely victims of the California economy. Even that was too pat. I wanted to make it forces beyond us; Tye wanted to make it a person beyond us. It was neither of those. It was who we were, or more to the point, who we weren't. I was splitting this blade of grass now, because if I was moving forward I couldn't live the lie any longer. I had to break it down to what I knew to be true.

"We were friends," I said, as I came to my feet, standing

up, unevenly at first, then steadily. "For a long time. Nothing happened. You have to know that."

She nodded, but her eyes were glued to mine. "Is this true?"

"Yes, it's true."

But as I slipped out the door and closed it firmly behind me, I asked myself, how true was it? In the underbelly of every truth there is some lie, a partial utterance, some interpretation we make our own. I was telling it to her as I saw it. Did Tye see it this way? Did Zeke see it this way? And now, did my mom see it this way? In the end, it mattered only how I saw and understood it. I was the one beholden to this truth now. We'd come west together, Tye and I, but now I was the one staking this claim.

PART VIII

MILL VALLEY, CALIFORNIA
2010

Two Years Ago

January 2010

Chapter Nineteen

It was January, and I'd been working exactly four months. Finding a job hadn't proved as hard as I'd thought. Zeke was right. I applied to four places on recommendations from Trish, of course, who'd given me every contact she had in the East Bay and then some. "Tell them to call me," she said. "It's not too far back for me to be a reference. It will make a difference. I know it will." It was a decent firm – private practice, because I wasn't going to do trial law ever again. I was building a steady clientele. I had flexible hours, which meant I could keep the kids' schedules intact. Yes, Mark was in day care more than I would have liked, but I'd made my peace with that too. If I was going to leave my husband, I would have to be more self-reliant, let alone financially solvent. Tye had gotten a job, ten months after losing the position at the ad agency. We were in debt; and the divorce hadn't helped any. But I was tough and the law had taught me a measure of confidence, or maybe I was regaining the confidence I once had, and lost.

I was at the therapist's one day, a remnant of our couples' counseling, on a lunch break from the office in Albany. We had counseled for months about Zeke. Little remained left for me to say: I had loved him; he hadn't loved me back – whether or not he was capable of it. Today the therapist wanted to know my work history.

"Why were you so long deciding to go back, Sara?" he asked me.

On his futon sofa, I balanced the box of Kleenex beside my leg and picked at my pants suit. I sipped my tea and held the mug close, nearly to my cheek, for warmth.

"I guess it was the Susan Holeman case – if I had to name it. And Tye too."

"Do you want to tell me about that?" he asked.

PART IX

RALEIGH, NORTH CAROLINA
1999

Thirteen Years Ago

August 1999

Chapter Twenty

I loved the law not because I enjoyed reading hefty briefs or spending hours in the library but because I was fixated on fairness – not to be confused with equity – in every arena, large and small. I knew enough by the time I was twenty-three and applying to Law School that there was no such thing as equality, despite all of our attempts to be an equal society. But I did believe things could be fair; and the jury trial system seemed to be one strategy toward achieving fairness. In a democratic society, I believed, it was the only way.

Things hadn't been equal growing up in my family. Even my mother admits that now. My two older brothers had widely disparate freedoms in comparison to mine and were granted every privilege I wasn't: they could stay out past curfew, spend the night with friends, and they had fewer chores yet made more money than I. Tough as she was with me, my mother let them slide – a lot. One day, as a result, I cracked.

Our father was out plumbing, and we were all three outside, our mother inside. She'd come home late from work. I was six, so Ephraim would have been twelve. Three weeks prior, Ephraim had figured out how to climb onto the roof from the pear tree at the far side of the house and he took my bike that afternoon and put it on the garage roof. He climbed back down, triumphant, leaned over and laughed right in my face. I turned and walked away, picked up a good-sized rock, and then hurled it at him. The rock hit my mother's prized kitchen window. Glass flew everywhere, chinks of it wedged in the refrigerator grate, narrowly missing my mother, who stepped outside when she heard her youngest crying. My mom, the arbiter of all things small and large, held me by the elbow and marched me into my room. She sat me down on the edge of my twin bed with the tufted-cotton bedspread, an abstract blend of orange, red, and brown – the glorious colors of the Seventies – and told me, "Not fair? Let me tell you something, Sara. Angry doesn't give you the right to hurt someone. And that is most definitely about fair." I was grounded for a week, while Ephraim ran free. It seems petty now; by a child's standard it was not. I never forgot it.

Years later, fairness became linked to hard work.

The day Trisha interviewed me for a position at her immigration law firm in LA, in 1992, we sat in her cramped office, stacks of depositions from floor to ceiling, because she didn't have time to set up her files. The phone rang constantly and Trish summarily ignored it. The receptionist came in dressed in a leather skirt and high boots; casual was an understatement, but Trish had no time to worry about standard office etiquette. A family sat in the waiting room, the child wandering around the lobby, such as it was, past the Lego set Trish had put out to lure kids away from, say, the filing cabinet with books piled atop it haphazardly high, and other more treacherous parts of the room. The man seated, his elbows on his knees, stared straight ahead; he was very dark-skinned, his eyes round and deep set. I didn't think he looked Mexican, and learned from Trish later that he was Peruvian. "Santiago's come a really long ways to work here. You wouldn't believe how he got here. The usual coyote story times about four." Trish shook her head; even she had been astounded. Shards of sunlight glanced across the linoleum floor from a tall wide window that looked onto a back parking lot beside a CVS store. You couldn't have found less glamorous.

Trish's staff was devoted. When she stayed late – which

185

was nearly every night, she informed me – they stayed late with her. She was lean with sharp features and looked every bit as Midwestern as she was, blond, high cheekboned. She paid no attention to her clothing, jeans most the time, unless she was going to court, when she dressed in heels that were precarious even for her. She rarely slept, and ate constantly. At the interview, Trish brushed a few crumbs off her desk, glancing wryly at them, then emptied her hands into the trashcan below her desk. "I'm going to need you to work really hard. Can you do that? Because otherwise it's not going to work. Everyone works hard here. It's not for the pay, you get that, right?"

We were there all the time. I worked six days a week, ten to twelve hours a day, and sometimes Sunday nights. I did everything from answering her personal line to meeting with clients with her to researching cases. At lunchtime I went to the Mexican restaurant on the corner, where no one spoke any English, and got us carnitas. On extra-long days, I bought us Mexican wedding cakes, the swirled, heavily breaded pastries they displayed in the glass cabinet beside the register. One constituted a meal in itself. Watching Trish that year, I equated the struggle for fairness with the challenge of hard work and long hours. Fairness could be reached through the law, as she modeled it – she won more cases than she lost – but it would likely come with a cost. That cost was time.

Most mornings in Chapel Hill, in my apartment, where Tye and I lived the year after we were married, I woke up early and read the paper, not because I wanted to follow the news – some sort of knee-jerk, politically correct kind of thing – but because I liked knowing what was going on in the world. The news was barely online, though Tye, working at the news station in Raleigh, was helping that cause along,

186

part of the new wave of live streaming, the Internet coming of age in the Triangle by the early Nineties. He took his news by the screen – he was in IT after all. I took mine over morning coffee.

On the 2nd of August, I woke early and slipped out of bed without waking my husband, grabbed a fresh towel, and stepped into the bathroom. It was Monday morning, and I needed to prepare myself mentally for the day ahead. I had a continuance to request on a trial, followed by a first interview on a new case. The shower steamed over me. I smiled, tracing a finger along the grout of the shower stall, as the water pummeled my shoulders. It turned cold suddenly; the downstairs flat, closer to the hot water tank, often fared better in the morning. "Son of a bitch," I said aloud. Then the hot water came back on.

"You talking to me?" Tye appeared in the doorway. "Can I come in?" His hair almost curled visibly in the steam; he'd cut it shorter because everyone was wearing it shorter now. I was barely accustomed to sharing my space. I smiled at his politeness, though, at the degree to which he never assumed my acquiescence. But this time he didn't wait for an answer. He slipped inside the shower stall and stepped toward me. He was crossing a boundary; not the shower or the privacy of my space, but some physical limit he'd not crossed before. It wasn't sex, but some step toward deeper intimacy as he held me close in the shower, steam enveloping us both. He wanted me – it wasn't just physical, he wanted some place I inhabited he wasn't certain he could travel on his own.

"Are you on this?" my co-worker asked me at the office, handing me a slip of paper.

I had just completed my first witness interview of the morning; it was a drive-by shooting of a teenager by a twenty-two-year-old, one of his close friends, who was high. The family members, all of them, were beside themselves. It was an onerous case; I knew I didn't want it and here was my colleague, bearing the news of yet another. We were told we had a choice, when really, we didn't.

"Why? Should I want to be on this?"

"Rough night last night?" Barbara – Beebee, as everyone called her in the PD Office – always cross-examined her colleagues about their personal lives because she had none of her own. "*What did you do this weekend?*" was her constant refrain.

"No," I said, deflecting. I was the master of deflection. "Give me the paper, Beeb. I'm on it." I picked up the phone, rang the number, and hung on the line.

Beebee gathered up her briefcase, turned on her heels and was gone. It wasn't a setting that coddled. I'd grown accustomed to its hardness. Being a public defender, it turned out, was nothing at all like I'd imagined it would be.

I picked up the phone, cradled it in my neck, and pulled out my notepad. This was the late-1990s and laptops at the PD Office were not yet the norm; the computers were old clunky MS-DOS Gateways that no one wanted. "Hi," I said, after ringing the number Beebee had given me. "This is Sara Greystone, I'm a public defender down in Raleigh…" Was I cut out for this? Some days I wasn't so sure.

The case was straight forward: the man who attacked Susan Holeman was her boyfriend, a chronic abuser, and Holeman's children had witnessed his abuse repeatedly. She was arraigned for assault, although the facts were stacked in her favor, in one sense, but not in all senses. She was African American, her abuser was white, and this was the 1990s. It didn't matter that the Civil Rights Movement, people in this state believed, had started down the road in Greensboro. Even if it *was* the New South, it wasn't yet "new" enough. This made the question of witnesses crucial. And the problem was that the kids were the *only* witnesses, which meant the five- and seven-year-old girl and boy would have to testify. I would have to put them on the witness stand to keep their mother out of prison. The types of abuse were horrible: burning, beating, attempted rape – all of it. The children were with the grandmother now. Holeman, by the time I met with her, had spent the morning weeping because she'd not seen the kids in three days and her mother refused to bring them down because she was angry at her daughter, who had spent years in rehab and had finally recovered (though not recovered enough apparently to steer clear of a lousy, loser boyfriend). There was every chance Holeman would lose custody of the kids to the children's father, on and off the streets as a user, also rehabilitated, ostensibly, or so he claimed. So the case was ugly in every direction.

I had seen worse: the case in which a man had chewed off the lips of the women he raped and killed – my all-time worst defense case ever. I had had nightmares for months going into it. The presumption that someone was innocent until proven guilty was a reasonable baseline until you had to apply it to the truly sick. Every time I sat in the room with him, I felt my hairline prickle. Making eye contact left me deeply unsettled for hours. Sitting across from me in the first interview, my client smiled even as he described the conditions he left his victims in. There had to be a word for individuals like that, but I was paid not to say them.

I still felt the weight of that case, when the parents of the young women eyed me in the courtroom as if I was the lowest of scum. One father refused to take his eyes off me as I sat with Mr.——, as if by visually berating me the father might take me down and lessen my case. I succeeded in keeping my client from the death penalty; he had boxcar sentences that totaled 72 years. He would never see time on the other side of the fence. But I still felt between every hard rock and rough place on that case. The DA himself had dressed me down that day for being too convincing in my closing comments. "You should have let the man fry, Sara. Honestly." So I got to feel horrible every which way. I didn't believe in capital punishment, but I never wanted to see that man again, his slick greying brown hair and the soft chin that broke into a wretched smile at the worst of moments, his arms crossed in the witness stand, the haunting grimace he threw me, victorious, when the jury returned the verdict. The father, who had stared at me the entire three weeks of the trial period, glared at me until he grew beet red and his wife tugged on his arm and he shrugged her off. That morning, he started mouthing something to me but I turned away, with a last glance at Mr.——, before they removed him in his jumpsuit back into the holding tank. Later that day they would pack him up to Central Prison in Raleigh and send him off to some maximum-security prison down the state.

I went home that night and drank half a bottle of wine, took a long hot bath, and cried myself to sleep. Tye was out of town so I had the apartment to myself. None of this was what I'd bargained for. But then what do you expect, when you learn the ropes under the toughest PD in the state, and this on top of one of the best law trainings I might have had anywhere in the country. I'd learned to be good, all right – but at what cost?

I spent a good deal of time researching the case. But inevitably, when the trial began, one never felt fully prepared; it was public defense and the caseload was high everywhere. We handled the preliminaries, picked the jury and, on the first day of the trial, moved through opening arguments. We had air in the courtroom but the intense heat outside made for heat in the hallways and everyone would feel the effects. Someone had eaten a sub at the security desk out front and it left a tangy unpleasant odor, I noticed, coming into the courtroom. The children were with a guardian and offered me feeble smiles as I walked in. I took my seat beside Susan, who wore her hair in a series of tiny braids with beads on the end. I pulled out my papers and whispered to her, "Stay calm, and try not to react, okay?" as the attending police officer led her daughter to the witness stand.

The presiding judge, Judge Anastase, after swearing in the witness, called both attorneys forward. "You need to watch yourselves today; I don't need to tell you that, but I will all the same," he said in a lowered voice. "This is a child testifying." He threw a glance at the prosecutor, Jim Archer, whom I had a particular distaste for. Archer was known for brutally extracting information from people. Socially, in a bar, he was nice enough but for someone on the stand, he could be deadly. He took every sentence and re-framed it to his own advantage. I had difficulty hiding my irritation toward him much of the time. I had, unfortunately, slept with the guy about six months into starting at the PD Office, one night after we'd all gone for drinks, and he'd never let me forget it.

Judge Anastase was known in Raleigh for his composure under pressure and his consummate fairness. His silver hair swept back off his head like a country western musician, and he gave the appearance of being slick or easy but he wasn't. He'd been educated at MIT, gone to Columbia Law School, and had returned to Raleigh,

191

where he was from, an altered man, if a Southerner all the same. He coughed, his smoothly shaved cheeks shaking, and then he cleared his throat, which usually signaled that it was time to begin.

Kelsey was in a striped yellow, pink, and brown gingham dress and wore her hair in pigtails with pink bows, tied carefully at the end of each strand; one side was slightly longer than the other, trailing down. The corners of her smile seemed to trail down, too, like the face of a jack on a playing card. Half of her face child-like, the other deadly serious. Her teeth were large, the way all children's front teeth are, and they were offset, so that none of them landed perfectly above the teeth below. She smiled at me, but the smile vanished as the prosecutor moved toward her.

"Kelsey," he said.

Her mother sat beside me, her eyes pinning down her daughter's. Susan barely seemed to blink. The courtroom was fairly empty, which made the voices more boom-y and ominous, though I knew the room would fill up over the course of the day.

"Kelsey, you heard what the man said about the truth, right? About telling the whole truth? You know what truth is, right?"

She nodded, somber.

"Okay, I want you to tell me the truth about what happened the day your mommy picked you up, Friday, June 4th."

She stared at him blankly; the day meant nothing.

He forced a smile, turned away, and then back again. "Okay, the day your mom came home to get you early from school."

He paced in front of the child. It seemed a strange way to open up his line of questioning.

"Yes, sir," she said, her voice quavering. This was the

South, and even a five-year-old knew to call a white man sir.

"What was your mother wearing that day, Kelsey?"

"Your Honor, objection. Relevance," I said, getting to my feet even before the words came out. Now I knew exactly where he was going.

"Overruled, Ms. Greystone. Mr. Archer, proceed."

Kelsey pressed her lips together nervously. "A dress, sir," she said.

"A dress? Was it a *pretty* dress?" He hung his arm off the corner of the stand, turned to the jury, and leered, directly at the men.

Kelsey shrugged, as if she knew he was leading her.

"Answer the question, please, Kelsey."

"Your Honor, may we approach the bench?" I asked.

"Mr. Archer," he said.

"Your Honor, this isn't an appropriate line of questioning. He's asking the child to assess her mother's physical..." I paused. "Prowess," I said, not knowing what other word to use. "He's entrapping her, or trying."

Anastase didn't respond, simply looked directly at Archer, who leaned in close to Judge Anastase's desk. I could smell his aftershave or cologne, its sweet sickly odor; the air in the courtroom was already too close.

"Mr. Archer, a more direct line of questioning, please?" Then he leaned back in his broad wooden chair, an act of dismissal.

"Kelsey," Archer said, turning back to the child. "Let's start again. Tell me what happened when your mommy picked you up from school early that day and took you over with her to Mr. Everett Taylor's home."

"Mommy took me into his house."

"And?"

"And I watched his TV."

193

"Did your mommy always put you in front of the TV?"

"Objection, Your Honor. Relevance?" I felt heat rising at the back of my neck.

"Overruled."

I frowned.

"Did your mommy always put you in front of the TV?" the court reporter read out.

Archer looked at Kelsey, who nodded, "Yes. Most times."

"And what happened, Kelsey. Tell us."

"I was watching," she said. "Then I heard voices."

"Voices? Whose voices."

"Mommy's and Mr. Taylor's."

"And?"

"They were having a fight." Her mouth twitched.

"Were they?" Archer smiled. A few people in the chamber snickered.

I bristled, fighting the urge to turn around. I glanced over at Susan, her face darkening. A chair scraped by the front door. The security guard rose to help steer someone to an available seat.

"How do you know they were fighting?"

"I heard yelling, sir."

"Whose?"

"My mommy's."

"What did she say? What was your mommy saying?"

"I'm—" She paused.

"Go on, Kelsey. Tell the court."

"I'm gonna take you out," she said, in a whisper.

Susan gasped. This was not a good start to the day.

At the break, before I was to cross-examine Kelsey, I tried in quiet tones to help Susan keep it together. "Did you say that?"

"I don't remember what I said. Sara, he said that shit to me all the time to lead me on, you know."

"What did he say?" I asked quietly. "I thought we had rehearsed this – gone over this hundreds of times, Susan. You've got to level with me or I can't help you."

"He told me he was going to hurt me."

"How was he going to hurt you? No," I paused, thinking aloud. "We're not going there, Susan. I'm not going there with Kelsey. I'm going to talk to her about the other incidents." I knew it was manipulative, but I felt I had to reverse the damage.

Susan's mouth tightened. A shudder ran across the woman's forehead. "Please," she said.

"I've got to, Susan, I'm sorry."

When the courtroom was silent again, and Judge Anastase had resumed order, Archer came over to chat briefly, but I cut him off. "Later, Archer," I said. I knew he was trying to blow my cool. Kelsey took the stand again, and I walked toward her, brushed against the wood before resting my hand in front of her.

"Kelsey, I have to ask you some questions."

"Okay, Ms. Sara."

"They might be hard to answer but you need to answer them anyway, okay?" Trisha had always done this: told the children what was ahead, to emotionally prepare them for the moment to come. When really there *was* no way to fully prepare them.

The child nodded.

"How often did Mr. Taylor come to your and your mommy's home?"

"About twice a week."

"Why did he come? Do you know?"

"Because he liked my mommy," she said, softly.

"Liked?"

"Yes."

"Liked her? Or would you say he loved her?"

The doors of the courtroom opened, more foot traffic only this time a woman with silvery-grey hair, hobbling on a cane, began walking steadily up the center aisle.

"Grandma," Kelsey called out. I bristled. Unbelievable timing.

"Kelsey, we need to keep going here. Would you say he loved her?"

"Yes," she said, still staring at her grandmother as she settled noisily into a chair.

"What happened when your mommy and Mr. Taylor were at your house?"

"What happened?" She was already distracted.

"Yes, what did they do?"

"I don't know. He came by and we had supper."

"And then what?"

"They went to Mommy's room." I could feel the tension rise in the room.

"And then what?"

"I heard noises."

"Like?" I took a deep breath. It was going to get harder, but I knew I had to keep going.

"Crying."

"Was your mommy crying?"

She nodded, and her mouth got very still and solemn.

"What else did you hear?"

"I heard a belt."

"Your Honor, objection. Lack of foundation," Archer said, as he got to his feet.

"Overruled. Go ahead, Ms. Greystone."

The fan above whirred, and I took another breath.

"Kelsey, how did you know it was a belt?"

Kelsey's voice sunk. "Because I saw it."

"And what did he do with that belt?" My breath stopped.

"He hit her with it." Kelsey fretted in her chair.

The jury, the women in particular, smarted.

"Once?"

Kelsey's face was streaked with tears.

"No, lots of times."

"Did this happen a lot? Kelsey, tell me the kinds of things you saw happen when he was there. Things that Mr. Taylor did to your mommy. Things that you actually saw."

Archer shot out of his chair. "Your Honor – I object. Compound question."

"Sustained. Ms. Greystone, clarify, please." He scratched his forehead, leaned forward in his seat and turned to face the child. He paused. "Keep going." His words were firm, but the expression in his eyes gentle.

"Kelsey, tell me the things that Mr. Taylor did to your mommy. Things that you actually saw."

She cleared her throat and said, "I only saw things in the living room," she said, "but he hit her."

"With his hand?"

"No," she whispered.

"What did he hit her with, Kelsey? I am sorry to have to ask this, but I have to."

"With a pan," she said. "On her face."

"And what else did he hit her with? His hand?"

"No," she said. "He hit her with a shovel."

"A shovel? And—"

"The poker. That thing by the chimney."

"Where, where did he hit her with that?"

"Across her face."

"Did you go for help, Kelsey?"

She froze, and I instantly realized my blunder. It wouldn't affect the outcome, but I'd place her in a role of responsibility she couldn't possibly hold at age six. "I'm sorry, sweetie," I said. I felt my temperature rise; why had I not seen this coming?

"Finish up, Ms. Greystone. Please." Judge Anastase almost spat out the words.

"What I meant was, were you able to go for help?"

"No."

"And why not, Kelsey?"

"He locked the door," she said, starting to cry. "He wouldn't let me out. I couldn't get out."

"Kelsey, one last question. I'm sorry, but did he hurt your mommy in the other room?"

She shook her head.

"So only in front of you."

She nodded.

"So, let me get this right. He purposefully locked you in so you couldn't get out."

"Yes."

"He made you watch."

"Yes."

Gasps shuddered across the courtroom, the whirring of the fan spilled over into the sound so that all you could hear was a gasp and a shudder, a gasp and a shudder, in a kind of rhythmic sound.

Kelsey's tears ran down her face. I felt my throat go thick.

"Thank you, Kelsey. That's all."

On the drive to Asheville that weekend, I took the curves too swiftly as we made the final ascent up the mountain. Trucks honked as they swerved into the far left lane, alerting us they were passing. The Smoky Mountains stretched to the east, rolling hills covered in dusty blue-grey firs and hemlock, a stunning sequence of dips and valleys and rises, the wisps of cloud blending into haze. We weren't at cloud level but it felt like it.

"I can't believe I've been here seven years and I've never been out here," I said. "It's stunning." Ordinarily we went to the coast, to Wilmington, where Lisa's family had a house. Sometimes Lisa would join us; more often she let us have the place to ourselves. I rolled down the window and shafts of cooler air from this elevation wallowed in all around us. A strand of hair got tangled in my mouth. "You know these aren't really mountains, right? Compared to the West that is."

"And the mountains of Maine? What are they, Sara?" He'd driven most of the way, but we'd swapped coming through Statesville, where we stopped for an ice tea.

"Foothills, honey. They're foothills."

He smirked. "How's the case going?"

"You really want to hear?"

"Sure, I want to hear."

"Monday I put the five-year-old on the witness stand." I sucked in my breath. It was 10:00 am; we'd left the Triangle around six under cloud cover. But it had cleared, the black tarmac on the road refracting the sunlight. It was painfully bright. I reached for my sunglasses.

"Didn't you say Trisha had had to do that before?" He was trying, I could tell. The night before I'd told him he never asked about my work, that he didn't seem all that interested. It was the closest we'd come to a fight in the first year of our marriage.

It was true: defending immigrants separated from their children through immigration law meant Trish sometimes had to involve the children in the trial. There was one particular case in which a twelve-year-old child had traveled across the border solo, on the top of a train, to meet up with his father. The story was heart-rending and made

199

headline news in the *Los Angeles Times*. And the boy was a poster child for the issue. The father spoke very little English. Trisha, who believed in and supported bilingualism, had all but insisted he practice his English because the jury would be more sympathetic. She spent hours in conversation with his child in flawless Spanish, although the boy was bilingual, because she knew it was the best way to ensure his full comprehension. Trish went on to win the case against the INS, securing residency rights for the boy. Outside the courtroom, the father broke down and wept in relief, the son cradling his father in his arms to comfort him.

"Yeah, she did," I said, my elbow out the window, buffeted by the breeze. "It wasn't always pretty. But her strategy was phenomenal. Unlike mine."

The car sped around the final curve, racing down the interstate; the black pavement seemed to envelope us. The sunroof on Tye's old beat-up Mercedes was open and sunlight streamed in, landing across our laps. I cradled a bottle of bubbly water in mine. The valley of fir, pine, and hemlock stretched for miles and a thin wisp of smog or haze crept all around it. Waves of mountains, smaller ones now and densely forested, on either side of the highway. The air felt crisp, sharper than in the Piedmont, and I drank it in.

"So what happened? On Monday, with the case." He had not asked that night, but then again I'd been home late.

I told him about the trial, including my gaff with Kelsey.

"Will it affect the outcome?" he asked.

"No, but it was a shitty thing to say to a five-year-old. Kelsey already has a yoke around her neck. She doesn't need me to make her feel more responsible. I just didn't think it through."

"You're being too hard on yourself, don't you think?"

The pavement was a blur as we sped down the interstate toward Asheville. Tye was silent as I finished recounting the scene. His mouth twitched, but he said nothing. As we pulled off toward the Biltmore hotel, the weekend away we'd planned for weeks, I turned to look out the window, at the twisted kudzu vine hanging from the trees, but all I saw reflected back to me was Kelsey Holeman's face.

At the Biltmore we pulled up to the magnificent stone front door to unload our bags. Tye parked the car while I rolled our luggage toward the south entrance to wait for him. The Biltmore hotel is on a small ridge, overlooking a sea of ridges across the Western Carolina landscape; stretching to the north and running southward are the Blue Ridge Mountains. Even on a hazy day, as it was that day, the sunlight pierces through clouds and reaches for miles, an endless horizon of endless trees. I traced the horizon, or tried to, as if in following its line I might find some sort of solace. The chateaux-style Biltmore – once the Vanderbilt estate and now a National Landmark – boasted extensive cultivated gardens. Its turreted-structure only heightened the differences between my world, or the privileged world I could enter at will, and that of the individuals I defended daily – a divide that did not trouble my husband nearly as much as it troubled me.

Tye arrived with the keys in hand. "You ready?" he said, with a grin.

I let him haul our roller bag up the steps and then we stepped into the splendor of the lobby: plush curtains, overstuffed chairs, ornate side tables, and massive oriental rugs.

"You okay?" He tucked his arm around my waist and kissed me. "You ready?"

"For what?"

"For a great weekend. A break."

I wheeled back around to face him and squeezed his hand

lightly. I was terribly distracted by the case but knew I had disengage from it. We needed this time together: our connectedness of late, it seemed to me, had grown paper thin.

In the room, he closed the door behind us and pulled me toward him. I blinked my eyes tightly at one point as he pressed against me.

"You okay? Are you up for this?"

"Yeah, I think so."

"Is it the day?"

"Most definitely the day. Not you," I murmured. I could tell he was grateful for that. I knew Tye didn't always understand me, and that sometimes that troubled him. I suppose it ought to have troubled me.

After we made love, we lay on the bed together. It was a sleigh bed, I noticed – bittersweet, of course, as it reminded me of Josef. The curve at the top of the bed was smooth to the touch, and the smoothness of the wood felt cool and refreshing after the heat rising between us. We showered and put on fresh clothes, and as I always did when I relaxed, I left a string of clothing across the room, as if by letting go of what I'd worn that day I might shake the memory of the courtroom earlier that week. Tye liked a tidier room and often picked them up after me. "You don't have to clean it up," I said to him, with a laugh. "We're on vacation, right?" He nodded, watching as I put dangly earrings on at the mirror, and then he looked away. I was suddenly glad to be here, to let loose here in the hotel; whatever I offered up in the rest of my life, I had to let it go now.

At dinner, I talked in animated tones and he watched me through the candlelight in the center of the table. The shadows danced across his cheeks, one moment in darkness, the next brightly lit. He had duck; I had roast lamb. We both ate with enthusiasm; I indulged in massive amounts of bread to wipe up the juice from the lamb on my plate. He seemed a bit laconic, while I had grown light, finally. He talked about Norm, his officemate at the station, who prodded him endlessly, and also Tom, his boss, a man in his fifties, with whom Tye got on quite well. But then he grew quiet again.

"What is it, Tye?"

He poured us both another glass of wine.

"You seem, I don't know – off." I had been the one that was tweaky and sensitive in the car. I thought we were at last re-connecting; now he seemed aloof and disengaged.

"I don't know, it just seems you talk about your work all the time."

I recoiled. I hadn't said a word about the Holeman case until he asked in the car.

"Look, I was in a crap mood coming up, but I shook it off, okay? We made love," I said, leaning toward him over my near-empty plate. "It's been a nice afternoon. We're here at the Biltmore. I think you're the one who needs to relax."

"It just seems we used to have more… fun somehow."

I stared at him and took a sip of wine, trying to digest what he was saying. The white tablecloth caught between my legs, yanking the cloth from under my wine glass and it spilled. "Shit," I said, and began mopping up the liquid with my napkin.

"Sara, let them get it. That's what we're paying for." He signaled one of the wait staff.

"I can clean up my own mess." Something in his manner was off-putting, as if we were there to have servants, not to relax.

After the wait staff had left, I said, "I don't really understand what you're saying."

"Maybe I'm having a mid-life crisis." He laughed abruptly, then stared over at one of the waitresses.

Oh brother, I thought. "What?" I said, pausing to watch him. "What is it?"

"Nothing."

"You're smiling."

"We just used to have more fun. I kind of miss those college days, no mortgage" – we had just put a payment down on a house – "no work life." We hadn't even known each other in college. Was it married life? I waited for him to continue.

"I feel like you work all the time, Sara." I must have made a fretful expression. "What?" he said, rolling the wine around his glass and taking another sip. "You look really put out."

"Tye, I'm a public defender. It requires a lot of work. You knew this about me when you married me. It can't be a surprise."

He raised a brow, scanned the room for: the wait staff? Some inspiration? Our corner of the dining room light was somewhat in shadow; the lights above put out a somber yellow glow and we were at a distance from the fire burning in the massive stone hearth. I wasn't sure why they had a fire going in August, anyway, unless it was to give the expansive dining room a cozy feel.

"It's this case. You're letting it eat you alive."

I gasped and shook my head. "It's a really tough case, Tye. It's the hardest case I've ever had. You think I like putting kids on the stand? You don't know how horrible that is." The wine was kicking in now and I began to feel emotional.

"Yes, but it's a case, it's not your life."

I stuck my tongue in the corner of my mouth, looked over at him steadily. "My practice is a really big part of my life. You knew this about me. It's a priority."

"And when we have a family?"

"You're the one delaying the family, not me. We'll get help. Or I'll stay home for a bit, or some of both." I didn't know what I was saying; I suppose I was trying to appease him.

"Good." He set down his fork on the plate, poured us more wine. "May the Susan Holeman case be your last. At least for a while," he said, and raised his glass to me.

"Don't you want me to win?" I asked him.

By moonlight we walked outside near the fountain. The sky had gone dark, the heat of the day giving way to nighttime.

"It's lovely out," he said.

I sat on the edge of the fountain, crossing my legs and holding myself tightly, rocking slightly.

The moon had come out with just a sliver missing. The rose bushes, no doubt carefully pruned by day, looked menacing by night. I shivered, though what little breeze there was felt softer and kinder than it would be come fall.

A smile crept across his face; Tye looked positively joyful. "Doesn't it make you feel so... Alive?"

He took my hand.

"Sara?"

I didn't respond. When I lifted my face to his, my eyes were moist. He didn't notice. How was it he felt so alive and I felt so deadened? I felt like an exotic bird and that the birdman had caught me.

I returned to work on Monday to find a message on my voicemail. We had new evidence and it was not in Susan Holeman's favor. At my desk, my ear to the phone, I prowled through piles of papers to locate a stray pen and listened to the message twice to make certain I had missed nothing.

205

A row of empty Styrofoam cups had made their home on the counter top beside my desk. I stared at the cups, scanning from one to the next, as if an answer might be contained in one of them. Beebee leaned precariously over the cubicle, waiting to chat. I raised my hand to halt her progress. Beebee scratched her head, hand on hip, suggesting her irritation. And then another deputy PD came up behind and slid past her to my desk.

"He wants to see you," he said, meaning the PD, of course.

I nodded, scrawled a few more notes on my yellow pad. "Not good," I said, dropping the phone back in its cradle. "What about?" I said to my colleague.

"You don't want to know," he said, clutching a worn organizer as he strolled past, its corners rolling up from too much activity or humidity or both.

I leaned back in my seat, held back my sigh. Grace under pressure. It hadn't come as easily as I'd hoped. This wasn't the Monday I'd had in mind.

"Was it a good weekend?" Beebee said, once she had me alone. She wasn't smirking as much as interrogating. Beebee liked me – I suppose everyone at the PD Office did. I didn't waste time calling people out; I just worked hard and kept my nose clean. Work for me was much like an attribute, a moment by moment way of being.

"It feels like 400 years ago now." I rubbed my hands over my face.

"Yeah, that's what it's like here," Beebee said, in a rare moment of unexpurgated candor. "Everything else burns away."

The PD himself didn't so much exude authority as imply the refusal to surrender authority. The binders and law treatises and folders were piled along the walls, spilling out from the overfilled bookcase – the scraps of food from lunch on his desk and plastic wrappers from the previous meal – it could easily be any meal at any time of night, because there was never time to clean up a work space littered over the decades, driven by one political agenda after another. It was the law so every PD fought his or her own version of that cause, a kind of uninvited warfare on the social dilemmas of the day, writ large against the politics of that particular time. But today was like any other day: butt-splitting hard.

I dropped into the chair opposite him, one of those 1960s affairs with the rounded back and straight legs, and balanced the notepad on my knee. Shoved in the corner was a circular bouncy for his toddler, who came in occasionally. Ray's children still woke him at night, and when he came to the office sleep-deprived all the staff steered clear of him. Had he gotten a decent night's sleep the night before? I wanted to know.

"You know why I've asked you in here?"

I nodded. "The Susan Holeman case?"

"Yes." He sighed, leaned back in his chair, the buttons of his shirt pulling away from the cloth so that slits of skin showed beneath his jacket.

"What do you want me to do?"

"What do I want you to *do*?" He said. "Jesus, Sara, what do you think?" He was just shy of sputtering.

"Take her off the stand."

"You're damn right, Sara. Do you know the heat I'm getting for this?"

My breath caught in my throat. He didn't care what the child was going through, he cared about the press. I looked away from Ray's steady gaze, his eyes had gone steely-grey, like the color of the sky beyond him. A jay raced across the sky, alighted on a limb in the window outside the office. Raleigh's stark, bleak office buildings slanted against the smoky blue of summertime. The worst of the heat was days away, we had just learned. I let out a slow breath.

"You got the news about the evidence?"

"How do you know about the evidence?"

"Everyone in the office knows about the evidence, Sara. Susan's going to jail. You can't stop it."

"Ray, we had a chance. What is more damaging for that child, a few weeks on the witness stand or not seeing her – or *seeing* her mother behind bars for seven to fifteen? You tell me, Ray." I smarted and stood up. "Now I have some calls to make."

He pushed back from his desk, his chair crunching Cheetos beneath his carpet pad. He raised a brow, then he spun around: to investigate the bird, or the buildings, or a blue sky none of us could find.

I did have a call to make, but it wasn't the one Ray thought I should. I called Trish. We hadn't spoken in six months but she was still a confidante and friend, and God knows there was no mentor for me in the PD Office – at least among the women – so I went to Trish when I faced a dilemma, professional or otherwise.

"You had to put her on the stand, Sara. You did the right thing," she said immediately, after I explained the case.

Trish had a matter-of-fact way about her. She never minced words. I paused, waiting. Trish always had an afterthought.

"So that prosecutor played hard ball, wouldn't let you do closed session with the judge, eh?" Her voice went high-pitched at the end, that Wisconsin twang. "You've got to get tougher, Sara, or those people will eat you alive."

I thumbed through the old raggedy Rolodex I inherited from the last public defender who inhabited my cubicle, and chewed on my lip, silent; I knew Trish was right.

"Okay, but what do I do now?"

"Is their testimony helping?"

"Only the girl's been up."

"And?"

"She did okay – except for when she repeated something her mom had said."

"Which was?"

" 'I'm gonna take you out.' "

"Jesus, Sara. These kids are going to take *her* out!" She paused. "Are you sure you want them on the stand?"

I explained these were the only witnesses, the only chance to keep their mother from going to prison. Trish said, "It seems like you've thought this through then."

"Well, problem is I've got new evidence…" I told her about the neighbor who had seen the couple going inside the house, playing around and flirting as they came up the walkway to the apartment building. He saw them holding hands and they looked like they were doing just fine. Unfortunately, it was right before the incident.

Trish made a clucking sound. "That's not going to make the jury happy. A jury doesn't like hearing they're getting along well, you know that." Battered wife syndrome was common in the court systems and usually the defense was a kind of temporary insanity or the need in a particular situation to defend one's self. "Sara, do you even have a case here?"

These cases were dicey. There was no hard medical evidence for insanity, other than a kind of post-traumatic stress disorder, and the self-defense argument came heavily into question if the jury heard the defendant and victim had been getting along. That was standard; the nature of the relationship being easily inflammatory, from playful and loving to violent or fatal in a heartbeat. This evidence could completely de-rail the case.

Trish wouldn't tell me what to do, she never did. She just said, "Be careful, very, very careful." I knew I would be on my own. I could throw in the case, as the PD wanted me to do, or I could keep fighting.

I wanted to keep fighting.

In the days that followed, the days leading up to the final days of the trial, I spent all my free time with Tye. On the weekend we walked along Franklin Street in downtown Chapel Hill, dodging students and moms with strollers and dogs, and disenchanted teens with earplugs, listening to the music they'd purchased the night before at the Cradle, the local music haunt. We went out to hear live music every night and hung out at our apartment, slept late and made love. Outside the heat blazed and even the activity on Franklin Street slowed, the air got thick with humidity, and the trees in the quad on campus stopped moving, not a leaf shuddered in the breeze, because there was no breeze, only silence in the heat. Summertime stopped you in your tracks; it was our version of winter in the Northeast. You had to give it up, and I gave in: to the heat, to the fact that I'd promised myself to someone I believed was a good man, if a man I didn't know fully yet, and to a court case I might have no chance of winning.

September 1999

Chapter Twenty-One

Most Monday mornings the office sounded like the cacophony of a mechanic's shop, but this morning exceeded the norm: phones ringing off the hook, incidents that had occurred over the weekend; a flurry of outgoing calls, panicked deputy PD's in pursuit of another witness because their case was coming up on the docket. It might have been the full moon; like hospitals, our activity level seemed to intensify then. People didn't usually talk to one another for hours; they were only waking up or had been rudely awakened, and it took time to roll into the day. The exception to this was Jay, our youngest PD, in his late twenties, who occupied the cubicle four stations over from me. Jay arrived hours before anyone else – even before me – and inevitably dropped by my cubicle to check in. He slid over the old coffee cups above my desk and draped his arms apishly over the ledge. He grinned jaggedly at me, and said, "What's shaking?"

"What's up, Jay?" I found him amusing. Though from time to time, when he came by to flirt, I would say, "I'm looking at my wedding ring. Do you see my wedding ring, Jay?" to remind us both where my allegiances lay. He had been a punker for years during Law School at George Washington University, and the demeanor was only slowly wearing off.

"You okay going into today?"

"Okay as I can be." I was gathering my papers, going through my briefcase. Ordinarily well organized, the weekend spent with Tye had blown my sense of sharpness; I felt dulled almost, and this worried me going into the courtroom later this afternoon.

We were in the conference room, such as it was, with no windows and a bare light overhead, and trashcan overflowing

211

in the corner – the essence of bleak. I sat huddled with Susan, who had spent the morning crying again, earlier in the backrooms with me, and had only now pulled herself together. She had told me, yes, they were getting along that morning, but that's how it always happened. He was incredibly loving and fun and playful and he called her *baby*, again and again. And then she'd say something wrong – just a little off – or the kids would be too loud, and he'd threaten to break their wrists if they opened the door to the wrong room. And she'd feel vulnerable all over again.

Susan was to testify, but Joseph would be put up on the stand first.

"Does he have to go up?" Susan leaned forward over her crossed legs. In our interviews she had spoken about the kids with delight and worry: Kelsey's intelligence but inability to focus, Joseph's capacity for focus but her fears for his future. A mother's consternation over a child's growth, strengths and weaknesses. They were hers, wholly, and she loved them, her adoration everywhere apparent.

I paused. What if I said no, might that change anything? I felt the tension icy across my forehead; I wanted the day to be over even before it had begun.

At our table in the courtroom, I said one last time, "The most important thing, Susan, is that you tell the truth. But stay with what we've rehearsed. Otherwise, he'll trip you up. He will fry you if you do, I've seen him in operation. You will give him the upper hand if you lie in any way. Do you understand?"

Being forthcoming hadn't been her strong suit so far, and this troubled me, as did the fact that, when the judge entered the courtroom and everyone rose, and the jury filed in, they avoided eye contact with us.

Archer flagged me when he came. I joined him in the

far corner of the courtroom. "We can do a plea bargain, you know that, right?" He eyed me up and down, waiting.

"What do you have in mind?" I asked.

"If she pleads guilty, we could get him down to three probably." I inhaled sharply. I looked past him as Kelsey Holeman's grandmother stood at the courtroom door, flanked by both children. I watched them clinging to her: should the grandmother be here today? The cane she leaned against, as she paused in the doorway, was made of a dark mahogany. The engravings were intricate and fine, yet visible even at this distance. She nodded wistfully in my direction, and Susan flashed her a small smile. Joseph's face was solemn, and the expression paralleled exactly that of his mother earlier that day. Three years would be an improvement over seven to ten, or fifteen, but still – was it worth it, if she could get off entirely? The case was so clearly self-defense, the abuse so severe and obvious, and so detrimental to her children, who had witnessed it. That Susan should have to claim she was in the wrong and do some time seemed patently unfair, and it meant three years separation from her children, which the kids already felt acutely difficult and damaging.

"I'll discuss it with Ms. Holeman," I said, with civility, but in a terse tone.

"Oh, come on, Sara, don't be a fool," Archer said. He looked me in the eye, close up. He, at least, had dropped the pretense that we had no former relationship. "Talk her into it. You know it's the right move."

As I turned on my heel, I felt him brush against me and it so enraged me I had difficulty keeping my cool. I'd managed so far to keep out of my mind our previous involvement. No one at the PD Office knew – even Jay, whom I counted as a good friend. Not even the PD himself, who knew ridiculous amounts about people's personal lives. It had been a brief affair, long before Tye and I met. We'd gone for a drink one evening in downtown Raleigh on a summer night, when even the breeze was hot against the skin, and you felt the humidity in your bones and it made you ache. I hadn't expected to like him, but he was funny off the job site and, though terse in his humor, he liked to get me riled up and then – because I was, I admit, vulnerable to a handsome man – managed to corner me as we left, stepping close to me in the alley beside the restaurant. I felt his hot breath against my neck. Even now I remembered his touch, but pushed the thought from my mind as I returned to my client's table.

"The prosecutor has offered us a plea bargain. He thinks he can get you three years. It would be better than seven to ten – fifteen, even – you know that, right?"

The color drained from Susan's face. "I'm not plea bargaining. I'm not going in. Sara, it will take me down to go there."

"Are you sure?" I asked. "You need to really think about this." The courtroom had filled now, and the judge was calling everyone to order.

"Damn right, he's not sending me to jail. That son-of-a-bitch is *not* sending me to jail."

I stifled a smile; today of all days when there was no humor in any shred of my body I felt the impulse to laugh. Susan was nothing if not vehement, one of her most attractive qualities. It made her a fierce mother.

"Joseph Holeman is called to the stand."

Joseph was thin and long and had dark hair cut close to his head. His lips had a perpetual smile, and you could tell that, even in adulthood, he would maintain his boyishness, a kind of freshness reserved for the truly innocent. But he, unlike his sister, knew what was at stake here, and you could read it in the stiffness of his motions. On the stand, he gave the appearance of a stilted scarecrow, he was that thin, and it gave him a striking vulnerability on the witness stand.

214

As he approached, Archer smiled too archly at the judge, who gave absolutely no response. I knew then Anastase was on our side. I just needed the jury. We could win this case; and the knowledge fueled me. However much I might have been tempted to back down, I knew now I wouldn't. If everything lined up, we would win this case.

"Joseph," Archer began, "how old are you?"

"Seven, sir."

"And as a seven-year-old do you understand what's going on here? Why your mother is on trial?"

"Your Honor, I object. He's badgering the witness," I said, but Judge Anastase shook his head and whispered hoarsely, "Overruled. Answer the question."

"Yes," Joseph said.

Anastase had developed a cold over the weekend. He looked weary today, and when he leaned back in his seat, he seemed winded almost by the movement. His cold concerned me, because it set a pallor on our interactions with the judge; the decision of when to object became more key. It would be important to move slowly, and the moments ticked by as Archer took the boy through the day in question, the day when his mother had slit the ankle of her boyfriend and impaired his walking permanently.

"What did you think of your mother's boyfriend?" Archer asked.

"I didn't like him, sir," the boy almost whispered.

"But he bought you gifts, right?"

Where was he going with this? I wondered. Archer was walking directly in front of the boy, pacing and not looking at him.

"Tell us about the gifts."

Joseph recounted the bikes and the Game Boys and the coloring sets, which Everett gave Susan for the kids weekly. Joseph didn't lie about the quantity; he told it straight. I could feel the compression in my chest; I didn't like this tack at all. And then he broke from this and hit to the quick suddenly. "Did you feel badly when your mother cut his ankle? When you saw all that blood?"

"Objection, Your Honor. Leading," I said.

"Overruled," said Judge Anastase. "Answer the question."

The boy visibly reeled, the contradiction of the two events raising his own discomfort so obviously. I kept my eyes on the boy, trying to make eye contact to support him, to help ground him. Susan seemed to sink lower in her seat. There were shufflings in the courtroom but no one spoke.

"How did you feel when you saw your mother cut his ankle?" Archer asked.

"It was scary."

"Were you upset?"

"Yes – no, sir."

"No?" This caught Archer off guard, and Sara had to fight a smile. The boy was sharp, really sharp, and he wasn't going to let Archer undo him. He was a good kid, and he wanted to see his mother this side of the bars. He seemed so much older than seven, and the thought of what had wizened him made me sad. Susan's eyes were glued to him, and she sat straighter now.

"Because he'd hurt my mommy," Joseph said, before Archer could ask the next question. Even he knew that Archer wouldn't ask why. He would have to volunteer it.

Archer began to say something, then stopped, and his next move surprised Sara. "That's all, Your Honor." Archer wasn't going to give that boy a chance.

When it was my turn at the witness stand, I approached Joseph slowly and then turned briefly toward the jury, everyone facing the child, except for the elderly white gentleman at the back. He was watching me, guardedly,

216

coolly and I looked away. He held his chin down, to gaze at me over the rim of his glasses, and it made his jowls loose and gave him a stern expression. I was most leery of the jury members in his demographic, they'd be most inclined to sympathy toward the prosecution, most likely to see me as the enemy – let alone Susan – as unseating white older male supremacy in the region. I didn't often fall prey to stereotypes among Southerners, but I intuited that he could be problematic and I let my understanding of this shape how I approached the witness. A conservative tack would be important, maybe even essential.

"Joseph, you said that your mother's boyfriend – Mr. Taylor – gave you many gifts, right?"

"Yes."

"Your mother said he helped pay for the preschool, right?"

"Yes."

"And you ate dinner out a lot?"

"Yes."

"That would be a lot to be grateful for, when your own dad wasn't able to do that."

"Yes, ma'am."

"Joseph, can you tell the courtroom precisely why you didn't like Mr. Taylor when he was so clearly so kind to you?"

"He wasn't kind to my mama."

I was silent, to let that stand, and then kept going.

"Joseph, I have to ask you some hard questions now." Susan wore an expression of utter concentration, a fierce frown on her face. I was beginning to break a sweat.

"Yes, ma'am." His mouth lengthened into a solid line.

"On the day of the event – of the incident – can you tell me precisely what happened? You were coming back from lunch."

"Yes, ma'am."

I paused. This had to stick or the case would be lost. "And you were walking into the apartment, your mother and Mr. Taylor were walking ahead of you, right?" Archer pegged me with his glare; he did this to all the public defenders, ceaseless watching.

"Yes."

"So you could see them. They were holding hands. We understand now – everyone understands now – that they *seemed* to be getting along earlier that day."

Archer leaned across the table, eyeing me.

I began to walk slowly in front of the jury, pausing before the elderly gentleman. "Now Joseph, did this happen often?"

"Ma'am?"

"Did it happen often that they seemed to be getting along right before something would happen? A fight, an altercation – some sort of conflict."

He nodded.

"Joseph, can you say yes or no please."

"Yes," he said. "A lot."

"So did you trust it, when things were going well between them. Trust him?"

Someone shifted in a chair and the screech of it, in the near silence of the courtroom, unnerved me.

"No, ma'am."

"Why? Tell us why you didn't trust him, Joseph – or trust these calm, playful, even loving moments."

"Because he was meaner after, ma'am." He dropped his gaze, staring at the floor.

"Can you repeat that, a bit louder?"

"Because he was meaner. He would do something worse after something special."

I felt my pulse pick up. "I'm not going to ask you to say

again the types of things you sister reported, okay? But you need to say one thing right now that he did, after he was nice to you and your sister and your mom. Just one, please. Give us one example."

There was a weariness to the boy now, not unlike the seventy-year-old man in the jury. "I remember one time he took a frying pan and hit her right in the face, and it busted her tooth."

"Had she done or said anything to him that warranted that, that would make him mad."

"No, ma'am. I think..." He paused. "I don't think he had reasons sometimes, Ms. Greystone. I think... he just wanted to hurt my mama."

I stared down at the floor, lifted my gaze to the elderly man's face, which was etched, his brow jagged. Sunlight from the window behind the jury box cast a thin yellowy light across him. And then he closed his eyes.

At the break, outside the courtroom, the children crawled in Susan's lap, taking turns on her knees, and Susan fiddled with the top of her zipper of her dress jacket, a nervous tic she'd picked up from wearing the jumpsuit. I had to work hard not to fantasize about a Visitation in prison where Kelsey would not be able to touch her mother. We were freakishly close to the end here, and I had to keep my focus strong.

"Whaaat?" Kelsey was saying to her mom on her lap, as her mother played with her hair. Susan twirled her daughter's hair around the edge of her finger. They were playing pretend curlers. Joseph, meanwhile, was sketching on my pad beside his mother. Beneath my single-word, under-lined entries – notes I took while the prosecution examined – Joseph had drawn a tree and beneath it two small trees, with the branches from the larger tree; it might have been an oak or a birch, stretching over the smaller trees, an arc of protection. I marveled at the metaphor he had so naturally created. He stood drawing, peaceably, until his grandmother reached her arm across the banister before her bench and called to him, to pick her up a canteen snack. She gave him three dollars, one for Kelsey and for Joseph, and for her daughter too. He dropped the pencil, took the dollars, and skated around the corner of the bench. "Don't be running in this courthouse, you hear?"

As he ran off, Kelsey wound her hair around her own finger, then reached up to wind it around her mother's, winding both their hair tighter and tighter, up to the top of her mother's head until she made Susan laugh. And the lightness of her mother's laugh brought a tone of relaxation to them all, however momentarily.

Susan Holeman was my first and last witness. Putting your client on the stand wasn't common, but Susan felt to me as much the victim as Everett Taylor. When she took the stand, I knew that she – not her children – and she alone had the capacity to take down the case. Susan had worked hard at moments to be truthful; she had shared story after story of the abuse, and talked for hours with me about the times in childhood when her own grandfather had beat them. No one in the family had escaped this particular kind of hardship. I had heard it so many times: the victim in turn perpetrated, though there was no evidence that Susan beat her own children. But violence was something every child in that family had been exposed to and, in that sense, I knew that the damage they'd witnessed with their mother was neither the first acts of rage they'd been exposed to nor likely to be the last. Violence had been a steady staple, like breakfast cereal and toast, or Sunday ice cream; inevitable, uncompromising, and never far off. It could, would, and did happen at any moment. Susan, in these interviews, spoke in low and quiet tones until she landed on certain topics: her own mother's turning a blind eye when her father beat Susan, her husband's absence and the dissolution of their marriage, and of course, Everett. Then her tone became harsh, like she had found a bitter taste to a fruit she couldn't expunge from her palate. There was no getting past the arch discomfort Susan felt at these moments. I knew these "sessions" – if not therapeutic – at least enabled some anger and sadness to be vented. They were purgings of a kind. I wished sometimes we could have been walking outside, at a track or a garden, a city park, to disperse the energy in the room. I often accompanied Kelsey with the guard back to her cell – not all defense attorneys did that. But I did it as a courtesy to acknowledge that where Susan resided at the moment was no different from the doorstep of a close friend, when of course we both knew it was as different as blue and red, or black and white.

That afternoon, when Susan testified, she didn't occupy her seat on the stand as much as shrink into it. Her terror was evident in the slump of her shoulders, the shifting in the chair, the frequent licking of her lips. Her eyes were glued to me.

"Susan, I'm going to ask you some hard questions here, and I need you to give as clear and direct answers, for the jury's sake, as possible. Can you do this?"

I needed to locate all potential sympathies for Holeman. The jury had to see her earnestness, her willingness to respond, a frank disclosure, ideally not overly emotional. That could have the reverse effect, I had found.

As I walked over to Susan, I studied the jury's faces: the elderly gentleman bore a scowl, and the young woman in the front row, in the white blouse and carefully turned-

221

down collar over a green-knit, preppy-style sweater, let out a long sigh, crossing and uncrossing her legs. I read her as more sympathetic. But then I turned my back on the lot of them; how else was I to make my way through this examination?

"Yes," Susan said, watching me closely.

"How long did you know Mr. Taylor?"

"How long did I know him?"

"Yes, how long did you know him?"

"Seven years."

"Seven years. Long enough to feel that you *could* know him."

Archer, trying to catch my eye, started to object, then stopped. He knew he would get nowhere. *He* knew where I was going, if no one else did.

"Yes," Susan said – and then started to say something, but it was better not to let her go on.

I had thought through this exchange for weeks. I had a friend from college who became a surgeon and he told me one time at a college reunion that he did surgery in his mind before he walked into the theatre. I believed that a good lawyer should do the same. No surprises, ever. That was the ideal.

"And how would you characterize your relationship? Tell us why you liked Mr. Taylor – Everett."

Susan brought her hands to her face, cradling her chin, and the action seemed to calm her and she stared at the floor before the stand and recounted the qualities of the man she had fallen in love with: his kindnesses, his fairness – generally – to her children, his treatment of her, how he liked to take her out and "treat her real good."

"Like what? What would that look like?"

"He bought me things."

"Did he demand anything of you?"

222

"Your Honor," Archer began. But the judge only waved his hand. "Counsel is legitimate in this line of questioning. Carry on."

Susan seemed empowered by this news, she knew the terminology by now. She knew when we had a green light, so she kept going.

"Not in the sense of what you might think," she said, meeting my gaze. I stopped before her hand, where it lay on the stand.

"He didn't demand sexual favors?"

"No, never. He wasn't that kind of man, Ms. Greystone."

"What kind of man was he, then?" I asked, and began walking toward the jury. "Tell us what kind of man he was. What did you *not* like about him?"

Susan had warmed up now and had seemed to shed her fear and though she didn't speak with strength, she spoke clearly and slowly, and she stopped shifting in her chair, but instead leaned back, arms crossed, as if cradling herself. "He scared me."

"How?"

Then Susan told me, in her own words, about the beatings: the first time, he held her down with one hand and slapped her back and forth until her nose bled, the next incident with the frying pan – the one her son had described, then the threats of rape, in front of her children. "It's like he became... another man." Her voice grew flat, and in the silence of the courtroom, as the members of the audience watched her, she paused, took a sip of water, and then, though I had not asked, she said, "He got real mean, really fast, and I never knew when it would happen, never knew how to stop it."

"You didn't go for help? You stayed with this man, Susan. Why?"

Susan closed her eyes briefly, put a hand out on the

wooden edge of the stand, as if to steady herself, and then said, "Because. Because – I loved him."

The silence in the room was deafening, a reminder that even in the most complex of life circumstances, in the array of choices an individual faces, there remains a simplicity. At her core, Susan loved him. In spite of who he was, because of who he was.

It would be an overstatement to say Archer ran to the stand, but he did take a little skip as if the lightness of his heels meant he was eager for the kill. He was a prosecutor, after all, and what he was about to do he'd spent years training to do and he wasn't alone in knowing he was good at what he did. He was the best Deputy DA in Raleigh, and everybody knew it. He stopped only to linger for a moment, walk slowly past the jury, and – like absolutely every one of his moves that day – this was fully intentional. You had to love going after someone to want to be in his prosecutor shoes, and everyone knew that he liked – actually enjoyed – overturning a court case. Who didn't? You might say. Except that Archer, more than most prosecutors, reveled in it.

"Ms. Holeman, Susan, if I may. Mr. Taylor – Everett – he was your lover, no?" asked Archer.

Her eyes flew open, even she knew this was not the term she would have him use.

"He was my boyfriend, Mr. Archer," she said, in a moment of unexpected boldness. I had to stifle a smile; smiles flitted across the face of the older gentleman, and the young woman in the white blouse nearly laughed. Archer hadn't expected this reaction, and he shoved his hands in his pocket, then gave her a false smile, before he approached her at the stand.

"Boyfriend, lover – whatever. You weren't married. Why not?"

I flew to my feet. "Your Honor, objection. He's badgering the witness. May we approach?"

He nodded. Judge Anastase was past words, whether it was the cold or his mind drifting onto other cases.

"This isn't appropriate. Her marital status isn't germane. They were seven years dating. Surely that's not a crime?" I said.

A flicker rippled across his mouth, set solemn, almost stern.

"Archer, where are you going with this?"

It was not a common question to ask a defendant, and Archer blinked. "Your Honor, I think it's germane. The jury needs to understand why they weren't married."

"This isn't a divorce proceeding, Your Honor, or a common-law civil trial. I can't see that it's necessary." I swept my hand beneath my hair; I could feel my heat rising.

Anastase looked from prosecutor to defendant and back again. "Okay, let's see where you're going. But you're not to badger her, Archer. You get that?"

Archer's brow flew up, his victory apparent. " 'Course not, Your Honor." His Southern accent crept in and I felt all the disadvantage of the non-Southerner. I wasn't part of the old boy network. They all said it didn't matter, but I knew that it did.

As I walked back to the table, I threw Susan a brief smile. But as I slid into my chair, Kelsey's grandmother, in the bench behind the rail, leaned forward and said, "Don't you let him take her down, you hear, Sara?"

If Archer's victory had shot her a blow, this added push from Susan's mother only raised my hackles further. The fans in the courtroom shuddered. I fought back my rising stress. The last rays of the day fell across the floor. This was the moment; if Archer got through to Susan, if he broke her down, we could lose this. She had to keep her cool. A

225

truck barreled down the road beside the courthouse; but in less than a moment, every one's attention became fixed on Archer, as he let out a shrill fine whistle. Not loud, just provocative. Susan looked visibly unnerved. He had her precisely where he wanted her, and when he wheeled around, he let it fire: "Why didn't you marry Taylor? He did ask you, right?"

"Yes," Susan said. "He asked me several times."

"And why didn't you say yes?"

Susan paused, caught my eye and at my nod, she continued, "Because he beat me," she whispered.

"He beat you, *rigghhht*."

She blinked, off-guard.

"But you loved him, didn't you?"

The fans whirred overhead. The grandmother stirred. And then she struggled to her feet, to join the children outside the courtroom. The resulting pause left me uncomfortable; something was afoot here and it wasn't good.

"Yes," she whispered again.

"Louder, please, Ms. Holeman," Archer said.

"Yes."

"But you hurt him. You took a knife to him."

Susan blanched.

Her mother said, "I'm not staying to hear this." Susan's face fell just watching her leave the courtroom. I fought back a gasp. This would throw her.

"Objection. Asked and answered," I said, hoping to shift the dynamic.

"Overruled." Anastase examined his nails again, then let out a long sustained cough. He leaned back in his seat, glanced over at the jury, studied their faces, and then turned back to the prosecutor. The air in the courtroom was still, the mixed smells of shoes, sweat, and stale snacks, filling the room at the end of a long hard day in court.

Archer strode to the table, picked up his notepad, and returned to the stand. "Okay, Ms. Holeman, on the day of the incident, tell us what happened. Every detail, please."

The courtroom fell silent as Susan Holeman recounted the events of the day in question. She leaned forward in her seat as she spoke and, to my amazement, Archer let her speak, with few interruptions and clarifying questions. But I knew it couldn't last. This wasn't Archer, not his style at all. He stood arms by his side, leaning against the wooden railing that separated the jury from the rest of the courtroom. The smirk on his face had vanished; he might have been sympathetic, the tilt of his head implying genuine concern, but then he leaned forward, and said, "Can you say that again, Ms. Holeman?"

"What?"

"What you just said? 'We were having an okay time of it.' That's what you said, right? That *you were having an okay time of it.*"

Susan's face went still and even from this distance I could tell he'd hit a chord. "He beat me, Mr. Archer. No, I was *not* having an okay time of it."

"Yes, but you said—"

"I said, that *day*. But you got to understand. Anything could happen in a day – everything. One moment he was Mr. Sweet, the next he was banging me with a pan. All due respect, do you not *get* that?"

The murmurs in the courtroom stopped, and the tone in Susan's voice was somewhere between cat snarl and a shrill catcall. Harsh, with an edge. I could feel my own tension rise. I tried to make eye contact, but Susan had been distracted since her mother had left the room. If Archer got her going, this would not be good.

"Yes, but you talked about all those *good* times, right?"

"Yes."

"All the times he cared for you and your children," he said. "Because he loved you, right?" He was leaning in toward her in a way that made me very uncomfortable. "And yet you took a knife to him."

"He came at me!" she yelled. "He was coming for me."

"You said he threatened you, but he was across the room."

"He was *not* across the room."

"Which was it, Susan? Tell us—"

And then she bolted forward, in rage, and began to yell, "Get out of my face. *Get out of my face!* You don't know who he was!" And as she turned a deep dark red, heaving, angry, rageful, Archer turned swiftly to the jury, and said, watching them carefully, "That will be all, Your Honor."

When I saw his facial expression, the sharp turn of his brow, the thin line at his mouth – solemn, serious, even worried, as he turned back toward Susan, I knew which way the jury would vote. The day was done. I felt the tingling in abject horror.

Susan Holeman sat at the stand and began to cry, her children nowhere to be seen, as if the separation had already occurred. Everett would go free, Susan would serve time. As if she knew what was about to happen, Kelsey Holeman's face appeared at the door of the courtroom.

"Come here, *baby*," Susan cried out to her. "*Come here!*"

That night I told Tye I needed to be alone; could he go out with Roy or Tom at the office? The verdict had come in three hours later; the members of the jury having barely gotten started when they'd already come to their conclusion. "Guilty as charged," the gentleman announced. I burned a candle at the low table in my kitchen and watched the leaves fall on an autumn night in Chapel Hill, less than two miles from where I had trained in Law. I had called my mother. I talked to Ephraim. I called Trish, who understood, but said to me, "Sara, it was a perfect storm. The grandmother, Anastase's cold, and that fucking Archer" – that bit made me laugh. I felt better for an hour after the call, and then I wept, openly, deeply, at my kitchen table as the candle flickered. I knew then I would go for the appeal. I had to do it, even though staying in this case would eat me alive. Susan had said no, instantly. But Anastase had pulled me aside and said, "Yes, you should definitely appeal." He smarted and said the words with vehemence – no one liked the new sentencing laws. And then, as he walked down the hallway with me, he added, "I don't know how you let him tear into her like that. But that was the moment. Archer's ruthless. Don't let him push you around. Let this one be a lesson. No kids on the stand again, ever. Not in my court. You get that?" As he turned to walk down the hallway, his leg pulled slightly to the left; he had one leg slightly shorter and a recognizable gait no matter what hour you saw him in the courthouse, or where you stood in direction to him. And the limp reminded me, in that horribly painful moment, of the limp of Everett Taylor, the limp caused when Susan Holeman had stood up finally to fight back against the man she loved.

PART X

ALBANY, CALIFORNIA
2010

Two Years Ago

January 2010

Chapter Twenty-Two

"Sara," the therapist had asked me. "Why did that case matter?"

"What do you mean, why did it matter?" I couldn't fight the defensiveness in my tone. I'd gone through half a box of Kleenex on his sofa. Why was he grilling me now?

"Lawyers lose cases all the time. My niece is one," he said. "She's lost all manner of important cases. Everyone does." His hand lay still on the edge of his upholstered chair. Then he began to tap his index finger lightly.

I watched the move in irritation. I was stretched uncomfortably on the sofa opposite him. I felt naked in my openness, hated him for asking me this question.

Above him was a painting of a long, wide, empty beach. I stared at it. "Because," I said, slowly, "because I didn't want to separate that mother from her children."

"Why?"

"Because I'd had separation in my own childhood. Because I didn't want to cause that kind of pain." I felt the tears smart behind my eyes. "Let me be clear," I added, "not separation to that degree. I would never make that claim. But distance." I inhaled sharply. "And I could only imagine how horrible that *physical* distance would have been."

"Your mother worked. Generations of women have worked and raised kids. How is that separation?"

"Jesus, this isn't about working," I said, exasperated. "Every mom works. It's because when she was with me, she was never with me." I paused, losing myself in that painting. "Because," I said, pressing my lips together, "she pushed me away, repeatedly."

"And?"

"And *what?*"

He paused. Then he leaned forward and said, "I'm sorry. I don't want to make you upset."

I laughed, bitterly. "Whoever wants to make someone else upset?"

"Your mother didn't want to make you upset, she didn't want to hurt you. Have you thought to ask her *why?*"

I felt the heat rise in me. Why was I railing at this man, sitting so calmly across from me? I wasn't angry at him – except that he was pushing me to feel all that I didn't want to feel. He'd have known this, of course. His face softened and I felt myself relax.

I studied the image of the beach in the painting, noticed the sea grass at its periphery, each blade sharp and distinct. "I suppose not," I said. "I never challenged my mother."

He smiled and said, "No, most of us don't. She won't fall apart, Sara, if you do. From what you have told me she has nerves of steel."

"Yeah, she is *nothing* if not steely. But what will it serve?" I asked. "She's come through cancer treatment, she's watched two marriages come down in her family. She doesn't need my residual grief."

After a time, he said, "So you returned to the practice but not trial law. Why not?" He was gazing at me intently.

"I can't go back to that kind of practice. It won't ever be the same."

"No, Sara," he said, "it never is the same."

"I guess not." I was breathing slowly now. I stole another glance at that image of the beach, wide and long, preparing myself, I suppose, for all that lay ahead.

PART XI

ALBANY, CALIFORNIA
2010

Two Years Ago

December 2010

Chapter Twenty-Three

Most days, when I started back at the law firm in Albany, I tried not to think about the Susan Holeman case. It had eroded my confidence as a lawyer like nothing else had, except perhaps my "failed marriage," as I had begun to call it. My mother told me not to use that terminology, but it was impossible not to feel that way when I tucked my kids into bed at night. "Okay, the marriage that didn't work. Does that sound better?" I asked Emily, one day when I called to get together for coffee. On the upside, moving to Albany brought me closer to her, let alone my parents, and meant I could drop the commute, even if it now felt as though, in more than a decade, I had barely progressed geographically, let alone in all the other arenas. It ought not to have felt like failure – all of it – but it did.

The hardest news wasn't mine. The boys had relaxed into our new life after about a year. It was rocky at first, after Tye moved out, but when the boys and I left Marin things took a turn. They liked being near my folks – we were in a small bungalow in Albany, a stone's distance away from the El Cerrito Plaza – and it was a relief for me no longer living in reach of Zeke Harris. The boys' dad was across the bay in the City, where he had found IT consulting work for Levi Strauss. Things were pretty even.

The hardest news was Ephraim's. No sooner had he and Barley finally ended things, but the partnership question that hadn't "fully resolved" reached its resolution – a result of the fall-out from the building industry decline, brought on by the subprime mortgage debacle. All the architecture firms in the area froze hiring or were laying off; he didn't lose his job, but as a new "partner" his salary was halved. I wondered if it was actually legal, but businesses seemed now to be doing what they liked to their employees. It was as if we'd never had a labor movement at all in this country.

"We'd like to take you on," Abe Morgan said to me when Morgan and Morgan hired me on, "but everyone here is contract." This was happening in the private attorney sector everywhere. It had its advantages: I kept my hours, I chose my clients, I didn't have to play the game. But it also meant purchasing insurance for the boys and me as – now that we were divorced and Tye was consulting – he couldn't claim them on his plan, if he had a plan at all. It meant also no pension. I was to build my own retirement. It wasn't ideal. But there seemed no other viable job option, so I told them yes.

Abe smiled generously and shook my hand. "Here, let me show you where you'll be working."

The desk was four feet wide, couched between old stainless file cabinets. "We're going to get some new cabinets in. We've got them on order," he said. The kitchen offered a seating area, a microwave, a small dishwasher, and an insurance company calendar on the wall with a faded picture of the Golden Gate. Recent issues of *Vogue* and *Esquire*, and today's *The Wall Street Journal*, were scattered on the dining table. He rested his hand on it and it wobbled; I stifled a smile, thinking of Zeke's extreme attention to detail. It seemed terribly old-fashioned, the entire set-up. "It's modest," Abe said, "but it works." For whom, I wondered?

So the morning I was to meet Larry for lunch, when Abe called me into his office, I didn't much believe him at first when he made me an offer to join the firm. I had only been on since January. I had a dozen clients within a month; mostly it was Trisha's doing – what hadn't she done for me? It was family law I was practicing: divorces, ironically, and estate planning cases. None of it particularly interesting, except I'd begun to work with intellectual property and estate planning; there were a number of university professors, artists and writers, who had complex estates to resolve due to copyright issues. It was moderately more interesting than the rest of my work. I didn't do long hours, because of the boys' school schedule, but I was efficient and hard working in the hours I was there. I didn't engage with the staff – just as I hadn't at the PD Office – and that had won kudos with my superiors. "Brian and I aren't getting any younger," Abe said, leaning back in his chair in our conference room. His brown jacket was flecked slightly with bits of dandruff, a strand of his greying hair swept behind his ear. He turned to stare out the slated blinds of the window that fronted onto San Pablo Avenue. "Think about it, Sara, will you?"

I told Larry about the offer over lunch, when we met at a sushi restaurant I often ate at while at work. I didn't have much of a social life because of the boys and working, so lunch out was an attempt to make up for it. Larry and I hadn't gotten together in a month or two, so he'd agreed to come over from Oakland. The interstate congestion – let alone the packed city streets – meant that everyone negotiated the driving question: *"You coming to me or am I coming to you?" "I need to leave by 2:30, otherwise I hit rush hour,"* etc. I arrived to find Larry seated out front, his legs outstretched, puffing on his cigarette.

"You know it's illegal now to smoke in restaurants, right?" I said, after giving him a peck on the cheek. "It's been that way for about two decades, Lar."

"Yeah, I know," he said, stubbing it out. "I'm just waiting. Isn't this just waiting?" He laughed his raucous, whinny-like laugh and I laughed with him.

We placed our order. Larry fidgeted with the menu and his place setting; he pulled off his cap and set it on the table, then on the seat beside him. I told him my news.

"Man, you have all the luck." This made me laugh. "No, I mean it. You've been there a year, and they want to make you partner!" He shook his head. "I can't even get a steady teaching job. Do you want it? I mean, I figure you want it."

"I don't know." I wasn't particularly passionate about it; I wasn't passionate about work anymore at all. It had been more interesting studying for the bar than it was having passed the bar and working. "But it's a job." I shrugged. "I've got bills to pay."

He cleared his throat. "You talked to Ephraim lately?"

I looked up. "What, what happened?"

"He's losing the house."

"He's losing the *house*?" The owner dropped our menus on the Formica tabletop; I stared blankly at mine. I was in shock at this news. "Which, his and Barley's? The place on Fourth Street?" I knew the housing decline had cost him, but hadn't fully understood the particulars on his partnership and the drop in his income. "You are kidding."

"No, he had an equity line. You can lose a house on an equity line. He knows that now." He laughed harshly. With one elbow on the table, he rested his chin in his hand.

"Ahh! I can't believe it." I stared out the window at the traffic. Outside the sun glinted off the tops of the cars. It was December and sunny, warmer than I'd expected. But the glare of the sun was too harsh, even at noon, so I'd left my sunglasses on. I took them off now, squinted at my brother. "Is there nothing that can be done?"

"He's met with all the Fair Housing people around."

"Good God, why didn't he come to me?"

"It's Ephraim, Sara. He's not coming to his baby sis." He raised his brows in play.

237

I laughed. "I can't believe this. Is he absolutely sure?"

"They were behind for about six months."

"What was their interest rate?"

"Ten percent."

"Ten *percent*? In this economy, with these low interest rates? Are you joking?"

"It was a shark loan. Happened during the second crash. Do you not remember that?"

I had the haziest of recollections of a re-finance they'd done some time ago. "I'd have gotten him something better. I really could have. That's just crazy. It was the Fourth Street purchase, wasn't it?"

"Yep." It was Larry's turn to stare out the window.

"What's he going to do? What are they going to do?"

"He's got Fourth Street – they're doing a short sale on Cedar Street. It'll cover some fees, that's about it. He's giving the Fourth Street house to Barley and the kids, and then he'll get a loft downtown – a rental."

"That house. Oh my God, that house." I teared up. "Mom's got to be beside herself. And Barley—"

"Hey, it's not a death we're talking about, Sissie," he said, chuckling. "Just a house. And look, these guys are lucky. They *have* a house. They have somewhere to go. I know two people on our block their houses are in foreclosure – and now they're on the lists for senior housing. They lost it all. We've not seen the end of it. It took a while to trickle down, all those balloon mortgages. But man, it's trickling now."

I looked around us at the sushi restaurant – professionals eating their meal in silence; and at the specialty foods shop next door; the extraordinarily expensive shoe store across the street, with its faded awning. "Is it worth it?" I asked my brother. "This?" I said, waving my hand in front of us. "This… place."

"Everyone wants a piece of it. Honey, you pay for the privilege of living in California," he said, squinting at me. "Don't you know that by now? 'Embrace uncertainty,' a friend of mine likes to say."

"I don't know," I said to Larry, after we'd placed our order. "I think that's code for everybody getting to fuck us over."

"That's good," he said, and laughed. "That's real good."

Over lunch he asked about Tye, how he was doing. He was the only one in my family, I had learned after we split up, who actually liked him and who understood why I had married the man. I told him about the job, his apartment. I suspected Tye was dating, but I didn't know for sure. We were doing okay now, negotiating around the kids. "It's amazing. Now that we don't have to live together, we don't fight anymore." He laughed.

Then he told me about Fran. They'd moved in together two years ago — I had applauded my brother at the time. "We're getting married," he said, hiding his smile.

"Larry, I am thrilled!" I almost leapt off the seat. "Get out. Why didn't you say so? You should have led with this. That's terrific news."

He shrugged, dipped his sushi in the wasabi, and popped it in his mouth, and then began fanning himself and taking gulps of water.

"When? Where?" I asked.

"Man, that stuff is strong." He inhaled loudly. It would be at the Brazil Room in Tilden Park up in the Berkeley Hills, he told me. It was price-y, but her parents insisted; it would be off-season in April to keep costs down. My brother Larry, getting married in the Brazil Room. It was too good.

"You told Ephraim yet?"

He laughed and shook his head. "Why do you always ask me that?"

"Because," I said, "you're his little brother. And you're making good."

The waitress came by to pour us more hot tea. Larry shook his head. "You know what he said at that Christmas Party, the one you held."

"The one I was such an ass at," I said. "That was a bad Christmas."

"He said she was too good for me." A flicker crossed his brow. He took his fingers to the last piece of sushi and mopped up his soy sauce.

"Ah! He said that? It's not true. I love Ephraim but he can be an ass sometimes."

Larry pressed his lips together. Then my brother sobered and said, "I can't tell him this, Sara. You have to tell him. He's had rock-solid shitty years, years in a row now. I am not doing that to my brother."

At the end of the meal, Larry insisted he pay. He said it was to celebrate my job offer. We stood outside talking and he smoked another cigarette. The owner came out at him, pointed at my brother and said, "You can't smoke here."

I took one look at the man and said, "Look, I come here every day, on days when no one else is in here. I don't see my brother every day. And he's not in the restaurant."

The owner threw me a glance, contrite. A man dressed in a pinstriped suit slipped by the owner, embarrassed by the altercation. My brother stared at me for a moment and smiled. "That's my sister for you, the tough lawyer," he said to the suit man. Then he laughed. When he hugged me goodbye, I held him close, smelling the sweat on his neck, the tobacco smoke in his hair, and said, "Thanks, Bro. Love you."

When Tye came to collect the boys that weekend, I pulled him aside on the porch as they gathered their things. The light was low in the sky – late December, a week before Christmas, which we had negotiated carefully each year since we'd split. It was only our second one, bound to be better than last year's. The sunset left rays of orange and mauve, escaping behind a strip of fog. It was chilly that afternoon. I had my overcoat on, fresh off of work, and I wrapped it closely around me to brace myself against the cold.

"Do you have a moment?" I said. "I was offered partner at the firm."

A ripple shot across his forehead; his eyes clouded, then he brightened. I couldn't tell if he was happy for me or envious. "That's good," he said. "I'm sure you've worked for it." I wasn't sure if there was something in that comment but opted to let it go.

Jacob, at age seven, already had his pack ready to go. Mark, only five, was pawing through the shoebox for his tennies, while his dad, a hand on the door, watched. Mostly I still packed Mark's bag, but he wanted to be older than he was and had insisted today I leave it to him. Their readiness to embark, their flexibility with this new equation, left me saddened, dumbfounded, and impressed in equal measures. Should children be this resilient? I knew they were; maybe we were the ones learning flexibility.

"I wasn't sure what it means if I take it. I mean, this is a long-term decision. Do you want to stay?"

The boys were on the porch now. "Go," he barked. I kissed them on the cheeks and they piled into his Toyota Camry. It was pretty beat-up from our seven years out here, but it was paid off; anything paid off in this economy represented a minor achievement.

"I've been meaning to tell you…" He trailed off.

I watched the boys over his shoulder, strapping in and locating their toys in his backseat. Were they okay? Daily I still tried to reassure myself. I brought my gaze back to Tye, who was watching my face anxiously.

"What?" I asked.

"The station has offered me a job. They want me to come back to Raleigh. It's permanent, full time with benefits. I can't say no, Sara. I think I'm going to go."

"You're going to go." I sputtered, nearly choking. It was like he'd informed me he was heading out of town for the weekend. "Do I have no say? I mean, our MSA says that either of us has to ask for permission to move. You can't be unilateral like this."

It still happened that we fought. If we'd gotten along, would we have needed to go our own ways? It should have been obvious, but I continually forgot it.

Tye hadn't been in the office that day so had beat the traffic across the bridge, but he would be keen to get back on the roads before they got bad again. I knew this.

"Okay." He let out a short, irritated sigh. "I want to go back to North Carolina. I want the boys to come. Are you coming? Now I've got to hit the road back to the City."

"Tye—!"

"What, Sara? You want me to take the initiative?" He smiled bitterly. "Well, I am. So deal with it."

"I have some news too, Tye. My mom went back in for a check-up and she's got another tumor. This one's inoperable." I blinked. I had just gotten the call a few days ago from Larry, because my mother hadn't wanted to tell me directly. "I'm not going anywhere until she's passed."

A shadow crossed his face. "I'm sorry, Sara," he said,

then turned to go to his car. Most people would say he wasn't. But I knew he was – about this at least.

That night I called Zeke. I don't know what came over me. Maybe the fact that I missed him. Or maybe it was only the conversations that I missed, the way he made me think hard and be truthful when I didn't want to be.

There was a long silence when he heard my voice.

"You're mad," I said. "I can tell."

"What do you fucking expect?" he asked, as if we hadn't had a year and half gap in our conversation. "Where the hell did you go? You vanished."

I laughed. "You have a lot of nerve, Zeke." I stood outside in my backyard, pruning the dead leaves on my camellia. It was my favorite bush and I cared for it when I could. "You're the one who blew me off."

"I was *seeing* someone." He still sounded outraged, which made me feel indescribably happy.

"Past tense?" I asked.

"Yeah, well, you know how that goes." He inhaled, then let out a long sigh. "The only problem with parking yourself somewhere is then you have to pay the meter."

I laughed hard, which made me instantly feel better. It was good to hear his voice. "You are too much. That's what we are to you, eh? Just a place to park yourselves? Zeke Harris, you are such an asshole. Why did I even *like* you?"

Outside the air felt fresh and clean; I was in a good mood because tomorrow I would have lunch with Trisha, who was in town for the weekend. But I wasn't in good spirits about my mother. I told him what had happened with Ephraim.

"Why on earth did he have that exorbitant interest rate? What was he doing buying that house on Fourth Street anyway? I could have told him not to." Zeke said this as if he had been in our lives, as if he'd been in my life.

I smiled. "Yeah, I remember when he told me that he'd purchased it, I was pretty surprised. They didn't know what they were doing at that point."

"Clearly," he said. He'd not asked about Tye – this would have been the moment. But I let it go. Talking about Ephraim led us to the building industry. I asked how he had fared. He'd been back in Chicago working, he said, because nothing in California had been moving; it was all at a standstill.

I didn't tell him about my mother. It would have made me too vulnerable, too wide open. When we hung up, I sat on the edge of my patio under a new moon and thought about all he had been to me and wondered whether it – he – was worth it.

But he had said one vital thing: "I don't even think this was about me in the end. This was about you."

"What do you mean?"

"This whole thing. What were you *thinking*?"

"What was *I* thinking?" My eyes flew open. He couldn't see me but I felt exposed all the same.

"I was your foil. Isn't that what they call it in Literature?"

"I'm in Law not Literature, you fool," I said.

"Well, plenty of storytelling in the Law, isn't there?"

Still, I suppose, Zeke was offering me some kind of truth.

"I mean, how available were *you*? You were out in some hemisphere, all on your own there, girlie. And I just reeled you in."

I stared up at the moon and laughed for nearly a full minute. I thought about Larry. It was precisely the kind of thing he would have said – and I'd have let him.

At lunch the next day, I told Trish about my mother's tumor. We were at Delia's, Ephraim's favorite restaurant on Fourth Street, under bright globes, with Vivaldi playing. An Italian waiter whisked by us, handed us menus, topped up our water in wine glasses and left the jug on the white paper that lay over the tabletop. The olive oil container, even the salt and pepper shakers, were immaculate and exquisitely chosen; we could have been in Europe. *This is what we're paying for living in California,* I thought, *for the privilege to feel privileged.* The front door was closed to the cold weather; it had hit finally.

Trish perused the wine menu. We'd not seen one another in about three years, since her last visit. She had more creases at the corners of her eyes and the ones beside her mouth had grown deeper. But her green-blue eyes were still bright. She wore her blonde hair pulled back in a ponytail and in her scoop-necked T-shirt she appeared remarkably Wisconsin for having spent two decades in Southern California.

"Want any?" she said, meaning the wine.

"Nah, I'm going to take a pass. I had more than enough the year Tye and I were splitting up," I said, and laughed.

We placed our orders, and after we'd talked about work for a few minutes – what could easily have stretched into hours – I told her about my mom.

"Inoperable. Ahh." She looked away and said, "I lost my mother two years ago. It is very hard, Sara. You've got to prepare yourself for this. No, maybe there's no preparation. It's your mother." She shook her head. Trish had always said things precisely as they were. "How much time?"

I pursed my lips. She put her hand on mine. "Four months," I said. "I don't know, maybe it's a good thing Tye wants to move back to North Carolina."

"Tye wants to move back to Carolina? What on earth for?" She dropped the menu on the table, looking around for the waiter. The music had changed to Beethoven's Fifth Piano Concerto.

245

"The TV station wants him back. They're offering him full time with benefits. It just hasn't worked for him out here." Actually, as I thought about it, it hadn't much worked for me either.

"But they want to make you partner at Morgan and Morgan. And your family..." Trish began moving her cutlery around, obviously agitated by this news. "It's not fair."

"When is it ever fair, Trish?" I said, with a laugh.

"Well, there's that," she said. "I guess you've figured that much out."

The following Monday I called Ray at the PD Office in Raleigh. It was Trisha's idea, of course. She'd always kept an eye to my progress, had never let me sit down.

I half expected him to be out, or away from his desk. I called him from mine at Morgan and Morgan, with briefs cleanly stacked on the surface. It was late morning, the rush hour traffic on the interstate near our office had let up. I could finally think straight.

"Sara? Sara Greystone? How *are* you? It's great to hear your voice!"

I hadn't expected the warm response. I'd not left on bad terms but I'd never much known what Ray thought of me and my work at his office. I'd been there seven years in total; Jay had outstripped me handily, as had Beebee and a few others, in longevity.

They were all gone now, he said. Jay had come out, joined the PD Office in Jacksonville, Florida, and married a former rocker he knew from college days, apparently. Beebee was in private practice in the Western part of the state. Ray spoke of some of the others, but honestly, I'd forgotten all but my immediate circle.

"None of them were as good as you anyway, Sara. You

were the one who put a new definition on the word 'thorough.' " He laughed. "I'll never forget the work you did on the Susan Holeman case."

I gasped. "Yeah, but we didn't win, Ray. You're forgetting that bit."

"We rarely win, Sara – you know that. Though you won a lot. But you can't let that be the gage. That's a fixed mindset. You fought for her. It was all you could do." He said it as if it was the most obvious thing in the world. He asked about my son; I told him about them both. "You practicing now?"

"Yes," I said, and spoke about Morgan and Morgan, although I didn't tell him they'd offered to make me partner.

"That enough for you? Civil cases? I'd have thought you'd be bored out of your gourd."

I laughed. I'd forgotten Ray's funny, frank ways. I found his straight-forwardness refreshing, something about the style of engagement in the Southeast still appealed to me, the way we talked about things for twenty minutes before we got down to business. His chair creaked as he went on about the current caseload and the new judges on the circuit court. "I'm thinking we're in for a wave of conservatism in the state," he said. "The conservatives are on this voter ID bandwagon now, and you can bet they'll want to redraw district boundaries. *That* never leads to good things. Not sure what that's going to mean for us here at the PD Office, but I sure don't like the feel of it all the same." I imagined him leaning his chair back precipitously against the window ledge, all that lunch debris scattered across his desk: what engagement looked like when you cared about your work. I nearly teared up at the thought.

When I said we were moving back – I didn't share the details – he said, "You coming back here then?"

"To your office?"

"Yeah."

"Is that an offer?"

"If you can stand the heat. But you can't let a case break you like that again."

I pressed my lips together tightly, and said, "Yep. I think my skin's just a bit thicker." I spun around in my seat, and caught sight of a hummingbird, its nose buried in the morning glory beside the brick wall beyond my window.

He told me to think about it. I told him I would. But I already knew my answer.

PART XII

RALEIGH, NORTH CAROLINA
2012

Current Time

October 2012

Chapter Twenty-Four

At Bodega Head, the air is surprisingly warm. It is October and early in the month, when the temperatures can occasionally soar. I don't get up here that often to the Sonoma Coast but I enjoy the drive, in complete silence, wending up past Point Reyes and Marshall. At the Head, midday like this, few cars are parked. Zeke wanted me to meet him in Tiburon to walk but I insisted we come up here.

He is parked already, standing against his car, legs and arms crossed, waiting. He looks just as I remember him. We walk first to the edge of the cliff where waves slam against rocks and spray filters up through the air leaving humidity that creeps into every crevice. My skin absorbs it readily. I close my eyes, and he puts one arm around me. He asks nothing more.

On the trail we walk side by side in silence for a time because it's grown windier and the waves below absorb all the audible sound I can manage just yet. My nerves are so frayed I am fragile, bits of me floating. We have to walk single file as the path reaches the edge of the bluff, where there simply isn't room for two. I am cognizant of this, wondering if it means something, if there is some cosmic "no" happening that I've not anticipated. Around the bend, he waits, takes my hand, and we walk together now.

"How is he doing?"

"He's okay." I think something has happened to one of my boys, but I cannot recapture precisely what it is.

He lets out a sigh, pulls down his glasses as we face into the sun.

"Can you take those off?" I need to see his eyes.

He slides them onto the top of his head, turns to me and smiles. I warm slightly, but still feel this tingling along every part of me. I can't see which way I'm meant to go.

"So no damage, right? He's okay."

"Yes, none." I sigh in relief.

Then he stops in the middle of the path, takes me in his arms and I begin to cry, every part of me is falling and I am falling back to where I know, the piece that I know, that I've known a long time: I am falling back in love with this man simply by being in his presence. I cannot help it. It is how I feel. And when I recognize this I am relieved, instantly, a relief that is bodily, that fills me.

"Are *you* okay?" he asks, and he is looking me straight in the eye.

"Yes."

He fishes for a Kleenex in his pocket. It's crumpled but I don't care, and then he smooths it out on the top of his blue jeans, above the knee, working it flat to the edge and each corner. I marvel at the precision. He smiles. "Here," he says. "Take it. You know that I want to marry you, don't you, when this is all over?"

"Yes," I say with a small laugh, though we've said nothing before about this.

"And have a third child."

"No, I get to have the child." I smile.

We talk about names.

"Evan," he says, "How about Evan?" It means: "young warrior," "God is good" and "good messenger" in Greek — all of which we like. But my favorite meaning, why I want us to choose the name, is because Evan means "rock."

We sit on the edge of the bluff in the grass, and he begins to make me laugh. Then I laugh, stronger now, because I know what is happening, what lies ahead, and I think even the boys will be okay with this. But for now, we wait, and walk into the headwind off the coast, the scent of the sage sharp, tickling my nose until I can breathe again.

I wake from the dream, and pad downstairs, alone, to the kitchen. I make breakfast for my boys and take them to school. Outside I feel the humidity on my skin and it prickles in defense of this new landscape. I drive up Martin Luther King Jr. Boulevard, as it is now called, to I-40, toward Raleigh, where I'm a public defender again. Maybe that isn't so bad. I don't have the man. I don't have a third child. I don't run a firm; but I defend people. And maybe that's my rock, I think, as I take the downtown exit.

Acknowledgments

As Ali Smith has said, "[N]o book exists without all the other books. It's a communal act to write a book."

I owe my first debt to Wallace Stegner's *Angle of Repose*, which inspired this work. But I owe other debts to those who offered me editing, general support, and technical or legal expertise. Any or all errors are my own, of course.

Thank you to readers of all or parts of the manuscript: Tom Jenks, Bonnie Nadell, Olga Zilberbourg, Kitty Walker, Jay Schaefer, John Dufresne, Michael David Lukas, Ian McGuire, Marli Roode, Susan Barker, Beth Underdown, Olivia Lee, Amy Resner, Elizabeth A. Brown, Cedric N. Chatterley, Heather Simonsen, Susan Rockefeller, David Barker, Katherine Armstrong, Sue Crowder, Lu Croft, L. A. Billing, Ursula Hurley, Szilvi Naray-Davey, Rosemary Kay, Helen Pleasance, Rhonda Carrier, and especially Geoff Ryman, M. J. Hyland, and Jeanette Winterson.

Thank you to those who provided valuable general or technical support: Valerie O'Riordan, John McAuliffe, Anastasia Valassopoulos, Kaye Mitchell, Judy Kendall, Scott Thurston, David Savill, Glyn White, Emma Barnes, Michael Butler, Madeline Rouverol, Dan Spiegelman, Sonia Auger, Olga Zilberbourg, Carol Edgarian and Tom Jenks, Michael Croft, Maria Hummel, Byron Schneider, Carolyn Chute, Cedric N. Chatterley, Caroline Knowles, Eric Anderson, Amy Resner and William D. Lee, Amy Naylor, Lisa Napp and Jack Bernhardt, Lisa Yarger, Connie and Truman Semans, Kathleen Robinson Letellier, Molly Couto, Zeena Janowsky, and in memoriam: Deborah Butler Spiegelman, Sandy and Bobby Ives, Robert J. Rowan, and Jean Rouverol Butler. Additionally, Sixers' members Ursula

Hurley, Kathryn Pallant, Tanja Poppelreuter, members of The Fiction Forge, Jen Barnes, Renee Whitlock-Hemsouvanh, Karen Kenkel, Lisa Redfern, Lee Hackeling, Joanne Bratsiotis, George Bratsiotis, Lucy McFarlane, Victoria Keeves, Janine Scott-Trumpet, Lesleyanne Ashraf, Shirley Nicholson, Steven Brearley, Bee Hughes, Queenie Ankrah, Karon Mee, and the Thatcher family, who housed me as I finished the early Michigan draft. A huge thanks to Andy Broadey for cover design (https://andybroadey.com/); Brooks Anderson whose artwork is mentioned in the novel (www.brooksandersonart.com).

On legal questions: Sarah Burton (Society of Authors, UK), Michael Gross (Authors Guild, US). On legal defense questions: Amy Resner and Kevin Robinson, and the National Association for Public Defense. Any procedural errors in the case, however, remain my own.

Special thanks to the Elizabeth George Foundation, the Albert Baker Fund, and particularly Gill James and Martin James of Chapeltown Books. Thank you to Bonnie Nadell, my nonfiction agent, who has stayed with me all these years.

I owe a special debt to my family. In the US: Sandra Rouverol, Paula Obrebski, Tessa Rouverol Callejo, William J. Black, Tina Warren, Eve Rouverol, Pam Wainman (and families), Carmen McKenna, and in memoriam: Jonathan Rouverol, Geoffrey Rouverol, Steven Obrebski, Beatriz M. Callejo, William S. Rouverol, Marian Robinson. In the UK: Rose Stallard, Paul Watson, Alice Stallard, Jane and Robert Stallard (and in memoriam Lancelot H. Walker, Dorothy Walker, Bettina Bracey).

My biggest thanks remain for, Lance Walker, who makes all things possible, and our daughters, Elena J. Walker and Sandalia M. Walker.

About the Author

Alicia J Rouverol is co-author of *I Was Content and Not Content: The Story of Linda Lord and the Closing of Penobscot Poultry*, which was called "compassionate and sorely needed" by The New York Times and nominated for the OHA Book Award. She lives with her family in Manchester, where she teaches at the University of Salford. *Dry River* is her first novel.

Please Leave a Review

Reviews are so important to writers. Please take the time to review this book. A couple of lines is fine.

Reviews help the book to become more visible to buyers. Retailers will promote books with multiple reviews.

This in turn helps us to sell more books… And then we can afford to publish more books like this one.

Leaving a review is very easy.

Go to https://bit.ly/3M8xMl4, scroll down the left-hand side of the Amazon page and click on the "Write a customer review" button.

Also by Alicia J. Rouverol

Chatterley, Cedric N., Alicia J. Rouverol with Stephen A. Cole, *I Was Content and Not Content: The Story of Linda Lord and the Closing of Penobscot Poultry* (Carbondale: SIU Press, 2000)

Most studies of deindustrialization in the United States emphasize the economic impact of industrial decline; few consider the social, human costs. *I Was Content and Not Content: The Story of Linda Lord and the Closing of Penobscot Poultry* is a firsthand account of a plant closure, heavily illustrated through photographs and told through edited oral history interviews. It tells the story of Linda Lord, a veteran of Penobscot Poultry Co., Inc. in Belfast, Maine, and her experience when the plant – Maine's last poultry-processing plant – closed its doors in 1988, costing more than four hundred people their jobs and bringing an end to a once-productive and nationally competitive agribusiness. Lind Lord's story could be that of any number of Americans – blue- and white-collar – affected by the rampant and widespread downsizing over the past several decades.

Other Publications by Bridge House

Face to Face with the Führer

by Gill James

Käthe wants to be a scientist. She sees herself as more than a housewife and a mother. And she is in her own eyes definitely not Jewish.

Life in Nazi Germany sees it another way however. She has to give up a promising career and her national identity. She has to leave the home she has built up for her husband and daughter. But she is not afraid of challenges. She enlists the help of a respected professor to help her fulfil her ambition, she learns how to use a gun and how to drive a car. But what will she do when she finds herself fact to face with the Führer or, indeed, with the challenges of modern life?

Face to Face with the Führer is the fourth novel in Gill James' Schellberg cycle.

Order from Amazon:

Paperback: ISBN 978-1-910542-99-6
eBook: ISBN 978-1-915762-00-9

Chapeltown Books

Invisible on Thursdays

by Peppy Barlow

Peppy Barlow is a playwright and screen writer who lives her life looking for meaning and material in all her experiences. In this book she and her friend Persephone/Lucia explore childhood memories - both good and bad - and travel with their children to Crete where ancient myths emerge to haunt them.

A very personal account of a friendship which takes Peppy back to England and ends with Persephone returning to the Underworld. Authentic, brave, honest, funny and touching - the author's voice shines out from these pages.

Author Peppy Barlow guides us through her turbulent and rich life adventures. Truly a life well-lived.

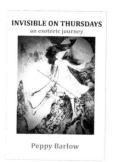

INVISIBLE ON THURSDAYS
an esoteric journey

Peppy Barlow

"I loved it… what a roller coaster ride. Living life as it occurred. For me there were laughter and tears in equal measure." (*Amazon*)

Order from Amazon:

Paperback: ISBN 978-1-914199-16-5
eBook: ISBN 978-1-914199-17-2

9 781914 199448